Kine was limp, his lungs bursting. A final plunge left him faint before the big fisher paused, beak on high, captive dangling . . .

Something stirred in the copse. The heron's head cranked, glance churlish, then the great bird was climbing, wings vast, stilt legs hanging, its *'Kra-aak'* of frustration the final knell of an evening of scanty profit.

Stiff and bruised, Kine lay doggo. The storm was close, thunder rumbling, and the pond hissed abruptly, rain churning its surface. On the bluff by the reeds, a dark form moved, its back humped. Another came, and another. A sheet of lightning revealed them: giant rats on the march, monster rats, a royal houseguard.

Also in Arrow by A. R. Lloyd

MARSHWORLD (First published as KINE)

WITCHWOOD

VOL II OF THE KINE SAGA

A.R. Lloyd

ARROW BOOKS

Arrow Books Limited
20 Vauxhall Bridge Road, London SW1V 2SA

An imprint of Random Century Group

London Melbourne Sydney Auckland
Johannesburg and agencies throughout
the world

First published in Great Britain by Frederick Muller 1989
Arrow edition 1990

Printed and bound in Great Britain by
Courier International Ltd, Tiptree, Essex

ISBN 0 09 953840 7

For the girls again

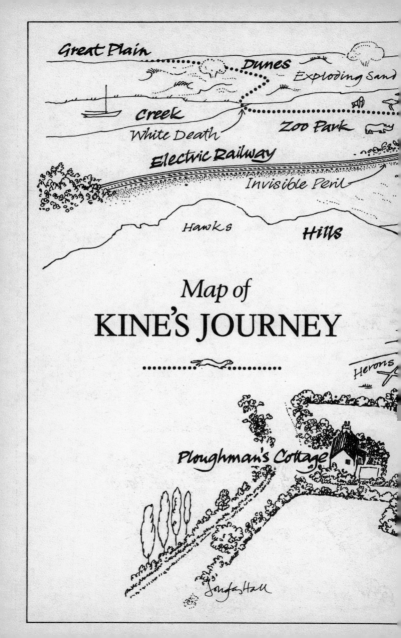

Great Plain

Dunes

Exploding Sand

Creek

White Death

Zoo Park

Electric Railway

Invisible Peril

Hawks Hills

Map of
KINE'S JOURNEY

Herons

Ploughman's Cottage

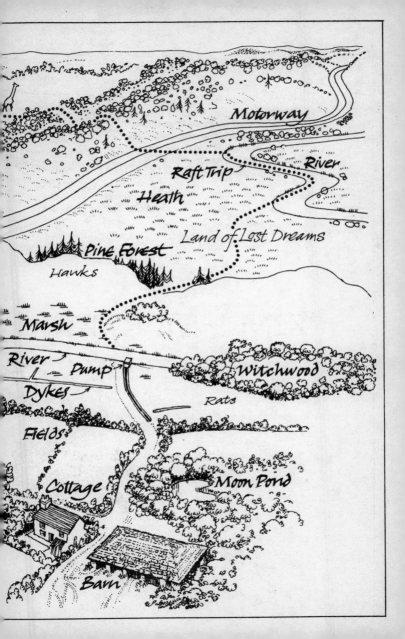

Yet still on mornings such as these
The mirage shifts our channelled course;
Streams run uphill above the trees;
The hero on the enchanted horse
Opens incredible doors.

Robert Gittings
The Fairy Tale

Contents

Prologue

The girl listened again. The sound came from the door, as if the dog was outside, but the dog was dead and buried. Poacher's patch-eyed terrier had died last autumn, twelve months after its master. There was no cat at the cottage. The nearest cat was her dad's, down the farm track. *Something* was scratching.

She turned her gaze to the rug, taking in the room swiftly: the once-filthy walls, now sprucely white-painted; the garden flowers in the hearth; the faded snapshot she kept of the old den's last tenant, Poacher glowering morosely from the cheap plaster frame, the small shrine on the sideboard.

The cantankerous tramp. No one else would have bothered, looked after his washing. Each day, towards the end, she had trudged down the lane to cook and clean for the ingrate, earning only his cusses. The old fool, she had liked him. The girl had always known Poacher and remembered his stories, anecdotes of his 'profession'.

Lifting her baby from the rug, she held the child close, still listening. Again, she heard it, the scratching. Or could it be gnawing? With a flick of a wrist, she turned the handle and pulled, so the back door swung open.

The baby burbled and waved, unsighting her for a second. Then her eyes met the other's. It had backed into the yard, where it crouched in the shadows, indeterminate and greyish. There was no move from the brute, just an insolent stare. Then, very slowly, its snout rose, the cleft top-lip curling, and two dull incisors were clear as she goggled.

Her startled scream made her angry. She felt her baby son stiffen and slammed the door loudly. 'There,' she said, 'it's all gone.' The thing was only a rat – there were enough in the country. 'Your mum's a great ninny.'

And yet, the rat had looked monstrous. It would have frightened the dog, had the dog been alive. It was unnaturally brazen. In a moment, she moved, stepping into the kitchen, peeping through the small window. There was no sign of the brute; the yard was deserted. Of course, the place was a sty and things looked weird in its shadows.

'Come,' she said, the child grizzling, 'let's see the sun shining.' She crossed the room to the front and gazed out at the valley. It was hot and the hedges, their utmost tips wilting, were strung with clusters of bubbles, like the suds from detergent.

Cuckoo-spit mystified her. Poacher had called it an omen, but he had been pagan, full of old superstitions. The poaching man's gnomish mind had encompassed dark fables: prodigies fleshed as toads, soul-mice, weasel-wars, witches. She gave the infant a squeeze, her hug warm and protective.

'There, my sweet,' she soothed gently, consoled by the brightness, 'cuckoo-spit – see it sparkle!'

Forget the thing in the yard. A rat, she thought, was a rat – however monstrous and evil.

Part One

THE RATS

1

All over the valley, blobs of frothy foam glistened, made by the frog-hopper larva, a teardrop-sized insect, from the sap of the plant stems. By mixing fluid with air, the bug had whipped up small bubbles in which to hide and develop.

Then, on the stalk of a grass, the first pinkish-green hopper emerged reborn from the globules and dried in the sunshine. It was airless that morning, the kind of hushed, inert day on which life held its breath against mishap.

The hopper shimmered. For one flicker of time, the bug existed in history as surely as Caesar; or the men from the longships, with their Black Raven banners; or the Saxons and Normans who had sailed up the inlet and passed through the valley.

Few others had followed. Today, the stream flowed sluggishly seaward, flanked by gaunt, stabbing herons and eerie marsh. On either side, in the heat-haze, blue-grey slopes declined inwards, marked by fields, copses, forest.

It was a valley of wildlife. In its tooth and claw fiefs, the white owl prowled his hunt-path as he had prowled down the ages; the rooks, in clamorous senate, enacted time-honoured rituals. There were few human dwellings: the ploughman's home on the ridge, and down the track the small cottage that once had been Poacher's.

Warmth engulfed the frog-hopper. For a moment, it twitched, its maiden leap in life signalled. An inch away, a shrew watched it, eyes like pinheads in velvet. There was a snap; the bug vanished. The pinheads gleamed and the shrew swallowed.

The girl's brief scream broke the silence. There was a bang as the door slammed, then something crossed the old track, making waves on the verges, coming on down the hedge, along its dark, thorny bottoms. Here and there, a twig cracked, and the pigmy shrew trembled. It caught a tendril of scent and drew back, the whiff powerful. The shape it glimpsed was obscure, for the shrew was myopic and already running.

The shape veered into the meadow. Grass was high, fit for mowing – cat's tail, timothy, couch-grass. It would have hidden a vixen. Only the swaying of seedheads, like plumes above some Mogul, marked an ominous passage from the hedge towards woodland. Now, a poppy was rocking, dripping four blood-red petals. Again, despite the air's stillness, spires of sorrel tossed wildly.

Flushed in fear from its ground-nest, a skylark towered, shrilling. As it wailed, came a crunching, a sound of shattering eggs and of yolk being guzzled. Grey-eared rabbits were ogling, sitting up, their heads twisting. In sudden panic, they scattered. The alarm was contagious. Pigeons fled with wings clapping; a pheasant whirred as it bolted.

And then, the beast drawing closer, the grubbing rooks sensed its presence, old birds calling to young, rising up in dense columns to form their dusky procession, the cawing 'Dread' of the commune. 'Rattun lives!' croaked the corvids. 'Rattun's back! The Lord Rattun!'

The man got down from the tractor and closed the gate. Rooks were bawling, scudding over in droves, and he shook his head slowly. Something must have dismayed them; it was too hot for such antics. He glimpsed the shrew by the gatepost. For a second, it paused, then made a sprint at the gap, for the far post and cover, its midget legs pumping.

With boyish impulse, Ploughman stooped, rough hands cupping the mite, but it slipped through his fingers, legging forward yet faster. The man straightened, grunting. He was no longer a boy. The girl had left home and married, moving into the cottage. He had begun to feel his age, a widower, now forsaken. Her engineer filled his place; she had a baby to dote on.

The shrew raced on down the verge. There, in a veritable jungle, it wove its way between columns, towering trunks of cow-parsnip; fought the dense thongs of stitchwort whose white stars submerged it. At last, deep in the covert, it came to the Life Tree.

Once a silvery giant, the willow lay in a pond, uprooted and barren. Poacher had called it his Life Tree, convinced it mirrored his fortunes. And in death it had obliged, for, with curious timing, the tree had finally fallen the very day he stopped breathing.

Now, the shrew scrambled upwards, tiny claws gripping bark, until it reached the bole's summit. Ahead, half out of the water, the great tree-hulk wallowed. Again, the pigmy ran forward, brisk with nervous compulsion. At the hole in the trunk, it put its head in and wailed. The bat-like squeal filled the breach, bouncing back, high and urgent.

'K-i-n-e . . .' it shrilled.

'*K-i-n-e* . . .' the hole called.

'Woe!' the shrew cried.

It echoed.

'Kine, come quickly – it's Rattun!'

'*. . . it's Rattun . . . it's Rattun . . .*'

Kine was far out of earshot. The hunting weasel stepped briskly, his pointed head darting, the supple neck swaying. From questing snout to tail's end, he measured ten and a half inches, ruddy-brown down the back, the narrow bib snowy. He was a flame, a hobgoblin, from a long line of hunters; Kine, a weasel name for centuries.

He was Kine the rat killer. He knew the trails of the valley, the secret runs of the rodents. The weasel missed little, a sleuth in his dominion. He knew the deep, earthy places, the badger's set, the mole's fortress, the stop of the rabbit and where the beasts had their warrens.

'*Tchkkk,*' he churred. He was cocksure. A hundred signs were clear to him. Kine knew the print of the mink, the hare's trod and deer's foiling. He could glance at a cobnut and know who had gnawed it: squirrel, woodmouse or field-vole.

Kine knew the sounds of the valley. He knew the hiss of barn owlets (like a drunken tramp snoring) and the call of the vixen, a siren by moonlight. And the woodpecker's yaffle, deriding the rainclouds. Kine knew the bark of the

5

heron as winter approached, and that the fanfare of geese, honking home up the levels, meant yet one more summer for Kine the survivor.

He was warm and he rested. The steamy heat of the marsh rose in skeins to the woods, where it hung, soporific. The rooks had lapsed into silence, high now in their turrets, wings spread, their beaks gaping. As they sunned in the trees, mallard dunked in the pond or sat out on drowned branches. The vale at noon was lethargic, and the river smelled brackish.

Even the weasel relaxed, chattering as he forayed. *'Tchkkk* – I am small but formidable.' He was not self-effacing. None, he thought, was more dashing, so accomplished a hunter. Kine made for the covert.

On its fringe, a vole sniffed, sensed the weasel and bolted. Its refuge was narrow, a twisting tube in the turf, branching into more tunnels. In a flash, Kine had followed. They disappeared and a bee droned. Then the weasel's head surfaced, popping up from a new hole. On the lean neck, it turned, like a periscope scanning, and once again vanished.

'Tchkkk,' the voice of Kine wheedled. 'Stay and dance with me, plump one; stay and dance with Kine the fearless, with Kine the rat fighter. Let me teach you the death dance . . .'

Ploughman lit up his pipe. The match flared in the dusk, playing tricks with the beansticks, which cast dark-fingered shadows, like the topmasts of wigwams. He was proud of his garden. The beans and peas had grown well. Some pest had nibbled his carrots, but not too severely.

It was still warm, insects humming. The cat came by with a mouse-corpse. It made the man think of Poacher. The fool had always maintained that when he died his soul would leave him in the form of a mouse, the soul-mouse of the pagans. Ploughman's lady had chuckled, her eyes full of mischief. The poacher's gab had amused her. But she had married the other.

And passed too quickly, he sighed, her daughter still toddling. That was a long time ago, and now Poacher had perished. The man gazed into the gloaming at the mist-haunted valley. If Poacher's soul was a mouse, he did not give it much chance, not out there in the evening.

By dark, the land was eerie. You could hear grunts and rustlings, feel the spirit of danger like weasel-breathing. At night, the hedgehog passed quietly, the stoat loitered grimly, each scuffle a feud, each squeal a life threatened. By dark, the valley had talons; the clans of tooth and claw struggled.

You might whistle by day, but walk the woods in the gloom when the owls watched like ghosts and your cheek felt the bat's wing – *that* was no time to whistle. Cross the marshes by night and you could feel the beast in you, your nape bristles rising.

Ploughman entered his parlour. There was bread on the table, left over from breakfast, and he fetched cheese and butter. At least, his own nights were safe, for loneliness did not kill, it just made the heart heavy. The cat appeared, purring loudly. He obliged it with milk, tipping some in a saucer.

Up the track, a light twinkled. They would be watching the telly. He sucked his pipe, gnawing on it. He could go, if he wanted; he could share supper with them. He was, thank God, independent.

The shrew awoke in the Life Tree. He had snoozed off in the hollow, awaiting the weasel. Now, he gave a quick shiver and blinked in the darkness. The willow chamber was haunted. When the tree had stood upright, a brood of kitts had been born there to Kine and Kia, the red hunters. Then, while Kine was away, marauding mink had surprised them, killing Kia and her young – all but one tiny kitten.

'K-i-n-e . . .' The shrew's pipsqueak trembled.

That bygone deed was unnerving and the pigmy's nose snuffled. There were dead leaves in the hole along with some kind of fur, an old and dessicated relic. A thin, brisk monster unfurled, its many legs moving. The shrew's snap was a reflex. The midget scarcely stopped quaking as the centipede squirmed, was demolished and swallowed.

Above the hole, a moon dazzled. The pigmy shrew

squinted upwards, blinded, awed by the light, the white flame of the cosmos.

'Who's there?' Kine's voice grated.

'Scrat.'

'Scrat's dead.'

'Old Scrat's grandson.'

'Another doom-laden midget?'

'Old Scrat was your friend.'

'All shrews are alike!' They stank, or Kine would devour them. He said, 'Come out of that hole, it's not a shelter for dossers; it's sanctified by Kia's memory, a place of weasel remembrance.'

Besides, the whole tree was sacred, for Kine a *true* Life Tree – he had been born in the crevice, in the womb of the wood when the willow was living. He remembered his mother. She had been an inspiration, as Kia had been later, a chattering spitfire.

He remembered the old days. His mother would scold him. 'Single file; keep together!' Those were the nursery safaris. All life, then, was sunshine: undulating in line down a ditch gold with tansies, butterflies on the fennel, breath of steers sweet and misty.

Later, losing his mate, Kine had learned the Blood Fury, the reckless wrath of the weasel. He had avenged the mink outrage then gone his way, a lone hunter – a dandy-hound, Poacher called him, a sprite of the death dance. He was small but formidable, and Kine did not dither.

'I am Kine, this is my land. Get out of the hole, shrew.'

Scrat climbed out. 'Rattun's land, Kine. The king is back, the Lord Rattun.'

'*Tchkkk,*' snarled Kine.

'Woe, the Rat King!'

'All shrews are pathetic.'

'I've met him,' the shrew squeaked.

'I hope you killed him,' Kine jested.

'No one kills the Lord Rattun. He's all-powerful, he's *doom*, Kine.'

'All-powerful?' Kine hissed it. The weasel drew back his head. 'Don't provoke me more, midget, your doom could be sudden. I am Kine the death-bringer and I answer to no one. There are no *powers* in Kine's country. The poaching man is a ghost; Kine has vanquished the she-mink.'

The shrew quivered. 'But Rattun . . .'

'Bah, Rattun, a rodent!'

'Woe,' moaned Scrat.

'A mere rat!'

'Woe and doom . . .'

'Depart, pigmy, before the rat killer strikes you!'

The weasel turned in the gloom, springing down from the trunk, and prowled by the water. Small beasts came there to drink. He was a master of ambush. 'Scrat!' he mused. 'Old Scrat's grandson!' A bright orb swam in the Moon Pond. Round the banks, it was black, the skirts of trees making caverns where waterfowl harboured. 'Rattun!' Kine's step was scornful.

All was still in the gloaming. Only the weasel's reflection in the pond shifted quietly, like a fish, as he bounded. Sometimes, he stood by the pond and, looking down at his image, hoped that Kia's might rejoin it. But Kia's spirit was shy. She came only in his dreams, quick and bright then, but fleeting.

Now, he was pestered by pigmies. All shrews were the same, inedible and neurotic. *Tchk-kkkk-chk* – the *Lord* Rattun! Kine had danced with rats often; they swayed and writhed in their death throes! He paused, far galaxies darkening while a flicker meant lightning.

Kine froze, his eyes darting. He had a sixth sense for danger and deplored the unfamiliar. The two dark poles *were* unfamiliar, strange stakes in the reeds, too full-girthed to be sedges. Nothing moved; it was silent. The gloomy stilts appeared lifeless. Then, with a gleam like the lightning, the heron's bill scissored down and the weasel was pinioned.

Suddenly, Kine was rising, yanked up from the ground and swiped back through the water. The heron dunked his furred prey as a matter of habit, to subdue and lubricate it. He would swallow it whole, perhaps alive, down that gullet;

a long and slow journey. Back and forth flailed the weasel, his drenched body spuming.

Kine was limp, his lungs bursting. A final plunge left him faint before the big fisher paused, beak on high, captive dangling.

The heron pondered a moment. The bird must now change his hold, flip the sodden prey lengthways, a prelude to gulping. It meant a break in his grip, and as it came Kine lunged wildly, all his waning strength summoned.

Desperately, he jack-knifed, wrenching free, looping downwards. The heron's stab raked a flank, then Kine was flat in the reeds, mud and silt oozing round him.

Something stirred in the copse. The heron's head cranked, glance churlish, then the great bird was climbing, wings vast, stilt legs hanging, its *'Kra-aak'* of frustration the final knell of an evening of scanty profit.

Stiff and bruised, Kine lay doggo. The storm was close, thunder rumbling, and the pond hissed abruptly, rain churning its surface. On the bluff by the reeds, a dark form moved, its back humped. Another came, and another. A sheet of lightning revealed them: giant rats on the march, monster rats, a royal houseguard.

2

The rain beat on the covert and crossed the fields to the Witchwood, the oldest part of the forest, much of which was decaying. Ancient hornbeams and oaks stood with tops like stags' antlers, their trunks hoary with lichen. Once a refuge for outlaws, the wood had been a wolf kingdom, a place where heathen rites flourished. Now, old branches stood withered, fossilized in the gloom, and gnarled roots lay uncovered.

Two youths loomed from the downpour. They wore their coats on their heads like monks' cowls, and were soaking.

'Well,' the first lad exclaimed, 'you've lost your flaming snares this time.' He was beefy and raw-faced. 'I thought you knew where you set them.'

'Thought I did,' moaned the second, a thin boy who snuffled. 'It's the storm; things look different.'

An owl shook in its shelter.

'What's that there – by them brambles?'

They gawped.

'It's a hedgehog.' The creature scuttled off, grunting. It seemed weird, other-worldly, a beast from prehistory.

'I thought you knew these woods backwards.' The big lad looked resentful. He rolled his eyes at the shadows. Trees dripped and creaked quietly. From funereal ivy, they stretched wizened fingers, white as bone where the rain gleamed. 'You said you came here with Poacher.'

'We used to come to the forest; he used to bring his old ferrets. It wasn't the Witchwood.' The thin boy sniffed. 'It was yonder. He wouldn't come to the Witchwood.'

'Why not?'

'Didn't like it. The old boy was superstitious.'

'More like, there's no rabbits.'

'I dunno . . .'

'Well, there isn't. There's no nothing in *this* wood, only

hedgehogs and toads. It's a petrified forest. All we'll catch is pneumonia.'

'Aye, let's go,' said the thin lad.

'Hang on, I seen something. There, what's that?'

'Where?'

'That rise there . . .'

The youths stared through the rain-rods. There was a bank in the gloom where the ground shelved up darkly – bare, moist earth roofed with scrub and pocked with black burrows. So numerous were the holes, it was like a giant ant-hill. And at each hole, or near them, sat a motionless body, hunched and brown, pale hands crooked, as if carved from the teak on some Far Eastern temple. Only the sharp eyes seemed living. And every pair watched the intruders.

'Thought you said there's no rabbits?'

'Them's not *rabbits!* I'm going . . .'

The sky was clear the next morning. For a while, at the wood's edge, droplets shone on the grass and on the damp webs of spiders, then the sun's rays dispersed them. The rooks had dropped into pastures to drill them for earthworms. A single bird stayed aloft, left in the trees as a lookout. Poacher had called him the Watchman, a grouchy, grey-faced old male whose head drooped morosely. Age had rifled his zest and the scene did not charm him.

Scanning the young rooks below, Watchman's dour eye was scornful. They knew it all, so they thought, with their strut and their lustre! Scarcely out of the nest, they thought life a flower garden, a constant splurge of wild roses, buttercups, oxeye daisies. They thought the woods always glowed with the June pink of campion; that the bright blue of speedwell and the yellow of cinquefoil ever brightened the hedgebanks.

They thought life a soft number, a warm green lane flanked by foxgloves, frothed with may and beaked parsley. Watchman glowered down his beak. They thought the rich, pliant soil, still wet from the rain, an inexhaustible larder of larvae and earthworms. Wait until the sun baked it, until the drought of late summer turned the clod into concrete!

And wait until winter froze them! The old corvid shuddered. Then each treetop assembly was a parliament of crisis, each voice weak with hunger.

They would learn, the rook brooded. He was, himself, beyond caring. Age had withered his interest in the endless debates of his garrulous species; the births, deaths and scandals; the matings, cuckoldings and worse. In one respect, he resembled the youngsters: after seasons of pairing, he was ending his life as he had started it, as a bachelor.

And now, Watchman peered down at the dirt-encased weasel. Exhausted, Kine had crawled to the Life Tree where, amid its disentombed roots, he was still sleeping deeply. A fleck of blood stained his snout. Scrat the shrew nosed him bleakly.

'Kine, wake up!' squealed the midget. 'Don't die when we need you! Kine, we look to your courage!'

'Speak for yourself,' croaked Watchman.

'A rat killer!' the shrew said.

'An uppity weasel; a small, bumptious braggart.'

'But a champion, Watchman!'

'Huh,' the rook exclaimed sourly.

'A prince of the death dance!'

'That beast?' It was crusty. 'What good will *that* do you?'

'Someone's got to do something. It's Rattun,' the shrew wailed, 'he'll spread his plague in the valley.'

'On the ground, dwarf. Too bad!'

'*Doom!*'

'For groundlings. Take a tip, learn to fly, Scrat!'

Kine stirred, an eye opening.

'Heron-fodder,' the rook cried. 'That's a poor fish, your champion!'

Scrat circled the weasel, his fidgeting nervous. 'Kine, they've gone to the Witchwood.' The shrew snatched a beetle. Cusps grinding, he added, 'With Lord Rattun. They've stopped there.'

Kine was sore. He stretched slowly. At last, he said, 'Let them stay there.'

'And *multiply?*'

'CAW!' the rook called. His gaze had turned to the cottage, where the front door had opened. The feeding birds took off briskly, a hundred fingered wings oaring, and the young man gazed upwards. The girl came out with the baby. She said, 'You won't be late home?'

'No,' her husband said, smiling. They walked to his van and he paused there to kiss them. 'Take care of the Dream Child.' They laughed, the joke private, and the infant blew bubbles. The van was white. On its side was the legend, *River Board Engineers*. The young man got inside.

The girl tossed her head slightly so long hair tumbled backwards. 'You won't forget the rat poison?'

'I'll bring some back from the pumps, it's not doing much good there.' Her husband grinned, looking handsome. 'The brutes downstream fatten on it. They say the strain's grown immune; we're breeding super-rats nowadays.'

'I reckon that's just what mine was – a super-rat!' The girl pouted.

'We'll see . . .' He drove off.

She held the baby up, smiling. 'Wave goodbye.'

'*Glub*,' the child said.

Taking a small hand, she flapped it. The little fingers were perfect, so pristine and plump, as pink as a mole's paw. 'Say bye-bye.'

The babe burbled.

'Bye-bye, Dad,' the girl prompted. 'Till this evening,' she added, twirling round in the sun so the child blinked and chuckled. 'See the rooks; aren't they noisy? Shall we look at the garden?'

It would get too hot later and she strolled in the grasses. They were cool on her bare feet, moist still from the night, and soaked her jeans at the ankles. Near a sapling of willow, she held the child tighter, stiffening. '*Silly* Dad,' the girl whispered.

She had said more when he did it: when he had brought it from the wood and planted it in the lawn, thinking that it would please her. 'A Life Tree, love, for the Dream Child!'

'A *Life* Tree?' She could have killed him.

14

'You don't *believe* it – not like Poacher!'

'I don't know . . .'

'What does that mean?'

What *did* it mean? And how could she have told him – him a townsman, an outsider? She had grown up in the wild, alone with Ploughman and Poacher, and the valley's spell gripped her. For him, an engine had soul, but a tree had no spirit. Who, then, was the pagan?

She had learned the traditions. Poacher never burned elder, believing bad luck would follow. Yet to dance round an oak was to find joy in marriage, and that *was* true, for she had proved it. She wanted no proof of Life Trees, and the sapling had riled her.

'Don't fuss, there's no problem.' Her man had grinned when she coloured. 'I'll pull it up and forget it.'

'No you *won't*, don't you touch it! It's done, let it flourish.'

She squeezed the child now. 'Poor Daddy.' At least, thank God, it looked healthy. The rooks were settling, gabbling. 'You know he wed a wild woman!' The baby beamed and she giggled. 'But *how* he loves us, my Dream Child!'

Tchkkk . . .' Kine had recovered. He hurled his scorn at the heron which stood siege by the river, then the weasel danced on, unabashed in his smugness, for he had cheated the fisher and that was no trifle. He was Kine the survivor; Kine, whose lives surpassed the cat's. His war chant resounded. He was Kine the heron-cheater!

Through the broad, dyke-raked levels, the stream's flow was lazy. Gnats hung in the heat and the flotsam passed slowly: twigs, a tangle of sheep's wool, an old can which listed. Kine tested the water then dunked his head, flicking droplets. The morning was quiet. The marsh seemed barely awake and its breath was hay-scented

This, thought Kine, was his kingdom; the vale was Kine Country. Kia had loved its green coverts, its slopes and its hedgerows. 'A good place,' she had called it one evening of thrush-song, and he had concurred. Now, as Kine marched the stream's bank, the white van trundled the ridge and a tractor was mowing.

Round a bend, youths were fishing. Their voices droned on the water.

'I went back for the snares.'

'You never went near them *creatures*?'

'Near enough – heard 'em squealing. Like a zoo.'

'They'd be fighting. I don't reckon it's natural, not for rats to be *that* big.'

'Nor I, but keep mum. We'd no right to be up there.'

Kine passed by under cover. The pair were inoffensive, unlike his late rival Poacher. The poaching man had known his business; the youths would catch nothing. Even Kine, who was no fisher, knew the best swims were elsewhere. The fish would be near the pump-house – witless roach, cunning carp, the fierce pike and the perch, which consumed its own offspring. Kine knew where they lingered.

There were few secrets safe from him. He knew where frogs went to sunbathe, a long hop from safety; where elvers shoaled inland, and where bank voles had nested, chewed grass used for swaddling. Tempting barrels of protein, the last swam like beetles, crash-diving when challenged, and Kine sometimes chased them. He also hunted the reeds, since rats and rabbits went in them.

Now, on the warmth of the bank, lay a scent no one relished. Two flat heads rose together, deceptively languid, and the adders hissed softly. 'Stay back, weasel,' the male said, and the female said, *'Bite him.'*

The painted snakes shifted slightly and Kine's dance was chary. *'Tchkkk,'* he rasped, 'This is Kine's land.' Their skin-glazed eyes were unmoving. 'I am Kine,' said the weasel, 'and you are unwelcome.'

'Bite him *now*,' hissed the female. 'Fill the weasel with poison!'

'If he does,' Kine responded, 'I'll tear the antidote from him. The cure's in his bladder. I'll suck his bile and recover.'

The male moved back, his coil flowing.

He said, 'I've no fight with weasels.'

'You should *kill* him,' his mate said.

16

Kine swayed, his gaze steady. He kept it fixed on the female, the flexile she-adder. The idle ripple of her scales beneath the bold zig-zag gloss concealed the speed she could muster. One lapse of his guard and the meandering serpent could strike like an arrow.

'I am Kine, this is my place. Leave now with my warning!'

The reptiles flowed, disappearing. From the grass, as they vanished, came a swishing rejoinder. 'And I, Kine, am the she-snake. Next time, weasel, you'll rue this.'

He made his way to the hayfield, where the tractor was mowing. It would disturb many creatures and Kine would lay ambush. He bounced, churring briskly. He had seen off the adders – Kine the snake-scarer! *Tchkkk*, the shrew should have seen him. Never mind about Rattun, if the dwarf wanted frightening, he should dream about adders. A valley of serpents – that was truly a nightmare!

He took the cut by the warren, plunging down into tunnels. Kine was at ease beneath ground, the earthy chambers familiar, the smell of rabbits enticing on clay-laden through-draughts. The engineering was complex, full of bolt lanes and junctions, but the weasel ran nimbly, scarcely slowed by the darkness. He ran by scent and skin-instinct, alive to touch, air, vibration.

At first, the footing dropped steeply, loam to clay, root to sub-root. Now the way became damp, the mud thick and adhesive, and the reek became heavy. Pad and claw took on cargo. Then he was climbing and twisting, passing stones, fibrous tendrils, and the blackness turned greyer. He was nearing the exit. There, Kia would wait when she had lived, sitting where the run surfaced.

The sudden heat made him gulp and he blinked in the sunlight. The tractor's throb had drawn close, dust and pollen erupting, the place sweet with mowing, grass in dense, seedy swaths, the severed stems fragrant.

'I thought you'd be along soon, Kine.' Another weasel was watching.

He sat back. Was he dreaming?

'It's Wonder, Kine.'

Of course, *Wonder!* She was the image of her mother.

They called her Wonder for surviving – the only one of Kia's brood – now a sleek, mature creature.

For a moment, he had thought . . . but then, the likeness was startling. 'Of course, it's Wonder,' he echoed. 'I thought you went with the heath weasel.'

The blue Ford tractor swung round, the mower's skirt swirling. Music blared from the cab, where a radio pounded.

'I thought,' said Kine, 'that you'd gone, left the vale with Young Heath.'

She laughed. 'He's not so young now, Kine.'

'A good weasel.' Heath had fought in the Mink Wars.

'Yes,' she purred, 'we still meet. I came back to check on you.'

Her father frowned.

'You've a mate, Kine?'

'I've Kia . . . I've a memory.'

'But no mate? A companion?'

'I hunt alone.' His voice sharpened. 'Such is the way of the weasel!'

'Not always,' she murmured. 'There are seasons and seasons.'

'Kine is a prince of all seasons.'

'A royal conceit!'

'Pride,' he told her. 'The pride of the hunter.' Modesty was for dormice, herbivores, berry-nibblers. Kine was small but formidable!

'Well,' said Wonder, 'you're blooming.'

'A master, still, of the death dance!' He paused, the tractor returning, spinning round by the wood, the standing grass now an island, getting smaller and smaller. 'And you,' he said, 'you're plump, Wonder.'

Her voice was coy. 'That's the kittens.'

'When?'

'Soon.'

'Heath's?'

She twinkled. 'Young Heath's! I must go, Kine.' She hesitated then added, 'You know, if ever you're lonesome, there's a world beyond the valley.'

'Beyond the vale!'

'Other weasels.'

'*This* is my land.' Kine scowled. 'It is held in Kia's memory!'

'Yes,' she said as she left him. He watched her go, lithe and bounding. She paused once more.

'Kine, be careful.'

3

The van lurched to the marsh. Its windows were down and, for a while in the sun, a brown hare sprang beside it. The big old buck ran half-throttle until, bored by the machine, he opened up and veered off, ears couched, flaunting his paces.

At the wheel, the young man whistled. He had come to know the valley, not with the fullness of the girl, who belonged as of birthright, but with an incomer's interest. His work's concern was the drainage, a web of pipes, dykes and ditches which led the rain from the slopes to the marsh and the pump-house.

There were many such 'houses' – small brick cubes – up the stream, each encasing a motor. When the flood levels rose, they pumped the water to the river.

The engineer stopped the van. Lapwings screamed overhead, their cries thin and urgent. One pair was persistent. They batted down round his head and, as he stood on the track, he saw the chick just in front. It might have been a small stone, the tiny prone form transfixed, the mottled camouflage perfect.

He placed the chick on his palm and still it crouched as if lifeless. Returned, at length, to the path, it lay doggo, unblinking. It was, he thought, like the pump: it would not stir until signalled, pump and chick automated.

To prove the point, he strolled off and watched the birds from a distance. Now, the adults grew calm, no longer sounding alarms but soft cries of assurance. At once, the chick was afoot, legging off through the grasses.

The man grinned and moved on, stepping into the pump-house. It was like passing through time. At the push of a door, the marshy valley had gone, a small, robotic cell shimmered. Fluorescent lighting bathed dials, mirrored in the floor's surface. Here, anchored by bolts, sat the big grey-clad motor whose own signal to stir would be flashed by electrodes which measured flood levels.

When the dyke water rose, the machine would start up, the pump heave into action. Every second it ran, a ton of swill from the marsh would be dumped in the river.

The engineer viewed it proudly then, reading the meters, made a note on a sheet, checked the fuses and belts and topped-up the grease feeder. He gave the engine a pat. It was seventy horsepower and had never caused trouble. If only all of the valley was as tame and compliant!

He laughed at the prospect – no more storms, floods, mud, vermin. But then, he mused, no love either – no wild, valley-bred wife, with her moods, superstitions! He grabbed a broom and, still smiling, swept a floor that was spotless. Poles apart were his passions, his unpredictable love and his dependable engine. He stored the broom and took stock.

There was a job still to do but he could not recall what. It was a job for the girl. The man remembered – the rat bait. Filling a bag from the box, he went back out and locked up, put the bag in the van and drove off with a whistle.

Kine ran on up the track. It was plain he was vexed, for his bounce was emphatic, his eyes dark with rancour. 'Kine is mad,' chirped the sparrows. They kept pace up the hedge, clamouring like a fight crowd. 'Kine can smell the she-adder. Kine does not like the adder!'

They were right.

He ran faster.

'Kine is angry,' they chattered.

'If there's a fight, we must watch!'

'A good fight,' sang the sparrows.

The weasel's nose led him forward. The scent was dense by the copse. She had not left as he had wished, and her thick smell provoked him. Round the pond, it grew faint then rose again in the nettles which invested the owl's home, the tumbledown barn, trailing on to the cottage.

'She's in the garden,' the birds cried. 'She's waiting for Kine there!'

The sparrows romped in their excitement, tumbling in the gutters. 'There'll be a fight; there'll be a fight!'

'*Glub*,' a voice said.

Kine halted.

He was still in the lane, the cottage hedge close beside him. Pushing through its dry vaults, he saw the child on all-fours on a rug by the sapling, where the lawn was shade-dappled. The human baby was harmless; he merely burbled and sprawled. But Kine did not like the other – the adder coiled in the sun within arm's reach of the infant.

'*Tchkkk!*' snarled Kine. 'I'm here, serpent . . .'

The snake's head turned.

'*Glub*,' the child said.

The weasel circled the adder. 'I gave you warning,' he chanted. 'This is Kine's land, I warned you!'

'You're a fool,' hissed the adder. 'You'll die when I bite you.'

'Try,' cried Kine. 'I'm a flame. Try to bite the death dancer!'

'*Blurp*.' The baby was beaming but the birds had grown silent. 'Hush,' the sparrows crooned, fluffing. 'Watch them dance; watch the death feud!'

The snake swayed, her tongue flicking. Beneath the flat, cross-signed skull, her eyes were cold, still as glass, and did not leave the goblin. 'Dance your dance; you'll grow tired, shrimp.'

'Kine is tireless,' he answered.

'Kine is *small!*'

'But a whirlwind . . .'

He dare not tire, and danced faster, seeming almost to hover, claws spread, his back arching. Rather than tire, he must strike, but he would not get two chances and preferred to confuse, to whirl round, to weave circles. 'Once he tires,' breathed the sparrows, 'she will fill him with venom.' Her languid rhythm would change and she would lash like a lance, poison-tipped, to her target.

Kine rose from all paws, a jack-in-a-box, sinking lightly, then turned, waltzing clockwise. 'Follow my steps,' he churred softly. 'Watch me dance; watch me closely.'

'I'm watching, weasel. You are tiring,' the snake hissed.

Engrossed, the baby blew bubbles.

Kine made to spring then swerved, feinting. 'You are the tardy one, serpent. Let me teach you the dance steps.'

'You are distant, come closer.'

'In good time.'

'*Nearer*, weasel . . .'

The girl was racing downstairs as the snake's fang erected, the lower jaw dropping, the poison-gland oozing. Armed to maim, the head darted, the sequence done in a flash while Kine, shimmying sideways, glimpsed the bolt as it passed him. Next thing, it retracted, the adder frustrated.

Kine churred his elation. 'The snake is swift; Kine is swifter!'

'We'll *see* . . . '

But they did not. At that moment, the girl, bursting into the garden, disturbed quivering sparrows and the duelling pair bolted, their flight paths divergent. The babe frowned, snatched up rudely. 'Oh, my darling, thank God! Come indoors . . .' The rug followed.

Kine made steps for the covert. Not displeased with his work, he marched with a swing, putting up with the sparrows who mobbed his withdrawal. 'A *fine* fight!' they disparaged. 'No blood and no killing! A fine battle that was!'

No doubt, the adder was wiser. He had shown her his paces, the nimbleness of the weasel. He had taught her a lesson.

'A poor battle,' the birds chirped, and three started brawling – a rowdy, countrywise trio – bundling down to the track where their wings sent up dust-clouds. Kine scattered them smartly. 'Wait,' he shrilled, 'for the next fight. That's if the snake is still eager. I'll show you a killing!'

In the shade of the wood, a grey dagger moth waited, wings folded, for darkness. Water crowfoot was flowering where a ditch joined the pond, and Kine sat by the rushes. Reed buntings were singing in stuttering concert. He ignored their tweek-tweeking. Kine had leaped like a demon! Who else could have dodged when the she-adder forayed? Like forked lightning, he pondered. He would have loved Kia to have seen him – and Wonder, their daughter.

What had Wonder besought him? 'Kine be careful.'

He snorted. Was that the way of the weasel? The weasel dared and was dashing!

'K-i-n-e . . .' Scrat's mini-squeal sounded.

The dashing weasel looked sheepish. He did not wish to hear gloom. Scrat and his fanciful fears! He slipped away through the herbage. As if there were not enough dangers . . .

'It could've been just a grass snake.' The engineer washed his hands. He had placed the rat bait in the yard, well away from the infant.

'My love, I *do* know the difference. You didn't marry a townie!'

'I know.' He grabbed his wife's waist. 'A wild kitten!'

'With claws,' she huffed. 'Put me down, I've got to get us some supper.'

'How's the lad, is he sleeping?'

'Go and see.'

He went quietly, tiptoeing upstairs. The child had thrown off his covers and lay, pale and serene, flat on his back, arms flung outwards. He was wholly relaxed, as only the young in sleep could be. At times, both parents were frightened by their son's vulnerability.

Downstairs again, the man poured cider. 'All's well . . .'

'Good,' the girl said. She drank as she cooked. 'I think we've bred a snake-fancier!'

'And they say nothing happens . . .'

'Who does?'

'At the works. They say the vale must get boring.'

'What do *you* say?'

'I tell 'em.'

'That you've a wild green-eyed kitten?'

'And super-rats and a serpent!'

He heard her laugh and the stove sizzled.

Outside, mist was forming, billowing in the twilight. The

engineer grew more thoughtful. 'Your dad must be busy, he never seems to come up.'

'I've asked him enough times. My dad likes his garden.'

'Aye, he's different from Poacher. Poacher neglected this garden. Still, we're getting it shipshape.' He eyed the flowers through the window. In the glow, sparrows dust-bathed. 'Damn those three on the border, they make holes like volcanoes!'

The girl joined him, voice teasing. 'Flit-cat, Peck and Farthing-feather!'

Her husband scowled. 'They want shooting. Was that tonight's bedtime story?'

'No,' she said, 'that was *last* night. Tonight, the story was Rattun: how the king takes a bride. It's an old one of Poacher's. How they seek a rat palace in which to rear all those ratlings!'

This was true of the valley: that any time in most weathers its temperatures varied – even those in one field – depending where they were taken. On summer nights on the marsh, some air pockets were hot; others, chill in the gloaming. Over there by the path, it was balmy and scented; near the copse, the shrew shivered.

Scrat distrusted the twilight. Antlered stag beetles droned, zooming over the reeds, and the mist rolled towards him. It crept up like a cat, pushing one grey paw forward then advancing another. Soon, the river ran white, overlaid by a broth that poured into the hollows and fingered the ditches.

Hedges drowned in the night-mist. Elsewhere, standing taller, trees reared crowns from the soup like dinosaurs browsing – some alone on the slopes, some in great herds where woods stretched. Scrat drew back from a thistle. 'Woe,' he moaned. Where was Kine? Scrat did not like the half-light, the hour of the hunters.

He could hear them around him, hear the *ping* of bat voices. Black shapes were zig-zagging, dismembering moths, whose wings drifted earthwards. A fox barked, the sound startling. In the mist, the beast paused, one foot raised, its ears forward. Then the fox-shape dissolved and a badger came snuffling, digging holes down the bank where wild bees might have nested.

There was a shriek as a stoat killed.

Scrat groaned. The dusk thickened. The marsh was quiet for a moment. Then, through its grey exhalations, a round white face trailed mist tendrils and Scrat glimpsed the barn owl. Silently, its wings lofted. As quietly, it plunged, talons spread, and a mouse died. 'Doom,' breathed Scrat, 'blood and murder!' If all the blood spilt seeped upwards, the mist would turn crimson.

If only Kine was there with him – Kine was bold and undaunted!

A far hum reached the dwarf, a grim drone from the Witchwood, rising, falling, like chanting. *'What's that?'* croaked the pigmy.

'Climb a tree, you could hear, shrew.' The Watchman stirred, squinting down, disturbed as he roosted.

'I'm not sure I want to.'

'Then keep quiet, rooks are sleeping.'

'I want Kine.'

'Kine's an upstart.' The rook was disgruntled. 'All weasels are upstarts.'

'That's the chant,' the shrew bleated. 'It's the chant of the Witchwood, the creed of the *chosen*.'

'Big fat rats! Let me slumber . . .'

'Rook, the creed – can you *hear* it?'

'I hear all.'

'Is it f-fearsome?'

' *"We the chosen,"* ' the rook drawled. 'That's what I hear, mumbo-jumbo. *"We of the blood defer to Rattun, Lord and King of the genus."* '

'Doom!' wailed Scrat. 'Go on, Watchman . . .'

'Will you hush?'

'I'll hush, Watchman.'

' *"Sixtyfold in a year shall each sow spread the chosen."* ' Watchman's tone was sardonic, his eye on the midget. The shrew had asked to be frightened. ' *"And Rattun's choice shall be queen."* ' The rook leered, warming to it. ' *"The Sow*

Queen of the master genus. And all her ratlings be feared. Then will the rat killer suffer. Then will the rat killer perish." '

Scrat gulped. 'The rat killer?'

'Kine the braggart. Now, *go*, Scrat!'

'Woe!' cried Scrat. He ran blindly. The rat killer *perish!* A teasel stem loomed ahead. At full gallop, he struck it, upending, legs kicking. Rolling over, he blinked. In the mist shapes were moving, four fat rats of the houseguard, the minions of Rattun. They shuffled by and Scrat squirmed. They were bound for the Moon Pond.

He ran again.

'K-i-n-e . . .'

Mist wrapped him. Spongey moss slowed his progress, as did the hooked thongs of goose-grass. Dandelions rose above, their blooms closed for the evening. At the pond's edge, he stiffened. A pair of dark eyes glared down and, though the shrew was short-sighted, the glint of teeth made him tremble.

'Stop there, Scrat.' Kine was earnest. 'I've had enough of you this time. You've pestered me once too often.'

'Kine, the chant . . .'

'I've been patient.'

'They're coming, Kine, Rattun's "chosen"! *Then will the rat killer perish!* Ask the rook, he'll support me . . .'

The weasel sighed.

'You must run, Kine!'

'*One* more chance,' Kine relented. He turned and slouched to the Life Tree. 'Don't say Kine is not gracious.' He paused, his nose working. There was a heavy scent present, a stench which trailed up the trunk and which Kine, stalking slowly, pursued to the hollow. He dropped inside.

Scrat's snout quivered.

'Tchkkk . . .' the hole said.

Scrat waited. The inner darkness spat anger.

'*Tchkkk-kkk!*' Kine erupted. He stood atop the bole, hissing. He was stomping, vibrating, his whole body bouncing. The shrew looked on, his paws rooted. The weasel was dancing, hopping on the spot, spitting. The Blood Fury had gripped him.

'They've been in!' Kine was outraged.

'I saw them, Kine.'

'They've defiled it; they've polluted the Life Tree.'

'Doom,' Scrat breathed.

'Kine's own birthplace . . .'

'Doom and woe!'

'Kia's sanctum.' Kine grew still, his eyes staring, as weasels will, still and trancelike. A weasel shrine! Time meant nothing. At last, he said very softly, 'Rattun's dead — note it, midget. As of now, Rattun's finished. You can broadcast the message. Kine will be in the Witchwood.'

4

A gale howled and the branch, weighty with leaves, snapped abruptly. It made a sound like a gunshot. The thrush lost her young. A wind in summer meant trouble: small birds blown from their nests, trees brought down across cables, devastation in gardens. Creaks and thumps filled the Witchwood. The dark, humped forms scarcely moved; the great rats were indifferent.

Sitting up by their holes, they watched Rattun emerge, to glower round from his platform. The grey-lagged tyrant was monstrous. From huge chisel-edged teeth to the grotesque naked tail-dock – that scaly, rope-like excrescence – the massive boar inspired terror, and those near displayed deference.

As roaring draughts ripped the trees, the brute's coat was wind-ruffled and stood on end, coarse and tufted. It made the whale-back look shaggy. Trunk-like legs were splayed outwards, the horny hands twitching. 'The weasel lives,' rasped the Rat King. 'The dancer must perish.'

He prowled the colony, louring, menacing in his movements. At each ponderous step, he cast a long, sullen glance that set the tribe shuffling backwards, subservient, fearful. He had a cruel reputation and few risked his anger. The heart of Rattun was steely, tempered hard as the traps which had tortured his forebears, and there was hate in the monster.

In droves, his race had died poisoned, or in the merciless gin-traps. Many, caught by their limbs, had gnawed a leg off to live, to escape execution, crawling home raw and bleeding. They had passed down their loathing; their anguished, three-legged hate of a world of rat tormentors. Others, pitchforked and bludgeoned, perished squealing defiance.

Persecutors had abounded. The fox, the owl and the

mink had all preyed on the species; cats and dogs had abused it. The long-necked heron took rats, as did stoats and the otter. But most hated of all, its size doubly insulting, was the light-footed weasel, the little red dancer.

The Rat King faced the wind's frenzy. Above him, rooks tumbled wildly, like debris in the gale, swept off course by its violence. The giant inhaled, his lip curling. All things changed; genes mutated. The hour had come of the reckoning – the day had dawned of the *chosen*, the master strain, of the Lord Rattun!

He spoke again. 'It was bungled; the weasel lives. This time, *find* him. I want an end to his nuisance.'

'We've seen the adders,' said Flit-cat.

'We could take you there,' Peck said.

'Then you could fight,' said Farthing-feather. 'We like a fight, a good dust-up.'

They launched themselves in the wind, tumbling over to prove it, a brawling bundle of wings which split again into three, each sparrow a champion. 'A good fight can work wonders.' They preened on the pump-house. 'Especially one with *blood*,' Peck said.

Kine sheltered below them. The gale had rucked up the stream, striking thick-walled reed alleys, whose mauve pennons fluttered. A moorhen, braving the waves, was almost lost in their troughs, her scarlet cap just afloat before a new crest enthroned her, her white tail plumes fanning.

Mallard circled the forests. Disturbed, they powered in the tumult, cutting through with quick stabs, fast and low round the vale, and Kine envied their swiftness. With such flight it would take minutes, not days, to search the Witchwood.

He said, 'I don't want the adders; you can guide me to Rattun.' Showers of spray shot the bank and he was drenched. 'Through the Witchwood.'

The sparrows fluffed. 'Rattun?' Peck said.

'Through the Witchwood?' chirped Flit-cat.

Farthing-feather looked sly. They shook their heads, squinting down. 'We never go to the Witchwod, no one does if they're smart. It's a toad hole, a graveyard. Whoever heard of a fight there?'

Kine was brusque. 'It's a *rat* hole. Show me where Rattun's earthed and I'll show you a killing.'

'But not a fight,' answered Flit-cat. 'We're not green, we know Rattun. You'd be out of your class, Kine.'

'And dead.' The birds twittered. They were boisterous urchins and hopped about sparring. 'The trouble is with a killing, when it's quick then it's boring. Try the Watchman, he's dozy.'

'Yes, try the rook, he might do it.'

'Try him, Kine, the rook's senile!'

Kine watched them bounce down a hedgerow, buffetted by the gusts. 'I'll have those three,' snarled the Watchman, his perch swaying gently. He was out of the weather, well screened by the covert. 'I'll teach those three what respect is!'

'I need a quick air search, Watchman.'

'Sparrows!' wheezed the rook grimly. 'Gutter hoppers and riff-raff!'

'I need to know where the rats are.'

'Oh, you do?'

'Which direction. I need to narrow the search; I could be days looking for them.' Kine paused. 'It's vast, Watchman, a vast and strange place, the Witchwood.'

'And Kine is small!'

'Rook, it's urgent . . .'

'Oh, I see – urgent, is it? You need the rook in a hurry? When you need him, you need him!' The inflection was cutting. 'Two points, Kine – first, I'm flattered. It's always nice to be needed. Second, find someone else!' He poked his beak at the gale. 'I'm going nowhere in *this*, least of all to the Witchwood. Nor should you,' he said, softening.

'I'm bound to go.' Kine turned slowly. He would search, find his own way. 'I've vowed that I'll be there.'

Watchman shrugged. 'That's your business. If I were you, I'd run for it, get away while you're able. Wonder's gone, you're alone. You can't fight against change and mere martyrdom's futile.'

Kine moved on. 'You *and* Scrat!'

The shrew joined him. 'It's doom, Kine.'

'What do you know, a *midget?*'

'More than you think,' the shrew bridled. 'I go unnoticed and listen. *You* should know – Old Scrat helped you; he spied in the Mink Wars!'

'But of course . . .'

'Old Scrat questioned the marsh frogs. They would have run from a weasel. He brought back *information*.' It was proud and Scrat's head rose.

Kine had stopped, his eyes brightening. He said, 'Old Scrat was a hero . . .'

The shrew's tail stood up bravely. He paced a ring, dwarf legs strutting.

'A shrew could talk to the toads, Scrat – they'd not be afraid.'

'A shrew is smart,' Scrat said, glowing.

'. . . toads who know where the rats are; toads who live in the Witchwood . . .'

'Who *what?*' The shrew crumpled.

'Think of your heritage,' Kine said.

'Kine, you're mad!'

'Nothing to it – quickly in, quickly out.'

'Of the W-witchwood? You're crazy!'

'Just bring word of the location then leave it to me, Scrat.'

'Doom and woe . . .'

'Scrat, *we'll* show them!'

The girl went into the garden. The gale had passed and its wreckage was strewn at the woodside: twisted limbs, trees uprooted. All the while she had feared for the transplanted sapling, but now she found it unharmed, saved, she thought, by being supple, and the stake alongside it.

Of course, her fears had been daft. So she had told herself often, ashamed of old superstitions long laughed at by others. As if the damned sapling mattered! And yet the sight of the thing, safely through its ordeal, brought relief. She felt joyful.

'Come on, my child, let's go out; let's check up on your

grandad!' She put the babe on her back and made her way down the track. The sky was blue, the air calm, and small birds had started singing. Where had they gone in the gale? Each, she supposed, had its niche, like the rabbits which watched, ears aslant, as she passed them.

Ploughman pondered his garden.

'Oh, Dad,' the girl said, 'your roses!' They had been ripped from the wall and hung down in a tangle.

'Soon tie *them* back.' His pipe glowed. 'Them and the beans. Could be worse.'

'We've been lucky,' she told him. She thought of the willow.

He took the child. 'Well, young fellow, I've something to show you.' Ploughman walked up the path to where his poultry were sunning. An old white duck showed her young, four small yellow ducklings. 'There,' he said, 'how d'you like them?'

The baby cooed.

'Aye,' the man said, 'handsome fellows, like you, lad!'

The girl beamed warmly. 'That's pleased him. You'd better watch out for rats, Dad.'

'I've never had much rat trouble.'

'You've not had super-rats yet!' Her slow grin was half-earnest. The backyard bait had been taken but no results proven.

'I've got the cat.' The man eyed her. His pipe smoke meandered, the slightest zephyr in charge where minutes back winds had rampaged. The valley was fickle. The baby chortled and pointed. He was entranced by the ducklings and raised his own gale of protest when passed, at length, to his mother. 'Oh no,' she said firmly, 'there's work at home, we're not stopping.'

'See you soon, boy,' the man said.

The girl looked bright. 'Come to tea, Dad!'

'I'm all right.'

'It's been ages. We've got the place really nice now.'

'Oh yes?'

'What does that mean?'

He shrugged, looking away. 'I got memories,' he grunted, 'longer memories than you have.'

'Of Poacher?'

'Aye, Poacher.'

'Come on, Dad, we both knew him.'

'I remember him better – all the years he lived up there.'

'Dad, he wasn't the devil!'

'He weren't no saint, my girl, either.'

'They're coming, Kine,' warned the Watchman.

The day was fading and the rook could see the squad by the marsh gate, five or six thickset shapes, before the hedge broke his vision. 'They're coming for you,' the rook said. 'I told you to run. There's still time, if you hurry.'

'Let them come,' said the weasel. 'Let them meet the rat killer.' To run would be a betrayal – of his land and the Tree, of the valley and Kia. Kine had sworn to kill Rattun. He said, 'The Rat King is *nothing!*'

'Please yourself.' The rook settled. Evening darkened the tree-tops, silhouetting late roosters, straggling birds who had dined well.

Kine slipped into the tree den. Several times, he turned round, leaving his scent in the hole, then sprang out, peering upwards. Along the great fallen trunk, many offshoots, once lateral, now rose vertically and mast-like. Nimbly, Kine climbed the nearest until the upright divided, providing a platform.

Aloft, the weasel lay still. The pond gleamed inkily below, stretching out round the trunk as the woodland light dwindled. The stars had yet to appear, but in the shade of great trees smaller galaxies shimmered, pale blooms in the dusk, constellations of hemlock, eerie planets of yarrow where folded dog-roses twinkled.

Stealthy steps haunted clearings. Mice were out round the banks and Kine could hear their jaws chomping.

The heron lingered to fish, grey and hunched, head in shoulders. His long neck whipped; a roach gleamed. Then the bird had dissolved, ghosting into the gloom, his place filled by mosquitoes. Their sharp-edged whine was bloodthirsty.

Kine crouched where the mast forked. Below, the hulk's deck grew dim and the hole lost its outline. He heard a faint scratch of claws and trained his sight on the root-mass. For a while, nothing happened, then a shadow slipped forward and several more followed.

He saw them, now, on the bole, half a dozen thick figures, broad-backed, their snouts snuffling. They were big coarse-necked creatures and Kine was awed by the posse. He might, perhaps, have been scared had he not been so angry.

'*Tchkkk-kkk . . .*' It was hissed.

A small white moth flew beneath him. The rats had crowded together, a dusky, heavy-tailed mob which came on in a rush, scuttling up to the hole and clustering round it. Kine did not doubt their purpose. They had come as assassins, sent to kill the rat killer. He heard their grunted frustration. The hollow was empty.

A minute passed. Still they searched, shuffling on up the pier where the deck became narrow. Kine scowled from concealment. He was smart, a hobgoblin! He watched them straggle back, thwarted. They were burly but dull; the master genus was witless. At length, they grumbled then left, trooping off down the bole, hauling into the night through the wood's dim grey columns.

One brute lagged, loath to leave, and the weasel's eyes glimmered. The rat returned to the tree-hole. At first, it sniffed round the trunk then its nose came up slowly and Kine, on his perch, looked straight into its nostrils. The rat said, 'You are condemned, Kine.'

'And you are witless,' Kine answered. 'You should've left with the others.' The weasel's gaze held the rat's as he sprang, plunging downwards. Kine struck the brute with such force that it spun from the tree-trunk.

Not far off, a coot started, while Watchman peered from his pulpit.

The splash was resounding. Way below, in the pond, a head broke the surface, leaving a luminous wake, and Kine regarded the water. He reached the bank in swift leaps and saw the rat pass the bluff. It was exactly beneath him when, again, Kine lunged at it, this time clinging fiercely. Locked together, they wallowed.

'Stay there, Kine, and I'll drown you!' The rat submerged, its legs kicking, and both creatures sank slowly, the gloom pressing on them. All the weasel could see was the moon on the surface, a crumpled disc which broke up, writhed a while and then mended. He gripped the rat, his lungs straining. It, too, would need air, he thought, locked in suspension, then slowly they rose, Kine's ribs tight, his eyes bulging.

Suddenly, he could breathe. A blissful breeze stirred the pond and they were rocking through shallows, the rat touching bottom. Pick-a-back, Kine clung on, dragged and bounced by the brute as it made for the sedges. The weasel fought for a death-hold. Clamping his mouth on the neck, he forced his teeth through thick hair.

'A few more steps, rat,' he churred, letting go. 'The nerve's punctured.' His foe turned turtle and quivered. It was quite still in a minute, the largest rat Kine had killed, as he boasted to Watchman.

'*Tchkkk*,' he bragged. 'A giant slaughtered!'

'Giant?' the rook cavilled, squinting.

'A giant is dead!'

'That's a small one – compared to Rattun, a midget.'

'Bah,' said Kine, 'you're a mile up.'

Scrat reached the edge of the Witchwood. It was scrubby and wild, the mere swampy and stagnant. Scrat took a few steps and halted, his mini-teeth gritting. Think of the valley, he winced; think of Old Scrat, the hero!

'B-u-f-o . . .' he piped. The sound scared him. 'Are you there?' This was murmured. He had no flair for heroics.

A great black bird left the mere, flying low, like a shadow. The shag swung round, heading seawards. A hummock moved in the earth, rising from a depression, and two coppery eyes shone. Scrat flinched. He said, 'Bufo?'

'Who's that?'

'Scrat,' Scrat whimpered.

The toad yawned. 'You've disturbed me.'

'I'd l-like a word . . .'

'I'm too busy.'

Scrat stared. She looked drowsy.

'Busy resting,' rasped Bufo, whose spring trek was over, her seven thousand eggs anchored. The thought alone made her languid. 'Can't you see that I'm weary?'

The shrew peered hard. She looked *toad-like*, her skin wrinkled and warty, greenish-brown on her back, her swagging gut flushed with yellow. The colours changed with her haunts and with her moods, which were fickle. Her present mood was a brown one. 'You find me ugly?' she dared him.

'F-far from it,' he blurted.

'The whole Witchwood is ugly; there are no butterflies here, shrew!' She flicked her tongue at an insect. The tongue was rosy and lethal. Old trees creaked as a breeze rose, the sound of branch chafing branch like a Jack donkey braying. 'Other toads,' she went on, 'find me sufficiently nubile.'

Woe and doom! Scrat felt queasy.

'Males fight over me, shrew-mouse!' As they had fought that last spring, more numerous than the females, their love cries resounding. 'A toad's embrace *lingers*, shrew-mouse!' Bufo stretched her short legs. She clamped her mouth round an earthworm. 'But what do *you* know of beauty?' The worm squirmed. 'What does Scrat want?'

'To learn where Rattun is camped; where the rat tribe has mustered.'

'To know where Rattun is camped?' She raised a hand to her mouth and pushed the worm inside slowly.

Scrat braced. 'That's my mission.'

'*What* mission?'

'I'm scouting.' He put his tail up, emboldened. 'I can't reveal any more, it's a secret assignment.'

'Who cares!' The toad gulped. 'I'm quite sure I don't,' said Bufo. 'Now, if you were discerning, an expert on beauty . . .'

'I'm not blind.' Scrat peered vaguely.

The toad puffed up.

'Well?' urged Bufo.

Doom, thought Scrat; doom and failure! 'A *subtle* beauty?' he ventured.

'Go on . . .'

'Well-proportioned?'

'You've quite an eye!'

'Ah!' Scrat brightened. 'And you've the eye of a lark, toad, and many pleasing complexions . . . I could continue at length.'

'You should call here more often.'

'I might,' lied Scrat, the thought shocking. 'But first, the rats . . .'

'Pah! Forget them.'

'I need to know where to find them.'

A green woodpecker laughed. The noise was mocking, demented. The bird made off, its flight dipping, then laughed again and the toad said, 'They'll find *you*, don't you worry. Give them time, Scrat, they'll find you; they'll find the whole of the valley. They'll multiply like the plague, Rattun's kind, who can stop them? You'd better mind how you step, for the Rat King is brutal.'

'Aren't you s-scared – in the Wildwood?'

'Why else hide in a hollow?' Bufo shrugged. 'Hide my beauty – what was your phrase? – *subtle* beauty. There's nothing *we* can do, midget, the master genus is with us. Why don't we talk a bit more? About my eyes, my complexion . . .'

Afar, the woodpecker hammered. The burst was quick, hollow-sounding, brief as a death rattle. Scrat's heart jumped, his head throbbing. Doom, he thought, he must run!

He held on. 'When you've t-told me. We can talk in good time. I *must* know where they are, toad.'

'I don't know, that's the truth.' She sank down and crouched, brooding. 'I've only been to the mere. I've made my trek and returned. I've been nowhere near Rattun.' The breeze had dropped; it was clammy. 'I'll tell you this, the hog goes there – the hedgepig goes that way.'

'The hedgehog?'

'On his night rounds. He has no fear, he's well armoured, a walking thicket of thorns. You'd have to follow the hedgepig . . .' Bufo paused. 'Scrat, where are you? Come back! Stay and talk, dwarf . . .'

Scrat was speeding, heading hotfoot from danger, from the toad and the mere, from the rank airs about them, all his pent-up fear churning, pumping fuel to his limbs. He did not stop until breathless, then gulped and plunged forward.

He scarcely glimpsed the shapes round him. The vast grey tree-stumps held demons; groping brambles were serpents. He passed a large, lustrous beetle as if food no longer mattered, his one concern to be home, away from the Witchwood.

At last, he reached the hay meadow. The copse and Moon Pond were near and the scents grew familiar. Scrat slowed down. He had done it! 'K-i-n-e . . .' he shrilled. The shrew strutted. He had accomplished his mission, found the way to reach Rattun. He was a shrew to be reckoned, a scout of some merit!

'K-i-n-e . . .' he called.

It was easy: simply follow the hedgehog!

5

The shrew was brisk, trotting proudly. 'I had to probe, Kine, to press her . . .'

'You did well.'

'There was danger.'

'There *is*, Scrat – for the Rat King!' Kine was fierce. 'Weasel danger! Now I know how to reach him . . .'

'Simply follow the hedgepig!'

'I'll be there.' Kine paced grimly.

Scrat looked up. 'He's d-doom, Kine. The giant is doom. Dare you face him?'

'*Tchkkk!*'

'Is it worth it?'

'Oh, let him go.' Dawn was breaking; the Watchman yawned. 'Does it matter? Let him play the white knight. One less uppity weasel!'

They were passing the cottage. In his cot, the babe stirred while sparrows roused in the eaves. Fluttering by the window, they bobbed in the gutters. The vale disrobed from night slowly, shedding darkness then mist until its greenness was naked – the greenness, Kine thought, of freedom, the wilds Kia had cherished. Wispy cloud streaked the east. High and sparse, it dissolved, leaving dawn without blemish.

'Another scorcher,' chirped Flit-cat.

'Nice day for an outing.' Peck bounced and they jostled.

Farthing-feather joined in. 'A nice day for a dust-up.' They tumbled down past the panes to the sill as the child watched. There, they sparred, chirping hoarsely. When they had done, Peck cried, 'Scrat's back. Look, he's there, with the weasel!' They bustled down to the hedgerow. 'What's on, dwarf?' called the sparrows.

'Kine's off to do battle.'

'A fight!'

'With the devil. With the monstrous Lord Rattun. A fight

of fights in the Witchwood. A duel of duels. Will you be there?'

Peck stalled. 'Will *you*, midget?'

'I've done my bit.'

'Ah,' Peck brooded.

'Fight of fights!' Flit-cat muttered. He preened his bib, the tone peevish.

'I doubt he'll get there,' Peck mused, and Farthing-feather said, 'Wood owls – I'd say the wood owls'll have him. Leastways, he'll be murdered. It's no match, Kine and Rattun. We might as well send the Dream Child. Now, a return with the adder – that would be a good dust-up!'

Kine pressed on to the covert and sat awaiting the sunrise. He watched the Moon Pond grow brighter. On that bank, Kia had perished.

'I'd come with you, b-but . . .' Scrat said.

'Go on, shrew, you've done well.' Kine was calm. 'I need peace, time for thought before leaving.'

He sat a long time alone. The first rays of the sun warmed the bluff and a dragonfly nymph, rising out of the pond, began to twitch on a reed stem. Bending its back so the shell split, it freed its head and the thorax, then unsheathed the wings slowly. It pumped blood. The wings opened. The plain nymph grew exquisite. At last, it flew, skimming, dazzling, its gauze-like sails irridescent, the slender sapphire hull brilliant.

Kine saw it skull with its fellows, jewelled craft in the sunshine. They hawked the pond for mosquitoes, darting over the Life Tree and whirring through sedges. In the warmth, flowers had opened, water buttercup and iris. Below the bluff, in flotillas, white lilies rode anchor, their crimson hearts a reminder that Kia's life had ebbed there – as Kine's might in the Witchwood.

The weasel had no illusions. Beneath his bounce of bravado, he knew the odds and luck's limits. He had danced with death now too often to think her merely flirtatious. Her game, at length, was in earnest. He cleaned his claws. Deadly earnest.

A weasel scent crossed the glade and he turned. Wonder eyed him. 'I saw the shrew, Kine, he told me.'

'I've a job to do, Wonder.'

'Why *you*?'

'I'll be back.'

'Perhaps,' she said.

'Kine is crafty!'

'A fool,' she cried, her eyes hot, so like Kia's he was startled. 'You're doing this for *her*, aren't you? She wouldn't expect it.'

'I'm doing what I *must*, Wonder. For I am Kine the rat killer!'

The female sighed. 'I'll come with you.'

'No, you're carrying kittens. Bring them up to be bold – if I should fail, to replace me. Train them well in the steps; make them formidable, Wonder.'

The Watchman cawed.

Kine said, 'Move!' and they dived for the ground-growth.

The girl swung into the copse, her child on her shoulders. 'There,' she laughed, 'there's the pond. See it splash!' She flipped pebbles. The baby flinched, eyes averted, then squealed for more, his arms flailing. 'Watch the ripples,' the girl said. 'There they go – watch the circles!'

She saw a red creature dart. Was it a stoat or a weasel? The tail was short, the size small, and she plumped for the latter. Dragonflies surged and wheeled. 'Look,' she fluted, 'horse-stingers!' Not that they stung; they did not, but it was Poacher's name for them. 'See how they shine – red, green, blue!' Hues as dazzling as gemstones.

She smiled, the baby's eyes widening. He had a hand in her hair, a wheaten lock in his fist. 'Hey, that hurts . . .' She released it. 'Just watch them fly – see that *big* one! I'll tell you a secret. They can fly backwards, like wasps.' Poacher had pointed it out. She would sit there when she was small, before the willow had fallen, and watch him fishing for tench while the Ploughman was working. Sometimes, squirrels would join them, shinning down from the trees, scratching round for old acorns.

Now, a male voice said, 'Got you!'

Her husband came through the scrub from the van at the woodside. She beamed. 'You're back early.'

'Come to clear out the rat bait. It's done no good, they're still coming.'

'What can we do?'

'I don't know. I'll ask your dad.'

'You could *ask*...'

'I could borrow his gun.'

'*You*?' She squealed her amusement. 'You in the dark with a gun? Heaven help us!' she hooted.

'I used one once at a fun-fair.'

'Who got killed?'

'Won a goldfish!'

The torch's beam glanced the tree boles. It struck the pond and spread flatly. 'Turn it off,' a voice grunted, 'you'll frighten the fishes. Sounds and movements disturb them.' A foot cracked down on a twig.

'*You* can talk!' huffed the torchman.

The youths advanced to the bank. 'Ugh,' croaked one, '*that's* not pretty.' He shone the light on the rat, its entrails torn, in the reeds, where Kine had finally dragged it. 'That's one of them beggars, them brutes from the Witchwood.'

'Over here,' said the big lad. 'It goes straight down at the edge here.' He wormed his way under boughs where an oak spread its skirts, their leafy hem touching water. It formed a dark pondside cave with enough bank to crouch on. 'Bring the net. Put that torch out.'

The thin youth groped forward. They peered in awe at black water. 'That's deep there, I reckon.' It might have been without bottom, and the two worked in silence, breaking up a stale loaf, dropping lumps on the surface.

For a while, nothing happened. Far away in the Witchwood, a dull dirge was drumming. Neither youth heard the chant. The bread consumed their concern, the soggy rafts near the bank, one of which wobbled slightly. A small fish was biting. Another rose, its lips nibbling. Then a shoal of fry joined them, young roach growing bolder.

Now, the crusts bounced and scuttled, flipping this way

and that as the unseen host guzzled, a silver flank sometimes glinting. 'Sardines!' The youths waited. The water churned, glowing faintly like the froth from propellers. 'Dozens of them.'

'There's hundreds!'

'Have the net ready. Watch . . .' Two large bubbles had risen. Suddenly, in the scrum, something large and dark heaved and a whole breadcrust vanished. 'There, that's a tench; scoop the bottom! That's a big old tench, that is!'

The thin youth almost fell in. He had the net in the pond, its short pole in one hand, the other clutching his colleague. Both boys pulled. The catch surfaced. Little pewter fish twitched as the net reached the bank and a fumbled torch glimmered. In the midst of the fry, a great cuirass gleamed darkly.

'We got him, the big 'un!'

The slimy tench did not move.

'Someone's coming,' one lad said.

The net was dropped. They looked round. 'That's rain,' said the other.

'It isn't raining.' They listened. The sound of pattering grew, like naked feet moving, as if a primitive army was on the march, barefoot. 'Shine the torch, I don't like it. Back there . . .'

The tench slithered. Sluggishly, it submerged and the black water gurgled. 'There – them eyes!' The beam wavered. Shakily, it traversed, coldly mirrored in pairs by the orbs in the covert. They seemed to shine on all sides, between the thick, dusky boles – small, cold eyes in humped shapes, like the shapes in the Witchwood. 'It's them brutes!'

'Let's be going.'

'They're on the path.'

'Chuck the bread. Hurl the crust to them, quickly!' It was munched. 'Now let's beat it!' Clambering up the bank, the youths lurched round the Moon Pond. There were rats in the reeds. 'Gawd,' the skinny lad croaked, 'they're shifting the dead 'un, making off with the carcass.'

'There's more ahead, listen to them!'

The pattering came again, and as they drew near the

track they could see the horde moving, darkening the dim lane. It was a wave, a black stream, a thing that surged like a tide-race. 'Sweet Gawd, it's a rat mob. I heard about them from Poacher.'

'Keep quiet. Let's get out.'

'I'm not stumbling through that lot!'

The stream split at the barn, going round it and through it, even over the roof, where the birds at roost panicked. Sparrows fled, flapping blindly. White wings poised, an owl glided, bemused by the monsters. A massive sow scuttled forward and nosed the night-curtained cottage. Covetous, she swung round, her envy borne by the sapling, which felt the rat's sharp-edged chisels. She tore a strip from the bark with a wrench of pure malice.

'They're breaking up.' The youths goggled. The rats were forming small parties, some scavenging singly, foraying up the track, slinking into the shadows. At last, they passed, a few stopping, digging in at the barn.

'Think we ought to tell Ploughman? He's got young fowls at his lodging.'

'Don't be daft, he'll be sleeping. He's up at work before breakfast; goes to bed when the sun sets.' The larger youth found a stick and thumped the ground with it, glaring. 'I'm going out down that lane, and any brute in my way . . .' He thumped again, this time harder. 'You'd best keep up, I'm not dawdling!'

'We've left the net.'

'Aye, *you* left it. You going back?'

They paused, white-faced.

'Going back? Are you kidding!'

A sparrow flapped in the dark. As they started for home, the frightened bird sought a perch, blundering round their heads before landing in thicket. The hedge enclosed Ploughman's garden. Flit-cat crouched amid blackthorn.

The old white duck was upset. She kept fidgeting quietly, not far from the thorn, and the unnerved sparrow watched her. Rats had got in the fowl pen. They had pushed under the wire and were threatening the Aylesbury, one rat prowling close until she rose and stove at it. In the gloom, pale and huddled, her ducklings were exposed.

Flit-cat saw the thieves snatch them. Then the infants were gone, dragged away into shadow, their distraught parent powerless. Fearful, Flit-cat hopped higher, creeping up through the twigs, wishing Peck was beside him, and Farthing-feather, their roost-mate.

He saw the humped shapes retire. But even when they had gone, straggling back down the track, he could not sleep in the thorn. He missed his two sparring partners, and the tiles, friendly gutters.

'Peck?' he croaked.

He was alone.

'Farthing-feather?'

The only sound was of boots, as the youths scurried homewards.

The girl went out before breakfast and crossed the grass in her nightgown. She had dreamed rats were swarming. Now, half-asleep, she was scared, fearful of a forewarning, the premonition which drove her. At the sapling, she stopped, her eyes averted, then rubbed them. She dreaded looking but had to.

'Oh Lord,' she thought, 'it's been injured!' She stooped and peered at the willow. Its rind was torn near the ground, a thin, vertical strip bearing signs of two teeth marks. Aloud, she breathed, 'Oh, my baby . . .'

The nightdress whipped as she ran. On the stairs, she tripped up, caught her balance and moaned. She was white, her lips parted, wide awake now and anguished. Bursting into the nursery, she stood at the cot-head. The child slept peacefully, smiling. She hugged her ribs; she was cold.

'Of course, the graze . . .' she remembered. There was a scratch on his ankle, a tiny hurt made while playing. She had dabbed it with spit. And now he slept like a pup, oblivious by the eaves, as Poacher had in *his* childhood, and countless others before – cottage children and kittens, fledglings reared in the roof, nests of mice, lambs made orphan and chubby-cheeked piglets. Life, then, had been one.

The girl sighed – he was safe. But over breakfast she mused. What if the tree had been stripped? A badly barked tree could die. She dared not think.

'Penny for them!'

It made her jump and she gawped, then raised a smile for her husband. 'I'll make the tea for your thermos.'

Glimpsing the barn through the window, she watched its roof while the pot boiled. There were two sparrows on it. They flew down to the ground, to some dark, shapeless object, hopped around, then ascended. Several times, this took place, and she said, 'What's got in them? Those birds – what's upset them?'

The man went out. 'I'll soon see.' He took his bag to the van, walking past the old barn, where he paused. 'It's a dead one.' He eyed the bird. 'It's a sparrow. Been mauled, it's a mess. Must have died in the night; been attacked while it roosted.' He drove away with a wave and the girl went in slowly.

Farthing-feather flew down. He touched Peck with his beak, gently nudging the victim. Peck was stiff. Flit-cat joined them. The living birds drooped their wings, hopping round in dejection. Peck's eyes were shut tightly, the pale grey lids closed like blinds, and his feathers were soiled as if he had been trampled.

'He had no chance,' muttered Flit-cat. 'There was no chance of a scrap.'

'It was no match,' said the other. 'No match and no warning.'

'He liked a fight . . .'

'A *fair* dust-up.'

Flit-cat gulped. 'There's *no* fairness. It was a horde; it was terror. I'd like – I'd like to get even. I'd like to see Rattun perish!'

Farthing-feather's cap nodded. 'We could've helped . . .'

'Kine could use us. He needs a couple of partners.'

'We could still help the weasel!' They turned to Peck,

the small bundle. 'We'll not give up, Peck, you'll see. We'll join Kine, we'll support him.'

The rook winged down. 'That's what you think! Kine's gone, he left early. I'd guess by now it's all over.' He shook his head. 'One less weasel. He'll be as dead as a sparrow.'

6

As Kine came to the forest, the sky clouded over; a sombre
roof dulled the trees. They loomed ahead gaunt and baleful,
their ramparts forbidding: the citadel of the rat, the shunned
and decadent Witchwood. '*Tchkkk,*' he churred, pressing
forward. What was a wood to a weasel? Was he not Kine
the dauntless?

'Prepare to meet the rat killer! Be prepared, my Lord
Rattun!'

A sheep had died, its bones bleaching. The skull was
bald and he paused, peering out through its sockets. Tawny
owls sat on boughs. When the sky wept, they ruffled,
innocuous until nightfall. Beneath them, glades decayed
slowly, mausoleums of past grandeur, great timbers age-
raddled, their courts dim and miry.

Kine advanced, the ground soggy. The nearby mere
reeked of rotting. It was a place of putrescence, ubiquitous
fungi. Blackcaps oozed as they festered. Others formed lips
on trees, pouting lewdly at the traveller, or grew like tumours
on roots. Some, flowerlike and opaque, importuned from
false gardens.

Bats snored in tree-hollows. Many trunks were decayed
and Kine passed damp, pulpy wood made exotic by insects:
the hanging house of the wasp and the ant's tree-stump
warren. Crawlers squirmed as he forayed. They would have
made Scrat a feast, the millipedes slow, archaic; the centi-
pedes swift and carnivorous.

Kine took stock. A ghost shimmered – the cast-off skin
of a newt - and he eyed the quag fiercely. Its mud stuck to
his paws, made him less than light-footed. He could not
dance with clogged feet, and he must dance soon, or perish.

And find the hedgepig by evening! It dossed, he knew,
by the mere and, at dusk, would start trundling. *Follow the
hedgehog!* Creatures moved by the water. A few rough ponies

were grazing, turned out round the lake where a rude path existed, worn by visiting graziers.

He looked back down its tracks. A hint of sweetness still followed, a haunting zephyr from home, and the valley's scents wafted. He hesitated then braced. It was not time to be weak; ordeal strengthened a weasel and he continued.

'*Tchkkk*!'

A gleaming flank slithered. The weasel froze, mud-encumbered, reminded of adders, but the serpent veered off. As it took to the mere, he knew his fears were misplaced, for it was harmless, a grass snake.

Tired and wet, Kine cast round him. He needed temporary shelter, a place to rest and get clean in. Ahead, an old horse-box beckoned. Weeds stood high round its wheels but the tail-ramp was grounded and dry straw lined the flooring. Climbing in, he lay down. The wheaten bedding was fresh and he rolled, his fur drying, then got rid of the mud which had made his feet heavy.

Fine grey rain screened the opening. He watched as it drizzled. A little waterfall splashed, trickling down from the roof, pattering on the ramp. A pile of straw near him rustled. He saw it stir and he hissed, on his feet, his neck bristling. 'Who's there?' The straw rose. Kine was poised. 'Come out slowly . . .'

The heap of bedding grew vast.

Kine pulled back, less assured. He was ready to bolt when the spines started showing, pushing out of the straw, and a big hedgehog surfaced. It took no notice of Kine. Instead, its drowsy eyes scornful, it turned to the weather, gave a grunt of disgust and sank back in the bedding.

The weasel purred. Luck had blessed him. led him straight to the creature. 'Sleep on, hedgepig, till dusk, then trundle your night-path. Kine will be right behind you!'

All the way to the rat camp, the redoubt of the Rat King! And then . . .

Kine napped briefly.

The rain had stopped when he awoke and he could hear frogs declaiming. There was a desultory drip as the roof shed its dampness, a *plop-ker-plop* on the ramp, of diminishing vigour. He searched the straw. It was warm. There was plenty of scent where the hedgepig had snoozed but the creature had shifted. Ducking under the stalks, Kine sniffed round, growing anxious. In disbelief, he searched corners. His guide had gone.

'*Tchkkk*!' He listened.

The sound he heard was no hedgehog – an engine was revving. He drew back in the horsebox. There was a movement outside and the ramp rose abruptly, formed the gate and was bolted. Kine was trapped. A jolt threw him. As he got up, the floor juddered. The horsebox was moving.

The sparrows followed the hedges, past the nests of wood-pidgeons where fat squabs crouched on platforms, past the dreys of grey squirrels, then took the path to the Witchwood. As they came to a corner, a battered Land Rover faced them, approaching at speed, at its tail an old horsebox.

So turbulent was the slipstream, it bowled Flit-cat sideways. Regaining course, the bird swore while Farthing-feather dived past him. 'You're not airworthy, Flit-cat!'

'More airworthy than you are! I saw you stall, and that tailspin.'

'I did not stall, I manoeuvred.'

'You stalled!'

'Right, I'll fight you . . .'

By now, the mere was in sight. It reflected the sunset, red as the blood Peck had spilled, and their badinage faltered. Climbing higher, they wheeled. 'Look,' bawled Flit-cat, 'a toad hole!' Landing near, they hopped over. 'Toad . . .' they called.

Bufo glowered.

'The weasel, toad – have you seen him?'

'Should I have?'

'He came this way.'

'Would I look at a weasel?'

'It's urgent,' said Flit-cat. Farthing-feather drew closer. 'The rats have been on the rampage. Peck was killed, our good comrade.'

'I warned the shrew.' Bufo paused. She cocked her head.

'Hark – the droning! Do you hear the far chanting? The chosen greet Rattun! It's just the start, there'll be worse. Is the shrew safe?' asked Bufo. 'I liked the dwarf, he's perceptive.' She plumped herself, her skin rosy, catching hues from the sunset. 'I think the glow suits me, don't you?'

'Listen, Bufo, where's Kine? We haven't come here to chatter. We don't care for toad talk.'

'You're like all sparrows, you're common. I find your manners distasteful.' She stuffed a slug down her gullet.

The sparrows flexed. 'Don't tease, Bufo. We're quite *unpleasantly* common; you'll find us worse than distasteful!'

'Yes, well . . .' The toad shrugged. 'I might've seen him,' she granted. 'I might've spotted the gnat-brain. He might've entered the horsebox . . .'

'And then?'

Bufo gloated. 'Then *nothing*,' she told them. 'He was shut in – and good riddance! It's bad enough here already; who wants a weasel intruding?'

'So we passed him,' moaned Farthing.

They turned their backs and flew off, chasing after the trailer, stubby wings pounding air until they ached from the effort. 'We'll never catch him,' puffed Flit-cat. They perched to rest, their beaks gaping. 'He could be carried for miles.'

Farthing-feather looked grim. 'We've *got* to find him,' he murmured. 'We promised Peck a revenge. We've got to track down that box, Flit, our champion's in it!'

In fact, the box was still rolling. As it sped by the marsh road, lapwings rose at its rattle, tumbling round it, protesting. Bovine herds raised black heads; white swans slept on reed castles. A snipe jinked up from a dyke as if each steer was a marksman.

Onwards jolted the box, slowed at last by the hills, bleak grey walls in the evening. Then, twisting over a pass, it lurched down the far incline, the valley behind but no end to the bumping. Kine was bruised. It was constant: bump, bump, bump, without let-up.

At first, the weasel had stormed, raging round in the box, caught off-guard by its closure. After that, he had jumped, leaping up towards daylight. There was a way of escape between the top of the gate and the roof of the trailer, a tantalizing rectangle, but Kine could not reach it. The only way was to climb, using thin laths of wood on the raised ramp as claw-holds. This, he had tried without luck, shaken down by the bumping.

Now, he lay on the straw, which took the edge off the jolts, and watched the square of sky darkening. Only the stars, Kine supposed, knew what worlds he was crossing; only the moon knew their terrors. His was a travelling prison. Only the straw knew his anguish.

He snarled, his lips parting. He was, he told himself, fearless (though conviction was dwindling). He was Kine the survivor. But in *exile*? He shuddered. The tremor stoked renewed rage and, in a spasm of fury, he hurled himself at the tail-gate. A fly batting a window could not have made less impression.

It went on for so long that, when it stopped, he felt giddy. He still expected the bumps, still imagined the rocking. He still felt sick in the stomach. There was a last wrenching jolt as someone unhitched the tow, and the journey was over. Kine heard the Land Rover rev, change its pitch, become distant.

The horsebox was inert. It was dark in the straw, for by now night had fallen, the only break in the gloom the square of sky at the back, which had a vague luminosity. As he watched, the square flickered, lit by far-away lightning, a common sight on the skyline most nights of the summer. At least it was familiar, and Kine took heart from it.

Challenging the raised ramp, he worked his way up the laths, his claws clamped to the ledges. The short climb was testing. Once, a vital lath missing, he jammed a claw in a nail-hole, inching shakily on. Higher up, he trod air, his back paws losing purchase. Dangling by his forelegs, he swung in space like a bat, found a ridge, clambered upwards.

Finally, he was there, at the top of the tail-gate. The world was dim, unforthcoming, a black void beneath him. It was a long way to drop but no choice faced the weasel.

The gate's exterior was smooth. He must jump or stay put, and Kine gave it slight thought, plunging down, limbs outstretched. For an interminable trice, he seemed to hang in the night, then vegetation engulfed him, soft and dewy, fall-breaking. He was sound, nothing broken.

He lay a while, breathing softly. He might be anywhere, Kine thought – a world from Kine's kingdom, from the Moon Pond and Life Tree. The land was still, its form hidden. It seemed a solitary region, full of indistinct shadows, clumps of feathery gloom which might be ferns – or might not be – and outlines of boulders. Or were they cud-chewing sheep? Or perhaps little hillocks?

Kine wished the sky had not clouded. At home, dark nights were no problem; he knew their folds and their smells; they had a depth he found peaceful. Here, the night was unknown and he longed for the starshine, some light on the phantoms.

Edgily, he lay listening. Sounds were changed by the land, the contours they travelled. Here, the music of owls, fluting out of the distance, had a curious strangeness. The noise of gnawing came faintly, some mini-beast feeding. Kine himself was not hungry. The emptiness in a gut deprived of battle with Rattun could not be filled by mere eating. Disgust soured his belly – disgust at his failure.

An aircraft throbbed, passing over. It seemed to rouse the night's wings, for there followed like spectres great squadrons of geese, their creaking pinions uncanny, their space-calling mournful. As their wing-beats vibrated, agitating the gloom, idle clouds stirred and shifted. At last, the vapours grew thin and, abruptly, the moon shone.

It bathed the box in cold brilliance and lit a rock near him. A second weasel sat on it. She said, 'My name is Chuk-Chukra, like the call of the partridge, who is swift. So is Chukra. They call me Chukra the huntress.'

Kine's gaze probed the moonlight. The land was vast in its flatness, now plated with silver. 'Where is this?'

'You're a stranger?'

'Kine,' he rasped, 'of Kine's country, the vale of the Witchwood.'

54

'I never heard of it.'

'*Kine's* realm.'

The other laughed. 'On which planet?'

'*Tchkkk*,' he snarled. 'And where's *this*, then?'

'Why, everybody knows that – the Great Plain,' answered Chukra.

'What great plain?'

She looked puzzled. 'There's only one. Are you teasing?' The female weasel surveyed him. 'You *must* have had a long journey!'

'I did,' he snapped.

'You'll be glad. Just wait,' she purred, 'until morning. There's nowhere finer to be. That's why the partridges live here, great coveys of redlegs. And skylarks in hundreds. Just wait for their dawn-song! Then there are harebells and heather, broom, bedstraw and crow's foot, and the scents when the sun shines: chicory, camomile. And the gorse in golden banks. And the skirling of curlews . . .'

'I've got to find the way,' Kine said.

'Oh, I'll show you the plain, Kine, I'm unattached. We'll go hunting. I'll show you the sights here.'

'Sights!' scorned Kine. 'I'm not *stopping*.' The moon had gone for a moment. He heard the female move closer.

'But you *must* stop,' she told him.

'No, Chukra, I'm leaving – first thing,' he said firmly.

She answered plaintively, 'Why? The Great Plain is a joy and it goes on for ever. It simply stretches and stretches.' Chukra frowned. 'No one leaves it.' She gave a smile. 'There's no reason . . .'

'I'll give you two: Kia and Rattun.' The tone was fierce, charged with passion. 'Good and evil,' Kine told her, 'the good to be honoured.'

'The evil?'

'To slay. Kine is bounden.'

'Kia and Rattun – who *are* they?'

When he explained, Chukra brooded. 'But Kia is dead,' she protested, 'and there are rats *here* for killing.'

'Not the Rat King.'

'Forget him.'

'That's not possible, Chukra. The dance is pledged; I must be there.'

'Oh, well . . .' It was glum. 'But you must rest – all that travelling . . .'

'I didn't trek, the box brought me.'

'The box?' she said, hope returning. 'But then,' she mused, speaking quietly, restraining her pleasure, 'you've no idea where you've been? I mean, you've no scent to follow, no landmarks to guide you. You've crossed worlds in the dark!'

'More or less.'

'Poor lost traveller.' Her eyes were warm. 'You're with Chukra . . .'

7

It was dark by the cottage. The midget wished it was dawn, when the rats would lie low. Now, instead, they came closer, their stench overpowering, and Scrat drew back, quaking.

He could hear muffled grunting. It polluted the gloom, coming on through the orchard with coarse variations, lewd squeals, slobbered mouthings. In ragged column, they shuffled, the mammoth Rattun amidst them, and Scrat glimpsed the sow rat, the big grey-lagged female.

They paused and droned. 'Hail the Sow Queen! The King has chosen,' they chanted. Scrat gulped; she was awesome. He did not care to imagine the broods she would suckle.

In the old cottage orchard, a broken flowerpot lay hidden, entangled in couch-grass. Peeping from it, Scrat watched, peering out round the fruit trees. Bounteous in the past, the trees stood gnarled now and barren, their harvest days over.

Scrat shook, whiskers trembling. Above his head, one starved apple, begotten in dotage, broke free and descended. It landed smack by the flowerpot, just missing the pigmy, who shrieked, his heart leaping.

'What was that?' hissed the Sow Queen. Sitting up on her haunches, she quizzed the tufted grass fiercely.

Once, Poacher's chickens had scratched there. A decrepit coop rotted, strings of bryony on it, their berries still green, yet to turn gold and crimson. The rats had stopped, their tails lumpen. While the shrew stared, eyes bulging, an unwise boar sniffed the Queen and Scrat froze as the Rat King, enraged, broke its windpipe. The choking rat gurgled briefly then dusky minions removed it, sled-dragging the body.

'Hail Rattun,' the rats droned, 'the Sow Queen is sacred! We of the blood defer to Rattun!' They fell quiet and Scrat, straining, caught the gist of hoarse whispers. 'The Queen has chosen her palace, picked the home for her ratlings . . .'

Snout high, she heaved forward. Her shambling gait was assured and the rats followed, grunting. She stopped at last and gazed up, her eyes on the cottage. It looked snug in the starlight, its roof sheltering windows dark save for the nursery, where the babe's nightlight glimmered.

The sow rat glared her envy. The den was warm, dry and peaceful. When she spoke, it was rasping. '*There* shall be the Queen's palace.' Her tail lashed the grasses. 'There shall Rattun's sons suck when the Sow Queen throws litter.'

Scrat could no longer see. The rats had moved through the orchard and the shrew, hesitating, left the flowerpot and bolted. Pellmell, the dwarf fled, making tracks for the covert. The droning followed him faintly. '*Sixtyfold in a year . . .*' He reached the Moon Pond and halted.

'*. . . shall the Sow Queen's brood flourish.*'

'K-i-n-e . . .' wailed Scrat.

The mite faltered. In his fear, he had forgotten – Kine had gone to the Witchwood. There should have been a great battle. 'Doom and woe!' He flopped limply. The tyrant lived, no whit chastened. The shrew's own eyes had borne witness. So what of Kine? Scrat's cheeks moistened. 'No, not Kine! Spare the weasel . . .'

'He spared himself,' a voice answered.

The rook blinked down through dim branches. 'He used his head,' wheezed the Watchman, 'I never thought that I'd see it – Kine come to his senses! He was always a hothead; I knew him back in the Mink Wars. I guess it comes to us all, we live and learn.'

'L-live and learn?'

'Even weasels. He's quit, shrew, like I told him.'

'*Quit?*' gawped Scrat.

'Left the valley.'

'But . . .'

'He's thought better of it.'

'It's not a bad land,' said Kine.

They had hunted and eaten.

Chukra laughed. 'It's the best land.'

'You were born here,' he answered. He watched the dawn rise behind her. It emphasized her sleek lines, lithe and strong, the neck snake-like. She had, indeed, hunted swiftly.

She said, 'We're all free to move. You've said that Wonder moved off.'

'But not *this* far.'

'What's the difference? Kine, you've nothing to lose, only foes.' Her voice pleaded. 'Who needs neighbours like Rattun? Here, there's all to be gained; everything you could want, Kine.'

'That may be,' he admitted.

The day's first sunbeams bedazzled and Kine could smell bracken. He had not flattered her country. The plain brimmed with richness. Amid smooth, mothering downs, nature welcomed the morning, sheep afoot on the barrows. Hares sat up in the sunshine. Shaking dew from their paws, they stretched and cantered at leisure, aware that none could outrace them.

Bitten grass spawned dwarf thistles. Here, butterflies hovered while great bees droned and trundled, and daisies were opening. Already, partridge were stirring, batting up into the wind. With a creaking tantivy, they hurled themselves a few furlongs, gliding down to fresh acres. As they passed an old chalk-pit, drowsy jackdaws erupted, tumbling over in space as if being juggled.

Here and there, a stream glittered. In cool, secretive curves, it would twist among kingcups, lissom as a trout, skimmed by gnat-snapping swallows. It was, Kine pondered, an idyll. What more could you ask for?

'What more could you want, Kine?'

'But what I *want* isn't important; what must be done is important.' He contemplated the female. 'You understand, don't you, Chukra? You belong to the plain; my home is the valley. I belong with its spirits, with Kia and my forebears, the ghosts of the Moon Pond, the souls of the marsh winds.'

'I understand,' Chukra answered. 'But, Kine, the future's important; not just remembrance – renewal.' He looked away, and she added, 'New generations are needed; without a future, the past dies. You need a mate, Kine, a *live* one.' So Wonder had told him! 'Swift and strong,' urged the huntress. 'Not to take the past from you but to share it, complete it.'

'When Rattun's gone.'

'Time won't wait. You've been alone for too long. And so have I,' she said frankly.

He raised his head. Dogs were barking. 'From the farm,' Chukra murmured. He watched them speed on the downs, wheeling out round the sheep, which they gathered for counting. He thought how Chukra had hunted, like a flame as she darted, and said at last, 'We're well matched. I'd like to stay but . . .'

She nodded.

He said, 'Some other time, maybe . . .'

'Kine, which way are you going?'

'Back down the tracks of the horsebox.'

'You won't get far,' she informed him. 'They peter out at the crossways.' Her smile was wry. 'My poor traveller.'

'*Tchkkk*!' Kine turned on her, snarling. 'That makes you happy!'

'Not happy. If you must stay, then I'm pleased. But sad, too, you don't want to. There's no chance you'll get home.'

'I'll find the way!'

'Kine, it's hopeless.'

'Nothing's hopeless,' he grated.

He racked his brains while she foraged. Above, the skylarks were deafening. A blackbird crowed on a wall and Kine hankered for silence. The dry-stone farm wall was crumbling. Its ancient rocks told him nothing. If they knew any paths then no oracle echoed, they imparted no guidance.

'I've *got* to leave,' he insisted. 'I *must* return to the valley.' What good was talking to stones?

He raised his eyes. The larks hovered. 'Kine the homeless,' they taunted. But they would see; he would show them!

'Kine lackland,' they warbled. 'Doomed to exile,' they carolled.

He clenched his teeth. They were wrong: Kine was bold and resourceful. He looked for Chukra's return – he had expected her sooner. A pebble rolled and he listened. There was a change of refrain, a troubled note from the larks while the blackbird gave warning, the high-pitched *Si*-call of danger.

The weasel crouched, senses straining. His view was blocked by the stones but something large was approaching, prowling down by the wall, and he remembered the sheep-dogs. It was worse: quieter, quicker. A pungent scent filled his throat and two ears rose like knives.

The cat was lean, a grey wraith, its rough farmyard coat matted. Claws unsheathed, it descended and Kine, caught as he turned, felt the blow on his backbone. Smashed down, he lay gasping. A crushing weight held him pinned, both the beast's forepaws on him. He thought his body must break and screamed mutely, maw gaping.

His assailant's head tilted. The cat had been hunting rabbits. Head cocked, it peered closer, inspecting the victim, its air slightly puzzled. Kine could feel its breath on him. The wall was slowly diffusing, turning red as his eyes bulged. He tried to focus his vision but loose stones kept revolving, swimming off into orbit. His sight was misting.

Kine gritted. A blurred shape spun towards him and became the she-weasel, eyes ablaze, dancing closer. '*Tchkkk*!' she hissed, 'I am Chukra! Lift your paws, farm cat, catch me!' Confused, the cat watched her. 'When you can move, Kine, the wall - there's a hole in the stonework.' She pranced away. 'Catch me, farm cat!'

The cat flexed then resisted. It seemed about to give chase but, instead, eyed its captive and dropped a grey muzzle. Beneath the nose, white fangs glistened.

Chukra flew like a dart.

Homing under an ear, she struck the startled cat headlong and leeched to the target. '*Eeeough*!' The cat panicked. Though scarcely harmed, it was stung and swung round, Chukra with it. Kine lay still, the weight off him. He could see the hole in the wall but was unsure of his legs. He tried to rise; they responded.

'Run!' he called, springing up.

The cat and Chukra were one, the female weasel tenacious. 'Let go, Chukra, I'm fit – I'll take the cat! *Now*! The wall hole . . .' He grabbed the beast's tail and tugged. The feline high-jumped. 'I'm with you!'

Hotfoot, the small creatures bolted, bounding into the stonework, worming deep in the wall where its substance had loosened. Kine flopped down, his lungs heaving. The cat was clawing the hole but the refuge was safe and Chukra gasped, 'It can't reach us.'

'You never mentioned a *cat*.' Kine caught his breath in quick spasms. 'The best of lands!'

'Nowhere's perfect.'

The scratching stopped and they laughed. It made Kine wince and he swore.

'Kine, you're hurt!'

'It's not much.'

'You're back's injured.'

'I've many lives . . .' He stopped short. It was no time to boast; he would have died without Chukra. Now, her tongue cleaned his wounds, and he said, 'You're a spitfire, a brave dancer, Chukra.'

'Just keep still.'

'You're like Kia . . .'

'And be quiet,' she mouthed roughly. 'You may be stiff, so be careful. No more risks.'

He moved slightly. The back was sore and he grunted. 'I'll soon get rid of the stiffness. I've got a long trek ahead.'

'You'd better rest.'

'Kine is hardy.'

'*Foolhardy*,' she snorted. It was a dream, this mad journey – he had no bearings, no clues, not the faintest direction. 'First, you rest,' she commanded. 'After that, you're alone.'

He sat up. 'What's *that*, Chukra?'

She heard the birds. They were corvids. 'It's jackdaws.'

'It's rooks . . .' Kine crept back to the opening. Cautiously, he stared out. The cat had gone and the skywall, bright and clear, was black-dotted. The distant sound of rooks rattled. In twos and threes, they came nearer, winged above then grew smaller. A sprightly pair rolled and tumbled, acrobatically sporting. 'They're changing feeding-grounds,' Kine said. 'They'll shift their roosts towards autumn. If only Watchman was with them!'

'Who's Watchman?'

'A neighbour.' Kine sighed. An old moaner – a batty, sour-faced old fowl. Oh, to see Watchman's grimace; to hear his gravel-voiced insults!

8

The engineer dodged the pot-holes, driving up past the covert. Rabbits slouched from his path, idly timing their hops with an indifference, he thought, they would not have shown Poacher. Poacher had been like a stoat, he had lived off the rabbits. A tractor blocked the van's progress.

'Just the man I've been wanting.' The engineer jumped out, waving. 'Here,' he said, 'let me help.'

'Working late?' muttered Ploughman. He was unhitching a power-tool. 'Trouble down at the pump?'

'Nothing much; soon put right. There'll be trouble at home, though!'

Ploughman leered. 'Treat her firm, son.'

'*You* never treated her firm. She ran wild.'

'Can't remember.' The sun had gone, the sky fiery. 'Lift that pin,' grunted Ploughman. He heaved the bar and released it. 'Got no memory nowadays. Getting old. What's your problem?'

'The rats.'

'Ah . . .' said Ploughman. 'She brought the child down and warned me. Funny thing,' he reflected, 'I'd seen no rats round all summer, not until the girl told me. She'd scarcely gone when they called and made off with the ducklings.'

'We tried the bait. It's not working.'

The older man lit his pipe. 'You must have rats with iron bellies!'

'They're super-rats.'

Ploughman squinted. 'Are they now?' he said slyly.

'Didn't Poacher speak of them?'

'Poacher, son? What did *he* know? Rats is rats to my knowledge. When I was young, we stepped through them, you'd hardly move for the beggars. Every farm was infested. That stuff you got . . .' He puffed pipe-smoke. '. . . that was what knocked them backwards. When that came out, we controlled them. It makes them bleed inside, that does.'

'Not *these* rats.'

'*Bah*,' growled Ploughman. He viewed the other askance. The engineer was all right, he thought the world of the girl, but he was green as the grass when it came to the country.

'What I wanted to ask,' the van-driver declared, 'was, could you spare your gun sometime?'

'The two-two?'

'If it's handy.'

Ploughman grinned. 'Aye, it's handy – that's if you are,' he chuckled. 'But that's a deadshot sport, mister, shooting rats with a rifle.'

'They're big enough; big as monsters!'

'Guns won't rid you of rats, son.'

The countryman shook his head. 'You'll maybe shoot one or two; the rest will carry on breeding. You'll not keep pace. Guns are useless, you've got to clear out the strongholds.'

'I've seen them round the barn lately.'

'I'll get the youths up one evening. We'll get some dogs and go at them. We'll have a bit of a rat hunt.' Ploughman climbed on the tractor.

The younger man said, 'Tomorrow?'

'Not tomorrow, it's Club Night. I go to the village.'

'Ah, well . . .'

'Next week, maybe.' The tractor roared. 'Aye, next week, son.'

Great tyres bit the verge and a mini-beast scuttled, avalanched by their back-spit. 'Doom!' squeaked Scrat, disappearing. A hidden grasshopper shrilled. To its stridulant music, an adder swayed in the wood, gulping down a plump mouse, the snake's jaws working round it. First one gripped, then the other. In turns, the loose jaw slid forward.

Scrat paused, fascinated.

At length, the snake observed smugly, 'Pity Kine's quit the valley.' She eased the swallowed mouse down with spasmodic rib movements. 'We had some unfinished business.'

65

'He didn't quit, Kine's no quitter!' Scrat was riled. 'Flit-cat told me.'

The adder sneered. 'Flit-cat told you!' She watched Scrat run. 'Kine's cried off. If he came back, I would kill him. It's *me* he's scared of, not Rattun!'

'He's scared of no one,' Scrat bleated. He careered round the pond. At the Life Tree, he stopped, drew a breath then ascended. Spires of bugloss flowered round him, vivid blue in the evening. He climbed above them, claws scrabbling, and reached the deck, peering down it. Masts towered dimly ahead. Three blurred shapes sat on branches.

'You're late,' groused the Watchman.

Scrat saw Flit-cat and Farthing.

'Now you're here,' said the rook. 'let's get on with the meeting.'

'Kine never quit!' the shrew gabbled.

'We all know *that*,' said the sparrows. 'We've explained it to Watchman.'

'I put him right,' declared Farthing.

'*I* put him right,' Flit corrected. He puffed himself, grey cap bristling. Farthing's black gorget pouted.

Watchman said, 'It was nonsense, I always knew it was nonsense – a weasel come to his senses! Where's the sense in a weasel?' One crabbed eye closed. 'Let's get on . . .'

'Kine's gone missing,' said Farthing. 'We're here because he's gone missing.'

'We're doomed,' wailed Scrat.

'Out of order!' Watchman glanced at the tree-tops. Glossy rooks idly flirted, making free with loose gestures. Things were not what they were. Once, debate would have drawn them. He had not spent *his* youth idling! 'If we're doomed,' he demanded, 'what's the point of a meeting?'

'What I mean . . .' the dwarf stammered.

'What he means,' sang the sparrows, 'is we've got to find Kine.'

'Then he should say so,' the rook said. 'In any case,' he complained, 'the point has not been established. Who says we need weasels?'

'Kine's a rat fighter,' Flit said.

'He's a *braggart*,' the rook drawled.

'He's our champion, Watchman! Name another contender. The weasel's small but he's fast, and he'll fight for the valley. He gives his all and keeps moving. We're for Kine in a dust-up.'

'He's a hero!' piped Scrat. 'Kine's a hero, a hero . . .'

'Silence, dwarf.' The rook scowled. 'Let's have order, it's late.'

He eyed the night-perches grimly. The goings-on there were shameless. He felt an urge to harangue, assert some old-fashioned standards. But who would take any notice? He was only the Watchman; to the rooks, an old dotard. He felt like showing them something – that there was still fire within him. He felt like making a venture.

'So you're proposing to find him?'

'With your help, rook,' Flit told him. 'You know the lands of beyond; you've the range to search quickly.'

'For instance, where?'

Flit-cat pondered. 'We thought we'd leave that to you. Beyond the range of a sparrow. We'll take the edge of the valley, search the hills and the ridges.'

Watchman sniffed. 'Where the hawks lurk!'

'*Pah*,' said Flit. 'What's a tussle? We'll search east first, then west.'

'We'll search north first,' said Farthing.

'East . . .'

'North!'

'Fight you for it . . .' They flew together, wings whirring, scrimmaging on the pier, flecks of down flying from them. Scrat moaned. 'Mind the water!' For several moments, they brawled then broke apart, smirking proudly. A rasping laugh shook the pond and a heron rose from it.

'Order!' Watchman reproved. 'I shan't proceed without order.' He quizzed the sparrows morosely. 'Who was the last to see Kine?'

'That was Bufo,' said Flit-cat.

'And did you question the toad?'

'She said he left in the box.'

'Did you ask where it went?'

The sparrows glanced at each other. 'Why should Bufo know that?'

'She might not,' allowed Watchman. 'But then, she might. No one's asked her. You didn't *think*. You've no brains!'

'She wasn't keen on us,' Flit said. He looked at Scrat. 'She liked *him* . . .'

'No,' sobbed Scrat.

'Yes,' said Farthing. 'She'd tell the shrew. The dwarf pleased her.'

Watchman stretched his wings slowly. 'Then I'm adjourning the meeting. You've not explored Bufo's knowledge. There's not enough information. When you've been back to her, tell me.'

'And you'll help?' asked the sparrows. They held their breath, their beaks open.

'The meeting's closed,' the rook answered.

There was fog in the morning. Dressing the baby, the girl said, 'See, it's all grey and cloudy and the garden has vanished.' She put the child into rompers. 'The valley's gone! Look, it's magic!' The fog itself would soon go, for the sun would dispel it.

Meanwhile, in the garden – in this nebulous garden – she let her son savour mystery. 'See, there's nothing around us; there's only you and me, Dream Child.' And a sun like the moon, a strange, circumscribed light she recalled from *her* childhood, the fog's inner spirit.

More than mist, she reflected, more even than night, the fog conjured alonenes, pleased the secretive in her. Unlike mist, which was ethereal, fog had substance, a body. You could smell it and taste it; you could feel it embrace you.

'See the cottage?' the girl said. 'Now it's there, now it isn't! Did you spot the two sparrows? Do you think they can see us?' The baby beamed. She said, 'Spa-rrow,' as if for someone lip-reading. 'Go on, you can say it.'

He eyed her thoughtfully.

'Wo-wo!'

'Good boy,' she said. '*Spa*-rrow.'

The girl had buried the dead one. Its small grave by the

sapling was not more than a cat-scrape. The willow leaves would fall on it. Odd to think, in the fog, that the cornfields were ripening, that soon the combines would trundle. Then, autumn's blaze, frosts approaching! The vapour thinned by the hedge and something stared in the greyness.

Her son chortled. 'Ga-wo-wo!'

'No, darling . . .'

She gripped him. The beast stood still, its eye beady. Very slowly, she stooped, one hand reaching a stone, which she clasped. The rat watched her. It seemed part of the fog, a huge deep-bellied sow, its nose high, gaze disdainful. The sight both chilled and incensed. The sheer arrogance maddened, as if the brute owned the garden, and her hand came up quickly.

'Get out,' she hissed, 'don't come *near* us! Stay away from our cottage!' She flung the stone with an oath and it rattled on thorn wood.

By now, the fog had swirled back. There was the swish of a tail as the creature dissolved, first a wraith then expunged, and the baby looked puzzled.

'Great brute!' The girl shuddered.

'Glub,' the child said. 'Ga-wo-wo!'

Her tension eased. 'Yes, love, sparrows – look, there they go, can you see them? Flying off in the fog. Where d'you think they'll be going? Perhaps to look for your dad.' She heard the thrum of the marsh pump. 'He won't have gone far today. He can't go far in this, can he?'

Farthing-feather passed near them. He took such neighbours for granted, scarcely sparing a glance before thrusting up steeply. Now, the girl's voice came faintly. '. . . time we got you a drink . . .' Then he had climbed through the fog and, bursting out of its gables, was blinded by sunshine.

Above, the sky was clear blue, while all round, like snow mountains, the vapour's roof glistened. He saw Flit-cat pop up. Levelling out, they drew close. For a while, they winged quietly, navigating by woods whose massed crowns broke the fog bank.

'We could miss him in that lot.'

'*I'll* not miss him,' chirped Farthing.

'If you'll not miss him, then *I* won't!'

The brilliance was stunning. Beneath them, white as swan fathers, sun-bleached fog capped the valley, its fluffy plumes gilded. Even the horns of the Witchwood, now ahead, were transmuted, standing out like gold chaplets.

'Always assuming he's there, Flit!'

'If he's not, it's just us. We'll have to chance our luck, Farthing.'

'The midget's better at wheedling.'

'I'd sooner tussle than wheedle!'

'He said he'd meet us. I trust him.'

'There's the rendezvous,' Flit said. He air-braked and dropped, plunging back into vapour. Again, greyness enclosed him and he twittered a call-note, touching down near the elm, as agreed with the pigmy. The elm was dead. It towered dimly.

'That you, Flit?' Scrat crept forward.

Farthing landed beside them.

'It's eerie,' Scrat said. 'I'm frightened. I can't see the toad hole.'

'Just keep calm.' The birds fluttered. 'We're here, we'll protect you.'

'I smell rats. I'm afraid.'

'*We're* not scared.'

'You can fly!'

'Oh, come now,' exclaimed Farthing, 'you've got the fog to conceal you. Who'd spot a shrew in the fog?'

'All you've got to do,' Flit said, 'is make up to her, Scrat, use your sweet tongue on Bufo. We want to know where the box went.'

'Doom and woe . . .'

'We're right with you.'

'Right *behind* you!' said Farthing.

'I can't see her . . .'

'Keep moving.' They watched the shrew probe the gloom. 'A few more steps, Scrat, keep going.'

'I can't see *you*!'

'Eyes front, pigmy.'

They heard his tremulous whimper. 'Yes, there's *something* . . .'

'What is it?'

'A head,' croaked Scrat.

'Rough and warty, orbs staring? That's Bufo! Remember, dwarf, keep her happy!'

'*Aeeee!*'

The birds listened. Scrat's wail pierced the fog bank. A moment later, he followed, racing back to the elm, charging on without stopping. 'Wait!' the sparrows squawked, chasing. 'Steady, Scrat, what's upset you?'

He paused, the pinhead eyes popping.

'Her head!' he croaked.

'Yes, you told us.'

'That's it . . .' He was quaking. 'A staring head,' the shrew spluttered. 'A warty head!' He stood snivelling. 'The rest,' he heaved, 'was n-nothing . . . f-flattened . . . t-trampled.' He gulped and said in a whisper, 'We're too late – Rattun found her.'

Part Two

THE LANDS OF PERIL

9

Kine left while Chukra was sleeping and took the track to the crossroads. In case she stirred, he went quickly, reluctant to face her. He would miss the swift Chukra. The wrench of parting was hard – best, he thought, not prolonged – and he made his way sadly.

Four lanes faced the weasel. Each lane lay in the sun and, for Kine, was a mystery. He chose the verge with the mallow, a splurge of palest mauve bloom, because the flower grew at home. The path led to the downs and the grass became springy.

Everywhere, sheep were grazing, great gloomy-eyed beasts. Had they heard of the valley? They looked bemused, the dull creatures - gummy, grass-nibbling brutes without a top-tooth between them! All they did was bite turf, taking dirt with the herbage, and chew. It was endless.

Kine could learn nothing from them, and yet he met none but sheep - bleak old ewes, staring, chewing. They flanked his path, dotted barrows, followed tails down the skyline. Once, he glimpsed a hawk wheeling and sensed his trail being dogged, being silently followed.

Anxiousiy, he lay low, hiding out in a covert, a little wood on the slope, where he found a quiet clearing. It was calm and sun-dappled. Yet, here and there, twigs were missing, the wounds on thicket still white, and he kept a sharp lookout. Something large had been browsing.

At length, the sound of steps reached him. Magnified by dead leaves, the noise came closer and stopped. Again, he heard it, *pat-pat*, and a fawn appeared, trotting. It came on full of verve, dark-eyed and light-footed, put its head down and froze. Might it know of the valley? As if it *could*, Kine supposed; it was too young to have travelled.

He felt the spray as it snorted. Then, with a leap like a frog's, the fawn was gone, bounding off, while a newcomer entered. This time, the scrub trembled. A towering beast thrust it back and, as Kine quit the glade, the fallow deer stamped a foot, looking round for her offspring.

Other sounds could be heard, perhaps more deer, and Kine hastened. He still sensed something behind him. Maybe the tension was telling, his natural fear of strange country – safety lay in the familiar. Standing tall, Kine cast back, neck outstretched, his eyes hostile.

All he saw were more sheep, their heads down, jaws in motion. Their chomping comment was scornful. 'A senseless odyssey, Kine; the plain and downlands are peerless. Why leave the she-weasel?'

'Because . . .'

But why waste breath on them? He was pledged and must search. It was his fate to seek Rattun, to dance with the Rat King. He only asked the way forward, some guide to direction.

Gnarled yews shared the hill, centuries old, like black shadows. Their ancient gloom made him shudder. He missed Chuk-Chukra the spitfire. Bold Chukra! Now the sheep were in motion, drifting uphill and past him. They filed from view on the brow and he pondered its secrets.

Cautiously, he advanced. In fact, the crest was a false one, giving on to a shelf, somewhat hollowed ahead and containing a dew pond. The flock was watering round it. Parched and weary, he joined them, refreshed by the moisture.

The pool was clear, free of weed. Small clouds scuttled on it, pale and fluffy reflections. Water-skaters were skimming; shiny beetles gyrated. It made him think of the Moon Pond.

'Kine!' The warning was urgent.

He glimpsed mirrored wings flashing and hurled himself to one side as the goshawk shot past, its claws spread, barred tail raking. Then, beating on, the bird vanished.

'It's a dangerous world, Kine!' He turned and Chukra was laughing. She said, 'You're easy to follow, your scent's quite distinctive.'

He shook his head.

'*Pleased?*' she asked him.

'But, why . . .'

'I've just told you – the world, Kine, it's dangerous. We'll be safer together.'

'But your home?'

'There are others.'

'As good?'

'I don't know. I've heard about this fine valley.' Her cackle teased. 'Let's look, shall we? Come on,' she urged, 'don't stand gawping. While you gawp, we'll get nowhere!'

They hunted that evening, moving on as the night fell. In the last gleam of day, the air was still, the downs hushed. Strange whisperings drifted. At first far off, they came nearer, a hissing blather which grew until, from over the hills, a cloud of starlings erupted, then more, the sky dotted.

Already looking to autumn, the clannish birds congregated, jabbering along powerlines, in the trees they infested. One tribe dipped to the dew pond, strutting close to its edges. Then again, they were up, a great tornado of wings calling all to its vortex. In unison, the host wheeled, stragglers swirling like dust motes.

Twice, it circled the deer wood. The final run-in was awesome. As one, the birds dipped their wings, plummeting as if shot, and fell into the bushes. Now every leaf seemed to shake as the roosting mob screeched, scuffling, jostling for perches before, as suddenly, quietening. The thousands were sleeping.

'Sheep and starlings!' Kine grumbled.

'You don't like crowds?'

'I distrust them. The ways of Kine are the lone ways.'

'Not *now*,' Chukra told him.

Her comrade frowned. 'This is different.'

'I'm glad,' she purred. Stars were twinkling. Chukra's dark orbs outshone them. 'I don't count two as a crowd, Kine.'

They crossed the brow and descended, the dew on their bellies. Distantly, headlights glared and the sound of trucks rumbled. A hoarse-voiced ewe called her neighbours. Closer, badgers were scraping, munching grubs, roots and earthworms. They looked up in the gloom, short ears cocked, blinking vaguely, bumbling shapes on the downs like small silky-haired bears; strange, preoccupied creatures, scarcely heeding their own as the striped faces rummaged.

Kine nosed the air quickly. There was the trace of a movement, a gentle southerly flow with a hint of salt on it. 'Smell that, it's good, Chukra!'

'A breeze?'

'The tang,' Kine said.

'From the south, it's quite usual.'

'I've smelled that tang in the vale.' He hurried on, undiscouraged. 'We're on the track; hurry, Chukra!'

'Wait – just look where you're going.'

He eyed the murk. It was boundless, but where the slope lifted from it an object leaped and subsided, glimmering in the greyness. It made sense to be cautious.

'What is it, Kine?'

'I can't see.' It leapt again, phosphorescent. 'Stay here, Chukra, I'll scout.'

He advanced. 'Kine, be careful.' A patter came from the grasses. There was a sound like a laugh, a teasing, chortling ring, and something cold struck the weasel. He shook the spume from his whiskers. 'Come here, Chukra, and see – it's a spring! Bubbling water. Look, it's flowing downhill . . .'

'Well, it's harmless.'

'It's *splendid*!'

'Wet.' She smiled.

'Much more, Chukra – a sign, a bright blessing!' Kine danced, flicking moisture. 'It's a guide,' he sang blithely. 'We've found a guide to the valley!'

'What makes you think so?'

'Here, listen . . .' The little spring slopped and gurgled. A lively rill tumbled from it. 'Don't you see, water *grows* – water grows as it travels.' Kine was thrilled. 'This will swell; it's the start of a stream. I know the stream, for I've seen it. Broad and deep! I've *swum* in it. I tell you, Chukra, I know it – it runs through the valley!'

'But Kine . . .'

'This will lead us!'

'Kine, there's more than *one* river.'

'*Bah,*' he said.

'There are many – three, at least, on the plain.'

'This is *ours*. Have faith, Chukra!'

He danced away in the dark down the course of the streamlet. It swirled and pulsed, mesmerizing. Puppy-like, the rill gambolled, swilling carelessly on. Now, it squeezed through small gulleys, waffling its impatience, or tumbled headlong down boulders. Here, it paused, spreading outwards, investigating flat patches. Then, the slope growing steep, off it rushed with a whirl, gliding, chattering, snuffling.

At its side, chased the weasels.

Where it rippled on stones, or sheeted smoothly down falls, it gained a luminous aura. Each glowing sluice led them on, beckoning in the starlight. From the shadows, it tinkled, its thin voice a pilot. Kine raced with it, elated. 'Come on, Chukra, this way!' He leaped and splashed, glancing back.

'Keep your head,' thought the female. He was impulsive, too reckless.

Three young foxes were sporting. She glimpsed them dimly and swerved, praying Kine would avoid them. They romped in rings, playing tag, a game of dangerous quirks when smaller beasts were enlisted. She was relieved to get past and hear Kine, his voice sanguine. 'We'll soon be off the hill, Chukra!'

'Then?'

'Follow the water.' The brook oozed, the ground flatter. Grass squelched. 'To the valley! All the way, you'll see, Chukra!'

He picked his feet up. They were paddling, the thrust gone from the rill, then the current gained motion. 'Over here – come on, Chukra!' The land had dipped, the stream quickening, funnelled back into rapids. Kine charged on by the torrent. A large, flat stone formed a tunnel. He stood on top, drawing breath, and watched the water purl under, its noises engrossing.

'Hear that, Chukra?' he churred. She joined the male on the sarsen. 'Hear it calling the vale? See its haste to arrive there!'

'I see its haste,' she acknowledged. It pounded into the tunnel. 'What I don't see,' she continued, 'is any water *emerging*!'

'Of course it is . . .'

'Where?' she queried.

Kine crossed the stone and looked down. The grass below was quite dry, not a trickle apparent. He cocked an ear and heard gurgling - it seemed far off, subterranean. He hung his head. 'It's gone, Chukra.'

'Underground.'

The male nodded. 'So that's that,' he said quietly. Turning back to the streamlet, he watched it pour into darkness. The sump beneath the stone echoed. Chukra shrugged. 'Kine, it's nothing.'

'I had high hopes.'

She smiled wrily. 'We've barely started,' she told him.

'Maybe it wasn't *our* river.'

'Who knows?' said the female. 'Besides, it's not gone forever, it's got to bubble up somewhere. It may reappear later.'

What reappeared at that moment were the foxes, tails streaming. One had captured a mole and, with this in its mouth, was being chased by the others, heading straight for the weasels. The smaller beasts bolted wildly. As they ran for their lives, a moon appeared, the hill silvered.

'Look, a hut – get in, Chukra!'

Diving under the door, they rolled in hay, pursuit thwarted. The shepherd's bothy was dry, aromatic with fodder. Kine looked up. 'You were saying?'

'Was I, Kine?' Chukra panted.

'That we've only just started . . .'

'That's true.'

'Shall we march, then?'

They trekked a long way by moonlight. The ground was flat now, broad farmlands, with occasional buildings. On sighing wings, plovers ghosted, their plaintive cries skirling.

There was no shortage of food, for small rodents abounded. Where the harvest had started, fieldmice feasted in stubble, sleekly plump on the gleanings. A combine stood by a gate, a tarpaulin roped on it.

A man and dog, out last thing, passed the gate at an amble. 'Hey, come here,' the man growled. The weasels crouched by the combine, a huge flotation-tyre near them. The tousled dog had their scent. They could see it approaching, loath to answer the call, then the voice beckoned louder. '*Here*, by God!' The dog scurried.

There was a whiff of tobacco, redolent of the dead Poacher, and Kine recalled his old foeman, the reek of his ferrets. 'Kine, you're dreaming,' said Chukra. 'Kine the rat-killer *dreaming*! They've gone, shall we travel?'

'No, don't move!'

Chukra flattened.

'The gate-post,' Kine whispered.

It towered darkly, moon-haloed, like a carved wooden totem. But the owl was no sculpture. Motionless on the post, it sat with claws clamped to oak, cast in black on the starscape. 'All right, Chukra, he's feasted.' Kine moved forward. 'He's snoozing.'

They took the verge by the lane. Chukra said, 'You *were* dreaming.'

'Of the past.'

'Oh . . .' Her teeth snapped.

'An old foe.'

Chukra brightened. 'The Rat King?'

'Poacher. He's dead,' said Kine, 'I outlived him. I am Kine the survivor.' But it was glum, lacking spirit. 'For what that's worth,' he reflected. A lot of good it was *here*, scratching round without guidance!

'You've work to do,' Chukra spurred him. 'Think of Rattun.'

'I'm thinking!' So fiercely, Kine scented rat. He raised his nose. 'Can *you* smell it?'

'Yes,' the female said. 'Listen.'

There was a sound in the ditch and a scrawny rat left it, scurrying from the weasels. Kine gave chase, heading

Chukra. 'It's a poor one,' he rasped, 'but we might as well have him.'

'Let him go, Kine – the lights!'

The rat had reached the lane's end. It plunged on to the highway. Headlamps flared. 'Wait!' screamed Chukra. Her voice was drowned by the roar as traffic raced from the gloom and, in the mêlée of lights, in the lurch of crazed shadows, she saw the male weasel pause then follow the quarry.

A moment's darkness ensued. Chukra flinched at fresh danger. A single lamp pounced and passed, the motorbike blasting. In the void it bequeathed, something jerked on the road and she ran to it, trembling. Its final movements were reflex. It was squashed on the tarmac.

Tchkkk . . .' The distant verge rustled. 'Come across,' Kine called tersely. 'Leave the rat, come to safety.'

'You fool!' Chukra joined him.

'One less rat . . .'

'*Fool*!' She quivered. 'It could as well have been you. I would've left home for nothing! Why d'you think I came with you - to drag your corpse off a road?'

Her eyes flashed. Kine admired her.

She said, 'Be *careful* in future.'

'Chukra, Kine's a survivor.'

'So you never stop saying. Once more, and I'll kill you!'

He laughed and marched with fresh spirit. They might be lost but she cheered him; the night was fine, the moon gracious. They stopped, at length, among trees, where a reservoir shimmered. Mallard glided to water. It frothed as they landed. Kine heard curlew and whimbrel. Somewhere near, ducks were lapping, bills busy in mire, and the weasels sought shelter.

They found an old hollow stump. Chukra gazed at the moonlight. 'I think we're still on the plain, Kine.' They heard the *whee-yo* of widgeon.

'We'll see tomorrow.'

A coot screeched.

'At least we're safe for the moment.'

'Perhaps,' said Kine.

There was silence.

10

Scrat awoke near the Life Tree. He rubbed his eyes and
sat listening. Something odd must be happening, thought
the shrew, feeling nervous, for rooks were still in the oaks
and the sun was appearing. By now, the birds should have
gone, quit their roosts to find food and not be milling above
with caws of impatience.

Things of that sort were scaring. It was a rule of the vale
– 'Woe!' breathed Scrat as he pondered – that the habitual
was sound, deviation suspicious. Life was governed by habit,
conservative instincts. Many beasts held to 'runs', loath to
tread in new places; others kept rigid hours, turning up on
time daily.

You could set a clock by them: the Vixen's prowl between
coverts; the barn owl's evening appearance; the foppish strut
of the pheasant, perambulating his colours. First light every
morning, the rooks departed to forage – every morning save
this, thought the shrew, his eyes rolling.

High above, wings were flapping, harsh croaks being
bandied. He heard a mutter – the Watchman. The grizzled
rook had not moved, still enthroned on his night perch. A
short way off, others glared, eyeing him down their beaks.
At length, one was urged forward, a bird of sleek self-
importance.

'Look here,' drawled the spokesman, 'you're late, late on
duty.'

'He's late,' the rooks chorused.

'Indeed,' the spokesman said tartly, 'too bad of you,
Watchman.'

'He's kept us waiting,' rooks chanted.

'Is he ill?'

'The bird's old.'

'Say we're hungry. Bestir him.'

Watchman scowled, his eye evil.

The spokesman said, 'Yes, we're hungry. It's most irregular, this.'

'Like old times,' sneered the veteran. 'You're too young to remember. I was *someone* in those days.'

'We really must have a look-out.'

'A look-out's no one,' mused Watchman, 'until he's missed, then he's someone.' He gave the other a leer. 'I'm quite important this morning!'

'It's high time you kept watch.'

'They think that's all I'm good for!'

'You're putting everyone out. I've no idea what you're up to.'

'Of course you haven't,' rasped Watchman. 'You've no ideas beyond breakfast – eating, swaggering, preening. You'll know better at my age.' His glint was malicious. 'I'll tell you *just* what I'm up to – you and that lot – I'm quitting. I'm flying off to beyond, to explore new horizons. You'd better find a new Watchman.'

The rooks were still. 'The bird's senile!'

'I'm off to look for a weasel, a brash, cocksure weasel; to lend my knowledge to riff-raff, common gutter-bred sparrows.'

'He's mad!' Feathers ruffled.

'At least *they* recognize wisdom.' Watchman's glare raked the commune. 'They know a sage when they see one. When I get back, I'll hold court, proclaim deeds, revelations. I hope you're there,' he wheezed drily, 'you're in need of uplifting.'

'He can't *go* . . .'

'He's our Watchman!'

Outraged rooks flapped and bugled.

'He's old!'

'In his dotage!'

A squeaky cheer drifted upwards. 'Bless you, Watchman,' shrilled Scrat. Watchman's rheumy eyes gleamed. 'The Watchman's going to find Kine, he's a saviour!' Scrat warbled. The ancient bird took off stiffly. 'Safe flight, Watchman, safe landing!'

'The senile fool,' rooks were blurting.

He disappeared very slowly, wings creaking like hinges.

As he shrank to a speck, a hush fell on the wood, several rooks glancing down, their darts piercing the pigmy. Scrat cringed, glee departing. Two or three birds came lower, fluttering through the boughs, and he ran with a squeal, diving into the thicket.

For a while, he lay low, a fallen branch giving shelter. The limb was rotten with age, its bark peeling in strips which curled as they mouldered. Something round-backed and grey left the bark, feelers twirling. Scrat grabbed the land-slater. His mini-cusps were at work, cracking through the grey shell, when another bug stirred and a whole platoon followed, groping out of the bark, plump terrestrial crustaceans of gourmand proportions.

The pigmy ate until he groaned.

Doom and woe, greed was punished! He squirmed, his gut aching. Shapes slipped by, long tails swishing. Monster shapes! The rats huddled. 'The barn,' rasped one. 'Don't go near. Tell Lord Rattun.'

They were four at the barn hunt. Ploughman brought the two lads and the engineer joined them. The youths had ferrets and dogs – a pair of small, eager terriers – and there were spades, forks and cudgels. The barn was fusty and dark. A smell of rats filled the building.

Between its great gloomy bays, the threshing floors had caved in and the ground was rat-tunnelled. Old sleeper-joists bridged the mines; a large food-bin lay rusting. At first, the ferrets were entered. When these returned soiled and bitten, the thin lad retrieved them.

Ploughman frowned. 'Rats?' he muttered. 'More like wolves! Fetch the spades. Put those ferrets away, son, we don't want them damaged.'

The men hacked at the floor where the dogs marked their quarry. Soon, the rodents were running, some killed, some escaping. Ploughman eyed the girl's husband. 'You were right, these are *big*!' Several made for the corners, climbing up the wood frame, disappearing in gloom or through cracked daub and wattle.

'We've seen bigger ones, mister.' The youths exchanged glances. 'You should go to the Witchwood, there's an army dug in it. You should see them there – monstrous!'

The tractor driver said, 'Witchwood? You've no rights to have been there.'

'Aye, well . . .'

'You'd no business.'

'We seen them on the march, mister – night you lost them ol' ducklings!'

Ploughman sniffed. 'Damn the Witchwood; no affair of ours, that's not. They can stay in the Witchwood. This is different, the barn.' He yanked the bin and rats scuttled. Dogs snapped. There was mayhem. 'To have 'em this close is bad. Next thing, it's the dwellings, you're under siege. *There's one* – stop him!'

The engineer swung his spade. He saw the blood from the rat, as bright and red as his own. It died belly-side up, the pale underpart broad. Others lay as if running, flung down by the dogs, or with trailing intestines. It was, he thought, gruesome work, but they had to be halted. The countryman was quite right. They would not stop at the barn; and the girl loathed the creatures.

'There's another . . .'

They missed it. It led the dogs from the barn – a scarred brute with one ear – and gained the field where the corn stood. 'They're onto him,' grunted Ploughman. 'They'll find him out in that wheat, for it's powerful is rat scent; it fairly beckons, a rat's line.'

There were at least twenty corpses. Another batch joined the pile as a large sleeper was moved and the terriers quarried. The farm veteran rested. 'It takes me back, does this caper.' He watched the youths. 'When I was their age . . . by heck, there were rats then!'

Humped forms were escaping. It was a scuttling retreat, across beams, along gutters, where shadows hid crannies. The dogs yelped, leaping up, but could not follow the climbers, those who made for the roof. The youths ran out, peering upwards, flinging stones in frustration.

'That'll do,' Ploughman stopped them. 'We've stirred

them up, they won't stay. They'll pull back for the present. They've had a thorough molesting.'

A single rat climbed the tiles and sat up on the coping. Sullenly, it glared down, like some rancorous gargoyle. The larger youth's mouth fell open. 'They'll tell their mates, you watch out.' He nudged his pal and grinned slowly. 'We're okay, we don't live here.'

'Thank the Lord,' Ploughman ribbed him. 'A pair of juvenile poachers! My life was plagued by a poacher. Just watch your steps in the woodlands.'

Afterwards, the girl thanked them. 'I hope you're right, Dad,' she mused, 'and the brutes take the hint. I've had nightmares about them. I'm sure they're after the cottage.'

The thin boy smirked, looking round, eating the cake she had baked and now served in the den while her husband poured cider. The engineer's voice was soothing. 'Don't worry, love, they've been routed – thirty dead at the least. These young men deserve feeding!'

'Glub,' the baby said, bubbling. He waved his arms at the callers.

'He's like our Flo's,' said the big lad. He made a clown's face and clucked. 'She's got five kids, our Flo has.'

'He likes you,' the girl laughed.

'I'm used to handling them, missus.'

There was a growl from the ploughman, his face flushed with anger. 'What's *this?*' he demanded. He viewed the snapshot of Poacher. 'What the devil's this mean, girl, stuck up in your parlour?'

'We found it, Dad, when we came. It had dropped in a corner.'

'What was wrong with the dustbin?' The veteran glowered, his fists clenching.

'Come on, dad, don't be sour!'

'I knew him better'n you did . . .'

'It's just a memento.'

'B'God, the man was a thief!'

The girl looked cross. 'That's unfair. He took a few mouldy rabbits.'

'A thief, my girl, and a heathen!'

'Well, drink up,' drawled her husband, his swoop diplomatic. 'The lads could do with more cake, dear.'

'Not for me,' blustered Ploughman. 'I'm not staying with *him* here. I've got work to be doing. *Huh*,' he said, 'a memento! I thought I'd seen the man buried . . .'

'Want a fight?'

'I'm too tired.'

'I thought – to celebrate,' Flit said.

The birds dust-bathed in the rose bed, earth particles flying. Their wings tossed up grit. 'I mean,' chirped Flit, 'it's good news. The old rook's gone to search. We could have a good-news fight.'

'All day, I've searched,' Farthing told him.

'And me!'

'So let's rest then.' They fluffed their feathers and drowsed. 'We've got to keep it up, partner.' They wriggled down in the pans, their heads turned to the sun. 'We'll look again when we've slept.'

'The rook can look a lot farther.'

'*We* can hedge-hop, the low stuff.'

'Yes, and zoom into gullies. We can beat up the daisies!'

It was warm, the soil arid. Farthing-feather reflected, 'We've done the marsh – next, the hills. We'd better start there tomorrow.'

'We've never been to the hills.'

'I'm not bothered,' said Farthing. 'I'm not frightened of hills.'

'Nor am I!' Flit raised dust.

'Nor of hawks.'

'*Bah*!' They ruffled. Earth-clouds rose; their wings fluttered. 'If Peck was here, he'd come with us. If anyone wants a fight . . .'

The engineer banged the window. Blasted sparrows, he thought, they made the place like the moon, filling flower beds with craters. He caught the girl's amused grin. 'Little pests,' he complained. 'I'll fix the hooligans one day!'

His wife hugged her T-shirt. Curled like a cat in the chair, she regarded the window. 'The one I'll fix is my dad, going on about Poacher. It's a bee in his bonnet. He never could abide Poacher.'

'Not surprised,' said her husband. 'Your dad works hard, always has. Poacher did nothing useful.'

'He joined up in the war, I saw his old service medals.'

'Poacher the hero!'

'Maybe that's what Dad envied. Dad stayed home doing war work. Growing food was important.'

'They just had nothing in common. You heard your father's opinion.'

'A thief, he said. That's untrue.'

The man laughed. 'Poor old Poacher. You can't deny he was heathen.'

'He was *not*!'

'Heck, a Life Tree!'

'A tree,' she mused, 'is God's creation. Poacher knew the tree's secrets. When I was small, he would show me: a weasel nest in a hole, the squirrel paths through the boughs, the lichen gardens and bird nests . . .'

She sighed. 'He showed me the nuthatch, her tree-door plastered with mud to a size of her liking. And scuttling tree-creepers, like brown mice on the trunk. And big moss-green woodpeckers. Poacher knew where they drummed.

'Poacher told me about them. When peckers move down a tree, they go tail-first like we would. Tree-creepers go head-first. He knew the old willow's secrets: where moths slept in the branches, where butterflies flirted . . .'

Her husband grinned. 'He missed one thing – where *we* courted!' he told her. 'How we lay in the shade and you squealed when I squeezed you!'

Poker-faced, she said, '*Dimwit*!'

'Poor old Poacher,' he laughed.

'Compared to you, he was Godly! Anyway, he's passed on; I reckon Dad should forget it. Down there on his own! It's daft he won't call more often; the man must hanker for someone.'

'Don't we all? A quick *squeeze* . . .'

'You great fool!' The girl giggled. 'Get off,' she squealed, 'you'll wake baby!'

11

The rook's dark wings oared slowly. He might have flown somewhat faster – would have done in years past – but had learned to pace a journey. For spells, he planed, sparing effort, then steadily winnowed. Below, the river grew small, a mere gleam in the vale flanked by dyke-patterned levels. At length, the marsh turned to slopes and, in turn, hills rose steeply, densely shadowed and wooded.

Watchman rose on warm thermals, pitched through bumpy air-pockets. He had begun to feel good, the routine chores left behind him. Lower down, a hawk hunted. He cruised regally onward. In the sun, he flew high; when it rained, he descended, threading clefts in the hills. Once, he perched in a thorn as louring clouds opened round him.

A group of starlings sat near, looking glum in damp feathers.

'Do we know you?'

He scorned them.

'Is it likely?' he cawed. 'An elder rook of the senate! An honoured sage . . .' An explorer!

Unimpressed, they took off, showering Watchman with moisture. He flapped his wings. 'Common tramps – vulgar starlings!' he shouted.

Soon, the heath was ahead. Beneath the rook, the heights passed, shelving down into pinewoods, a belt of close-ranked plantations, to scrubland and heather. Little clusters of birch grew in stunted oases, their silver poles spindly. Over vast tracts of ground, even that much was absent, the sandy heath blackened.

Dropping closer to look, Watchman saw racks of fire-brooms. Many of them were empty. Others, newly replenished, kept incongruous guard on a sea of cold ashes, the charred stumps of thickets. There had been an inferno.

Where growth survived, little moved. He saw scant signs of fauna.

A small lizard appeared, froze a moment and vanished. A magpie crossed the scorched kingdom. The bird looked thin, starved of pickings. Watchman followed a path, a foot-worn trail between dunes, and saw a lean creature on it. The tiny animal veered, foraging in the ground-growth.

The old rook dipped a wing. Youthful prowess recalled, he spiralled down, slipping air, and was convinced, flattening out, that his find was a weasel. Not Kine, to be sure, but a tender apprentice, little more than a kitten. As Watchman's shadow engulfed it, it paused, staring upwards. Then, the bird landing near, the small weasel's teeth glimmered.

Suddenly, others joined it. Blinking, Watchman saw four, all juveniles like the first, in a row, milk fangs threatening. He could not tell them apart. Wonder sprang from the heather. For a moment, she hissed then, eyes puzzled, said, '*Watchman*?'

'You're Kine's daughter,' he grunted.

'Good old Watchman,' she echoed. 'I never thought . . .' She beamed broadly. 'And these,' she purred, 'are my kitts, just beginning to hunt. Aren't they dandy?'

He scowled.

They snarled and Wonder said proudly, 'Wonder's dandies – bright dancers!'

'Quite so.' Little upstarts! 'And where's their father?'

'Oh, Watchman . . .' Her voice grew thin. 'I fear for him. The fire destroyed half our land, running wild through the scrub, and Heath left to explore for we needed fresh country. He never meant to go far; just beyond the scorched heather. He said he'd find us a Dream Land.'

She paused to brood, adding quietly, 'A Land of *Lost* Dreams, more likely. You see, he never returned.' The female weasel smiled sadly. 'I've only *them* now, my dandies.'

'I see.' The old bird coughed gruffly. He had a soft spot for Wonder. Good old Watchman, she called him! 'That's bad,' he conceded. 'There's – um – something else, Wonder.'

'Kine?' she said.

Watchman nodded.

'Kine's dead!'

'I don't think so.' Not Kine the survivor. 'We've no *reason* to think so.' He told the tale as he knew it. Wonder listened in silence. At last, she said, 'And you're searching: you, Flit-cat and Farthing? You're doing that for a weasel? I'm proud of you, Watchman.'

Proud of him! He glowed warmly. 'This Land of Dreams . . .'

'Lost Dreams, Watchman.'

I'll keep an eye out in passing. I want to search the Great Plain.'

'You can't go *that* far,' she cried. 'There's no return from the plain. It's an unthinkable journey.'

'Tosh,' he croaked, 'sparrow chatter!'

'The lands you'd cross are alarming. The Land,' she said, 'of the White Death!'

Watchman sneered. 'Starling gossip!'

'The Land,' she breathed, 'of Exploding Sand.'

'Exploding sand? It's unheard of.'

'It's what *I've* heard. There are more – the Realm,' she said, 'of the Shadow; the Invisible Peril. I've heard of many more terrors.'

'Exaggerations!' the bird said. 'There are dangers in all lands.'

'To cross on foot would be madness.'

'Then Kine is qualified for it. He always *was* mad,' said Watchman. He preened and growled, 'Trust the Watchman. Experience triumphs – the wisdom of age.' He glared at Wonder's four dandies. 'Age,' he wheezed, 'the great *improver*.' He stretched a wing. It had stiffened; stiff old joints. Keep them moving!

The combine-driver killed time. Then when the dew on the corn dried, he climbed to his platform. Glancing over the hedge, he glimpsed two small, darting creatures advancing behind it. You did not often see weasels, he thought, to such advantage. Grinning, he watched then donned goggles. The man touched the starter.

In the lane, Kine marched bleakly. Families of flycatchers flipped past, country gipsies. Their roving air-dance seemed aimless: like his own trek, haphazard. 'It's almost autumn,' he churred. 'We're getting nowhere like this. We could be travelling in circles for all we know, Chukra.'

They kept close to the hedge, where the cleevers were tangled. Stalks of straw, signs of harvest, had blown from the cornfields. Sights and scents cheered the female: the close-packed fruits of the arum, the dry nostalgia of stubble. The scarlet pimpernel's flower had its small, bright face open.

'It's warm and sunny,' she jollied.

She could quite happily settle, she thought, in such a country. Not Kine, of course, he was different. She eyed his dour visage.

'For how much longer?' he snapped. 'The season is changing.'

Beneath ubiquitous elder, messy purple-stained ground showed where birds had cleared berries. The haws, much slower to ripen, still hung in red clusters. Above them, sun-lovers gathered, broods of swallows and martins on phone wires, on power lines and old buildings. 'If we could just find a sign, just the smallest clue, Chukra.'

They crouched low by a wall as a load of bales passed them. It scraped the ivy from bricks, leaving small adhesive roots, hairy fingers still clinging – the graffiti of nature. Unimpressed, Kine rose glumly.

'It's my fault,' he confessed, 'I should never have brought you.'

'Kine, you didn't,' she cried. 'You left without me – I followed! I want to be where you are: hiking on, Kine, or stopping.'

'There's no stopping.'

'All right . . .'

'The quest continues, no matter!'

'Cheer up, then, I'm with you!'

They turned through crisp, uncut corn, pressing on down the drill lanes. Overhead, ripe wheat rustled, a golden grail in the sun which penetrated in slivers to long, narrow highways concealed by the crop's depth. A flock of small birds shot skywards. Alert, a rabbit sat up, a bulging orb briefly glazed by its cleansing third eyelid.

'What's that?' Chukra listened.

A thrumming roar filled the corn drills. It seemed to sound from all sides, reverberating and pounding so that Kine's 'This way, quickly!' was countermanded by Chukra and both weasels dithered. The earth was shaking and Kine hissed, 'Which way *is* it, Chukra?'

'I don't know.'

'We can't *wait*.'

They tracked cautiously sideways, pushing through the corn columns. A towering dust pall had spread. In its shade, the noise thundered, now so close it was deafening, a howl of destruction. Teeth chomped – wheat was falling. 'We're moving into its path!'

'I can't hear . . .'

'*Kine*!'

He turned.

The combine loomed like a tank. Belching grime, it came on, a red wall on the corn, biting into the gold, leaving drab stubs behind as the weasels watched, rooted. They had no time to get clear. Kine's mind raced – the loose tilth!

'The mole hill!' he shouted.

They dived, cleaving the mound, squeezing into the tunnel. In the dark, they lay still. There was a moment of quiet, of overwhelming soil odour, then the earthquake began, filling in the mine's entrance and loosening its ceiling. The farm machine pounded over. The very darkness vibrated. Earth tumbled from walls. They held their breath and it passed. 'Are you safe?'

'We're blocked in.'

'This way,' Kine said.

He scrambled on down the tube. Loose earth clung to his coat; he felt the soft grope of roots. A worm was toiling ahead. As Kine charged, it contracted, contorting its segments. Soon, fresh air filtered in, a second shaft shedding light, and they emerged near a hedge, the machine's rumble distant.

'Let's get on.' Kine shook briskly.

Chukra said, 'I'm for resting.' She threw herself on the verge. 'When you're weary, it's dangerous. We let the combine surprise us. I think we both need a pause.'

Kine set off. 'Are you coming?'

She caught him up. 'If you say so. But tramping blindly won't help – simply getting exhausted. I think we need to take stock. I think a pause is important.'

'Only one thing's important.'

'Oh yes, I know . . .'

'To slay Rattun!'

'Go on then, which way next, Kine?'

'Down the hill – I smell water. If we could just find that stream.' They came quickly to mire and he said, 'This looks hopeful.'

They made their way by the ridge, a fold of land fringed with reeds and tufts of tall dark-green grasses of rapier thinness. It was a bleak, spongy country, the firm causeway narrow. Either side, they saw sedges, draughty osiers huddling, occasional aspens. A wading-bird watched them pass, its shades precisely attuned to the drab, silty background. There were dead stems of hemlock and menacing teasels, bizarre, other-worldly.

Chukra viewed the scene glumly. 'It's a swamp, Kine, a bog!'

The bog seethed.

'Wait,' Kine cautioned.

Reeds moved, their heads tossing. They slid apart as he stopped and a beast, streaming water, hauled forward, head cranking. The weasels froze. It was fearsome, several times their dimensions. They watched its neck tower and turn and, as the mouth's cavern gaped, Kine could feel his skin tingling, the Blood Fury rising.

He snarled, recalling the Mink War, the death of Kia and her kittens, the sacrifice of the weasels who had fought the marauders. The reek of mink caught his throat; he could taste it and loathed it. '*Tchkkk*,' he spat. 'Let us pass.'

The mink's button-eyes stared. The beast was slick, almost fish-like, but when it shook its coat bristled, bushing densely and fiercely. The tail scattered water. 'This,' it said, 'is a mink path. And who are you, little stranger?'

'I am Kine the mink fighter.' Kine took a step. 'The death dancer.'

The other laughed. 'A bold upstart!'

'Gru's slayer,' Kine answered. 'Vanquisher of the she-mink.'

'Death dancer, you say? Then dance a while for me, shrimp – dance a while before dying!'

Kine made a few skipping passes, the mink's cold gaze on him. His own eyes were for Chukra as she slipped through the reeds, quietly flanking the other. He quickened pace. 'I'll dance faster. Watch me, mink, I'll bemuse you!' He whirled and hopped like a sprite, all the time making play while the small female shifted. At last, she crouched to the rear, where the mink's tail was flicking.

Kine paused, his breast pounding.

'You've stopped,' the mink drawled. 'You're finished.'

'No,' churred Kine, 'we've not started.' He braced himself. 'Ready, Chukra?'

The female flew like a bolt. She struck the mink on the back, tooth and claw clinging grimly. As the startled brute reared, Kine drove for its throat, leeching under the jaw-bone. Confused, the mink blundered wildly, neither weasel relenting, then twirled its tormentors. By turn, it tossed and gyrated. Finally, unsuccessful, the creature lurched to the morass, by now in panic.

As it submerged, Kine let go. 'Put your head in the bog, mink!'

'It won't come back?' Chukra joined him.

'Not while *we're* here! Are you fit to march, Chukra?'

'When you're ready,' she told him.

He gave a nod of approval and they went forward toge-ther. The path was now a mere ribbon, obliging them to step singly and wade in places. 'Kine,' the female said shortly, 'we can't get very much farther. We're out of luck.'

'The river's got to be somewhere.' He pressed ahead.

'No one's *said* there's a river.'

'They will,' he muttered. There was a whistle of wings and wild duck overshot them. They came in flights, quacking loudly, and Kine exclaimed, 'The ducks say so! Dozens of them,' he exulted, 'all proclaiming a river. They say so, Chukra!'

'They say there's water, that's all – a great mire, that's what brings them. They're congregating for winter. It's not a weasel place, Kine, it's a wildfowl kingdom.'

'We'll see,' he said, his voice stubborn.

They said no more until, a few minutes later, the track expired.

12

She placed the child in his cot and watched him sleep, thumb in mouth, where it had been while she spoke. Wide-eyed, he had listened, his thoughtful gaze on her face, as if the words cast a spell – as if the spell of the tale, not her tone, made him drowsy.

'Soon,' she mused, bending over and gently straightening the cover, 'you'll stay awake for my stories.' They had been wheedled from Poacher: yarns of marsh sprites, hobgoblins, kingfishers, frog-princes. 'And *then* what'll your dad say?' the girl wondered, smiling.

What he said now was whispered, an arm round her shoulder. 'He'll grow up full of nonsense. Fairy tales!' he exclaimed. 'A fine start to the career of an engineer of world standing!'

'Oh, you've no imagination.'

He grinned and led her downstairs. 'I'll use some now; I'll cook supper!'

'You *will?*' The quick hug was grateful. 'Then I'll slip down the lane. Another dad needs a call, a few sharp words from his daughter. Sat alone down there, sulking!'

'Unless he's found a good woman.'

'Now who's dreaming up stories?' She slipped a coat on and paused. 'I'll come back hungry,' she warned, 'you'd better make it a feast, an *imaginative* blow-out.'

'Cheese omelette?'

'Oh, well . . .' Glancing back from the gate, she saw him watching and called, 'Don't go swilling that cider. Keep an eye on the Dream Child.' The handsome head gave a nod. As if he needing reminding! He had his own fairy stories – an engineer of world fame, another Isambard Brunel!

Tales like that had sad endings. Expectations were fragile. The girl felt safer with Poacher: fantasies of the Rat King, yarns of sparrows and shrew-mice. Of all Poacher's stories, only the witch tales dismayed, and those she kept deeply buried. Everybody of sense was afraid of the Witchwood.

Purple-eyed in the dusk, a hare watched her trip past, bustling under the poplars. The evening track was high-flanked, edged with overblown growth, gloomy burrs, wilting hogweed. Somewhere there, between dwellings, the bones of old envies festered, the clay of old ructions. Her dad had no right to raise them, to go on slanging the dead. He should let bygones be bygones.

A shrew popped out of the grass and crossed in front of her, beetling. Its urgency made her smile. Perhaps the dwarf was in flight from the snake on the bank, where the ground remained warm and twisted roots hid smooth coils. The adder moved as she watched, sliding into the gloom, and she cursed being startled.

'Stay away,' the girl willed. 'Keep away from us, serpent; don't you dare touch my baby.'

She reached the gate, still on edge. It was grey, a light burning, surprisingly in the front. Her father lived at the back, the kitchen more to his taste, the front parlour unused save on special occasions – when the landlord came by or, more rarely, the doctor. Now, her hand gripped the latch but never opened the wicket.

There was a face at the window, a woman's face, lean and raw, the eyes staring. Then the curtains were pulled with a swift double action that left the girl flabbergasted. From earliest childhood, she could remember no female but herself in Dad's parlour. It had not changed since her mum, whose knick-knacks filled it, had died.

And yet the face had been real. If she doubted it now, the silhouette from the lamp was plain proof on the curtains, the dusky outline sharp-featured. She felt her nails in her palms and found her fists tightly knotted.

Dad's parlour was special. She saw the room in her mind: the glass gimcracks, white doilies, the little straw harvest dolly, a table-mat her mum had crocheted – a mum she always envisaged as tidy and dainty, serene as the room was. The witchlike shadow grew vague. As it dissolved from the drapes, the girl half-stirred to go in but turned instead, her gorge rising.

In dismay, she fled homewards. Small dark shapes skipped the path. Rabbits ducked into holes. They ran, as she did, blood racing. Where a tin shed stood rusting, the sound of claws drubbed on metal. Her hair bounced on her shoulders, and now, as if in sly mischief, pipistrelles flitted past and an owl, its flight hushed, loomed from nowhere and vanished.

For a while, her eyes wide, she paused outside Poacher's cottage. When she was partly composed, she pushed the door, her mouth opening. The sound came out as a croak.

'You're soon back,' said her husband. He glanced again. 'What's the matter?'

'What's the matter?' bawled Flit-cat.

Farthing waggled his wings. They were skimming the hills, over scree and starved bushes. Stunted trees grew lop-sided, all their growth to one aspect. 'Sparrowhawk in the sun. Keep alert.'

'Bah!' said Flit-cat. He pulled up over a ridge, bustling down a bare plateau. The hawk was high, flying level with angled wings and closed fingers. Flap-flap-glide. A hawk scouting. 'Prospecting,' Flit said. 'No problem.'

'Not yet!'

Flit-cat snorted. 'I'm not frightened.'

'Nor me.'

But they watched the hawk as it soared, wings now rounded and broader, the small, fierce head peering. The black-barred underside shimmered, denoting a female.

'We've no cover,' said Farthing.

'Could make for that hawthorn.' They banked and steered for the hedgerow. 'Just in case.'

'A precaution.'

The rough old hedge drooped with berries. There were finches along it, some green, some more brilliant. 'I wonder if they saw Watchman?' The sparrows joined the throng briskly. 'He must've crossed the hills this way.'

'Anyone seen a rook – a single rook?'

No one answered. Instead, with sudden commotion, the flock of finches took wing, bowling Flit-cat and Farthing from their path as they bolted. 'Rook? Who cares about rooks?' flung a bright bird in passing. 'Just get out of our way, there's a sparrowhawk prowling.'

'Cravens!' Flit smoothed his feathers.

'Yellow bellies!' bawled Farthing.

'I'd like to give them a dusting.'

'Tweek their fancy tails for them!'

They found a branch and sat waiting. Farthing peered. 'She's descending; she's coming down at a rate. We'd better watch ourselves, Flit.' The hawk had plunged like a stone. Now, her hunting ground mapped, she pulled out, still at speed, clipping over the thorns to flush prey from its shelter. Farthing whistled. 'That's *fast*.'

'All dash and no cunning. She'll get a fight if she wants one!'

The hawk had banked, wheeling round, carried wide by her swiftness.

'We ought to shift farther down, there's more growth. We'll be safer.' They hustled off through the haws, stubby wings churning bravely. 'Watch your back, she's returning!'

With scything grace, the hawk caught them, coming low, lean and deadly. Farthing threw himself sideways, pitching into the thorn as a glaring eye passed and the bird's slipstream hit him. He saw the yellow-rimmed orb, claw-tipped legs and then feathers – a little cloud of brown plumes where his partner had scurried.

'Flit?' Farthing's voice trembled.

The racing bandit had gone, powering on down the hedge. The feathers sank to earth slowly. Farthing perched in the thicket. 'Flit?' he breathed, glancing round. Something stirred in the hedgebottom and through a jumble of twigs he saw a small, forlorn bundle with sparrow-brown markings.

'Flit!'

The shape moved a little. It shook and lost some more feathers. Slowly, Flit left the ground and came up through the thicket. 'She'll get a fight,' he gasped, glowering. He ruffled fiercely. 'I'll show her!'

'*We'll* show her!'

'She's turning, Farthing – we'll teach her ...'

'What's the ploy, Flit?'

'The thorn lure?'

Farthing nodded. 'I'm with you.' They sat up high on the bush where the sharp spurs were thick and watched the hawk stream towards them. With every wing-thrust, she grew, coming on like a bullet. When they could see the strong bill, the tenacious expression, Flit gulped, 'Hold on, Farthing ...' Long legs raked, talons splaying. '*Now!* Get down!'

The sparrows dropped through the thorns and heard the hawk strike the thicket. She gave a screech of dismay and reared up, legs entangled. 'Got her!' Farthing exclaimed. The hawk's wing-beats were frenzied. By the time she was free, the smaller birds were away, bumbling down to a wood where their safety was greater.

'Nice skirmish,' mused Flit.

'Yes, but hardly a battle.'

'D'you *feel* like a dust-up?' They wrestled, chirping and flapping, brimming over with gusto. The sky was red in the west and, as they parted and preened, migrating swifts sported round them, their mouths full of insects. 'Tell us,' Farthing demanded, 'have you seen an old rook, a lone rook, on your travels?'

'He's far away,' the swifts answered. They filled the dusk with black crescents. 'He must be old as the hills. He'd had enough when we passed him; he could barely stay airborne.'

Flit looked grave. 'Poor old Watchman. What d'you make of it, Farthing?'

'We'd best hold council with Scrat. We'll find the shrew in the morning.'

As the evening grew dark, a glow-worm shone in Plough-man's garden. The small, pure light lured the shrew who, turned pale by its spell, became a sugar-mouse creature. But was the bright bug a meal? Scrat pondered its segments, the rearmost three of which gleamed. The thought of glowing at night did not appeal and he left it.

There was a scream from the marsh – the first since dusk. Scrat took cover. Overhead, broken clouds, hunting east in lean packs, made the night doubly daunting. A thickening mist swallowed fields, diffused the glimmer from windows.

Scrat crouched by a flower-tub.

If only Kine was about! Kine would swagger and brag but his bravado inspired, made the shrew feel intrepid. Now, there was no one to turn to, for Watchman had flown and Flit and Farthing were searching, away in the hills. And every sound made Scrat quake, especially those of the screech-owls.

He heard the turn of a latch and a door partly opened. Ploughman's cat rippled out, stretched and glared. The shrew shivered. The green-eyed cat was a ghoul, a relentless dwarf-catcher. Scrat had seen its small prey set in rows, cold, uneaten.

The cat vanished.

Muttered phrases ensued, then raw light splashed the tub and a dim apparition, dark-cloaked, reached the gate, swirling off in the night, and the door was shut on it. Scrat fled. He was shaking. Kine, he thought, would have sneered, and he wished himself bolder, a scorner of demons. He wished himself a death dancer.

'Have courage,' he muttered, 'behave like a hero!' Was he not Kine's lieutenant? Who had visited Bufo? Who had made special missions? 'You're still Kine's spy,' the shrew mumbled, 'keep your eyes and ears open!'

Yet when he did, his legs weakened. The shrew saw lewd, groping branches, grey with age, mist and lichen; faceless giants, vaporous phantoms. There were fiends where stones crumbled and devils in tree-stumps. Here and there, fleeting moonlight, irradiating the murk, created nebulous spectres which shimmered in openings. He preferred *not* to look.

And when he listened, he squirmed. The wind which droned through the thickets brought tidings of evil. The draughts brought squeals, whimpers, moans – the nightly dirge of the doomed – and Scrat did not care to listen.

'Woe and woe!' The shrew scuttled.

Poacher's den appeared dimly, shadowy and unreal, then dissolved to a glow where the child's nightlight glimmered, a charm against mischief. Shuddering, Scrat went faster. Eerily, the mist writhed, stealing trees in the dark and absconding with paths so he seemed to be borne upon dank exhalations, the drab hems of witches.

He almost struck the barn headlong. Snuffling round to the threshold, he thought of hiding inside. The old floor ran with beetles. But, though the rats had been cleared, he could still smell their spore and drew back with a tremor. Oh, for Kine the rat killer, whose boldness encouraged!

Something moved and he ducked. It was a stone from the rubble dug up on the rat hunt. Disturbed, it had tumbled, dislodging earth with it. Scrat's mini-head rose and he blinked, staring inwards.

The moon was bright at that moment, slanting through the great door, and in the mist-laden brilliance piles of soil and old sleepers formed desolate mountains beside dark, spade-torn craters and the holes dogs had worried. Amid the refuse and diggings, spots of dry, blackened blood still bore witness to violence.

Doom and woe! Scrat was rigid.

Atop the largest earth-mountain, a peak wreathed in vapour, stood the Rat King and Sow Queen, surveying the ruins. In their fury, they swayed, made macabre by the mist, squealing hate from the rubble, squealing plague on the valley . . . plague on *them* and the Dream Child.

13

The two weasels marched slowly, retracing the swamp path. Kine's mood was depressed, for turning back was offensive, against all his instincts. Kine the fearless went *forward*. And yet, such terms made scant sense when 'back' and 'forward' were guesses, merely flukes in a maze which had long-since confused him.

'You're right, Chukra, we're lost.'

'Don't despair.'

'It's frustration . . .'

'Kine, I know what it is. If you were not what you are, you could settle in style. You could live on the plain, or the corn lands, and prosper. Instead, you strive to get home and face death, to face Rattun. What it is, Kine, is madness.'

'Perhaps.'

'I admire it.'

'You do?' he said, slightly brighter.

'Luck will change.'

'Yes.' He paused. His gaze was fixed on the skywall. 'Do you see something, Chukra?'

She gazed exhaustedly, nodding. There was a spot in the distance. Like a tadpole, it grew, imperceptibly sprouting . . . black wings . . . dark tail feathers . . . 'It's a rook.'

'A lone corvid!' Kine gawped. 'It's *him*, Chukra!'

'You mean . . .'

'We've been found!'

The bird flapped and cawed faintly. Chukra said, 'Are you sure? He's not in much of a hurry.'

'He's old – good old Watchman! Down *here*,' Kine cried, dancing.

'He hasn't seen us.'

'He must have!'

'By the trees,' Chukra shouted. The rook lurched and

stopped striking. He oared again. It was feeble. 'Kine, he's all in, he's wilting.'

'*Here*, Watchman! We're here . . .'

'He'll go past.'

'No, he's turning!'

Staggering, the rook banked, planing down in great jerks as if losing control then regaining it wildly. 'The tree,' screamed Kine, 'on the causeway!' They could see him in detail, raking beak clamped in anguish, eyes fixed on the alder. He picked a bough, now, feet spreading.

'Too fast, Watchman, you'll miss it.'

'Poor bird . . .' Chukra flinched.

Somersaulting through branches, the rook sped on, plumes awry, crashing into the marsh grass. There was a flutter. Kine groaned. The fingered wings were spread-eagled, orbs half-closed, the bill gaping.

'Kine?' the rook croaked.

'You found us . . .'

'Kine, the uppity weasel?'

'Take it easy,' Kine told him.

Watchman gulped. 'Take it easy? You think that's how I found you - by taking it easy!' His eyes closed, then flickered. 'It was epic, Kine, epic . . .' His head tilted abruptly. It lay lop-sided and sightless, the beak opening wider.

Chukra peered. 'Is he dying?'

Kine said fiercely, 'Not Watchman – he can't. The rook's timeless!'

'He looks bad.'

'He's tough, Chukra. He's our guide, he can't *die*.'

'Make him say something, Kine.'

'Yes, Watchman, say something!'

'Make him tell you the way.'

'Yes, the way – don't die, Watchman!'

A rat-grey eyelid slid open. 'Listen, Kine . . .' The sound rattled. 'The lands . . .' the rook intoned feebly. It was the husk of a whisper. 'Note the lands you must travel . . .'

'Yes, the lands. Tell us slowly.'

'First . . .' The voice trailed away. 'You won't believe what I tell you . . .' The wheezing whisper came fainter.

'First, heed the rumble of thunder, the sound of explosions. Cross the Sands of Explosion, then cross the Land of White Death to the Realm of the Shadow . . .'

'Yes, go on.'

There was silence.

'Then find the Pass . . .'

'What pass, Watchman?'

'. . . of Invisible Peril.' The old bird gasped. 'Kine – the otter . . . take the line of the otter . . .' His eye was wide. It closed slowly. 'I must rest . . .' He lay still and Kine, glancing at Chukra, said, 'There's not much left in him.'

'He's just a pile of old feathers.'

'We must stand guard, this is mink land.'

'Kine, wake up – wake up, quickly!'

He had drowsed. 'Is he dead?'

'No,' said Chukra, 'he's breathing. It's not the rook. Can't you hear it?'

'What?'

'Far off . . .'

Kine heard rumbling. It had the anger of thunder. He felt the earth itself tremble. 'Explosions,' he murmured.

'The Land of Explosions!'

Kine jumped up. 'Like he told us – first the sound of explosions. Then cross the sands. That's it, Chukra, that's the sign, the call forward.'

'You must go.'

Kine was startled. It was so clear and insistent, so awesome a challenge: march towards the explosions! He paused then said, 'And leave Watchman?'

'I'll stay with Watchman,' said Chukra. 'He'll need to build up strength slowly. If he recovers, he'll guide me.'

'If he dies?'

'Don't find problems. Go, Kine, before the sound stops.'

'But *you* . . .'

'Go!' snapped Chukra.

'We've grown together; we're partners.' He had got fond of the huntress, come to relish her talents. They had baffled the cat and confounded the swamp mink.

'It's you who's pledged to meet Rattun. It's *your* affair,' Chukra told him. Her eyes belied the indifference; they were pining already. 'There's no time to make speeches.'

'I'd come back for you,' Kine said. 'That's if . . .'

'Kine, just *hurry!*'

There was a long, distant roar and Kine said with his throat full, 'Now or never!' He gritted. He had no choice, he was thrice-pledged – to the vale, Kia and his forebears. He was Kine the rat killer. 'Take care, Chukra,' he muttered. 'The rook will mend; he'll scout for you.'

'I don't need looking after.'

'No,' he said.

'*You* take care, Kine.'

He turned and left – at first slowly, then with gathering purpose. A final glance, thrown behind, showed him Chukra's slim neck raised where Watchman was lying, and Kine went on faster. Tenacious rook; dashing huntress! A part of Kine's heart stayed with them. The rest addressed his design: the quest to regain his homeland and vanquish the Rat King.

Bounding now, he thrust on, his line fixed by the rumbling. Cornfields passed and deep pasture, then spinneys and scrubland. He ran by tracks, ditches, hedges. And all the while a clear sky, as the thunder grew louder – the two unreal in conjunction – increased his foreboding.

Small birds flew against him, staring down at the weasel. 'Turn,' they piped, 'don't go that way!' Their tone, thought Kine, held conviction. He was a maverick traveller, bound alone towards uproar, sounds which ripened in violence until the ground he trod shuddered. 'Turn,' the birds cried, 'turn back!'

But he could only go forward, for that way lay the valley, a journey of dangers, the ordeals named by Watchman. He could not quit at the first, though he did check his pace and advance with more caution. Ahead, a thin neck of wood, mostly whippy young poles, crossed his path and he paused, weighing up the best passage.

The noise ahead had expired. In a hiatus of silence, the world again seemed at peace and his ears had stopped pounding. Relieved, he made for the poles where, no longer sound-guided, he romped by sense of direction to a wire-guarded frontier and tested the footing. The scrape he dug was loose, gritty.

'*Tchkkk*,' crowed Kine. It was sandy. A land of sand. His eyes glinted.

Sunny dunes glared back quietly. Ranging into the distance, clad with sparse, arid grasses, they looked less daunting than dull, despite the War Department warning – this lost on the weasel – with its red on white legend.

KEEP OUT – WEAPON TESTING.

Kine danced under the wire, Kine the scorner of danger. Exploding sand! That was nonsense. The dunes were becalmed. The wiry grass barely twitched, a few small movements his own, where he jostled a stem, stirred a trickle of sand-grains. Between hummocks, the sky's dome, bird's egg blue, was unsullied. It was serene, Kine reflected, devoid of commotion.

Perhaps a shade *too* serene. Not a beast or fowl squabbled, not a mouse or shrew loitered. It was a rule in the wild to beware when life vanished. A browsing vole would have helped, a robin's song to relax with. One bird, a lone redshank, did pass, fast and slanting, its eerie *tu-ee* unnerving.

Nothing else broke the quietness. Kine threw his own voice ahead; the churring call was unanswered. The mounds were still, the bowls brooding. Here and there, puny shrubs, dry and stunted, cowed bleakly. There were odd pans in the ground, as if large holes had been filled – or almost filled – by loose sand. And, in strange twisted shapes, lumps of metal lay near, like petrified reptiles.

Kine began to feel jumpy. The breathless hush went too far, became intangibly charged, a conspiracy of silence, as if the dunes were in league to effect some terrible stroke, embroil the traveller in ambush. He tried to keep on his toes but the soft sand dragged at him.

A far-off thump stirred the air. The sound was dull, deeply muffled, but broke the spell with a jolt and Kine paused, almost grateful. Struggling on up a slope, he heard a screech in the distance. Again, he stopped, the sound closer. The screech came on, now *crescendo*, a screaming roar, and he ducked, lying flat on the sand dune.

He was stunned by the explosion. Sand half-buried the weasel. Still bemused, he wormed free and heard more thumps and screeches. They came in double effect, then in multiple salvoes, whining, shrieking, exploding. All round, sand erupted, mixed with scattering sub-soil. Reeling, Kine fought the debris. He was blind, his ears ringing.

A piercing whistle then thunder!

Mortar bombs ripped the hollow, some ahead, some behind him. Should he turn and run back or lurch on seeking cover? There were no burrows, no mole holes. Shrapnel whined, the sand stung him. Bombs chewed monstrous black chasms or, exploding as air-bursts, hurled searing-hot fragments.

Plucked up by the blast, the small creature whirled forward. The land was fountaining muck, befouling the heavens. Kine pitched headlong in grass, rolled the length of a slope and sprawled, dazed, at the bottom. There was some scrap-iron nearby, an old tin sheet from a roof, and the weasel crawled to it.

Semi-conscious, he sheltered, the cannonade raging. With every salvo of shrieks, his corrugated roof trembled; at every bomb-burst it lifted, falling back on his bruises. As shrapnel flew, the tin rattled. The sound was something like rain; a rain that punched holes in metal. He eyed the holes and crawled forward. He would be killed if he stayed; better perish advancing!

Better still, *defy* peril, for was he not a survivor? '*Tchkkk*,' he churred, 'Kine the fearless!' He stumbled into the bomb fumes.

The air he breathed reeked of burning. Shrapnel hummed. Grass was smoking. He tried to sprint but moved slowly, the sand disobliging. For every length he went forward, he seemed to slip as far backwards, or tumble sideways, blast-hammered. Explosions skittled him over. Avalanched down a dune, he lay smothered in filth, spitting gravel and grass-roots. Again, he rose, scrambling on.

110

Crump-wzzzeee . . . A fresh salvo, more missiles appro-aching – screech, whine, the fierce onrush. Freeze and wait. Tremble. *Blat!* Kine stretched cautiously, blinking. He felt no blast, saw no debris. The bombs had burst far behind, their obscene muck-spouts harmless.

The next were even more distant.

Hope rising, he paused. He was undamaged, he marvelled, the uproar receding. A last stray bomb made him flinch. Tempering his elation, it goaded flagging exertions, but the thunder abated. Again, the sands became quiet, a land beaten and broken. Between the dunes, like a mirage, a new vista opened.

The scene was bright, life-affirming. Sunshine twinkled on water, a small coastal inlet, seabirds dining on mudbanks – dunlin, gulls, oyster-catchers. There were wet sands and rock-pools, oarweed, crabs, shrimps and limpets. A little pool fish, the shanny, stared and suddenly vanished.

Out to sea, on white sails, a stately gannet was cruising, its dagger-beak slanted.

The creek was shallow, tree-skirted. Above the trees, cattle nibbled, the fields rising steeply; below, mud-flats shimmered. On the flats, dunlin drilled, doubling forward and checking, flashing up in close ranks to wheel, land, double forward. It all made Kine feel uncertain. This was congenial country, not the path the rook promised.

14

The motor fired and then idled, its driver's head through the window. He stretched a hand to the child's and gravely shook the small fist. 'See you later, you two, mind the witch doesn't get you!'

'That's not funny,' his wife said, and pulled the babe to her. 'It's a serious matter.'

'Poor old grandad,' the man said.

'Poor old *nothing* – just wait!'

'I thought you said he was lonely?' The engineer gave a grin. 'Seems he's found a companion. That's no crime. What's so shocking?'

The girl looked fierce. 'She's a hag.'

'He can't expect a princess,' laughed her man, 'like his daughter. You'd not expect a blonde kitten.'

'She wasn't anyone normal; she was brazen,' the girl said. She made a pout and protested, 'Standing there in Dad's parlour! She'd no right, her or no one – least of all a witch woman.'

'That's not reasonable, is it? Some old dear you've not met. . . .'

'Some old dear!' the girl mimicked. 'You didn't see her like I did. I dread to think what Dad's doing.'

Her husband blipped the van's engine. 'You couldn't grudge him a chum.'

'She'd no right. That's my mum's room!'

'You can't remember your mum.' He shrugged and said, 'It's an age. He's lived alone half his life. Hell's bells, he needs *someone*, a lady companion.'

'Oh, you . . .' the girl grumbled. 'You think I don't know a face? I know a witch when I see one. I'll tell you this, there'll be trouble.'

'If I don't move!' the man reckoned. He gave a wave and smiled slyly. 'If I don't get on my broomstick . . .'

The van chugged off, the girl glaring. She hugged the babe, seething quietly. 'Sometimes,' she said, 'I could kick him. Yes, my child, *kick* your father!'

She eyed the valley's calm beauty. It made her sigh, the peace soothing, and she strolled by the wood where ripe blackberries clustered. Some, late flowering, still bloomed, drawing insects in droves, the last ball of their lives for many bright, flitting creatures. Green-tailed flies sucked the fruit; turquoise demoiselles hovered, or sat on leaves, their wings shining.

The infant ogled them, burbling.

'Yes, my dear, aren't they lovely . . .'

Massive dragonflies rhumba'd. Clad in gold, scarlet, pink, they graced the levee and passed, making way for fresh dancers. Painted butterflies waltzed: tortoisehells, commas, brimstones, blues, admirals, peacocks. Entranced, the child watched them gather.

'Soon be winter,' the girl said. 'It's their last sunny party. They're showing off their fine things. Then the leaves will come tumbling.'

She loved the valley in autumn. Already some trees were changing, the limes and chestnuts bright chrome while the oaks held their depth, a foil to hazel and birch with their dappling yellows. Amid the grass, fallen leaves, small and spring-like in colour, might have been clumps of primrose. Soon, the woodlands would blaze, afire with coppery red, the plough's umber waves round them.

Her autumn dream held a tractor, growling loudly then silenced. Ploughman stretched and climbed down. 'How's my boy?' It was hearty. He caught the girl's eye and paused.

She glowered, her chagrin revived, shooting back, 'How's your *woman*? That's more to the point, Dad. How's the witch at the window?'

'Ah,' he said, 'I've been rumbled.' Ploughman stroked his chin slowly. 'You're right,' he owned, 'you've described her. A proper witch *she* turned into.'

'You don't deny it?'

He cackled. 'It's plain enough,' he wheezed, laughing, wiping his hands on his trousers. 'She weren't so bad back at school; least, your mam always liked her. They were children together. She left the village soon after. I'd not have known her, not nowadays.'

'She's come back?'

'Aye,' he pondered. He said, 'She turned up at bingo then called to inspect me. Natter-natter, the ratbag! You should've been there, my beauty. She put the evil eye on me!'

'Oh, Dad . . .'

He grinned broadly. 'I got her out. Now the door's barred.'

The girl felt bad. 'I was worried. I thought you might . . .'

'Me and *her*?' He reached and took the child from her.

She said, 'I should've known better.'

'I don't know.' He looked sheepish. He kissed the boy's head and mumbled, '*I'm* the one who should know better – ranting on about Poacher! I'd no right, girl, that's sure. It's high time I was learning.'

'Call it quits,' the girl told him.

'Aye, the old witch – forget her.'

'Yes,' she said. 'If she'll let us.' It was, she thought, far from certain.

Ambling home, the girl smiled. She sang songs to the child, who squealed softly with pleasure. As they passed, their sounds dwindled: snips of verse, chortles, giggling.

> '*Anything like the sound of a rat*
> *Makes my heart go pit-a-pat!*'

In the wood, the rats paused. They pushed on to the Life Tree. The path they chose shunned the sunlight. Instead, it led them by vaults, dingy crypts in the growth where opaque fungi lurked and slugs slept in dark dungeons. The pond was still, weed-encrusted. It had the look of a grave, the great tree settled low, as the rodents stole round it.

For a moment, they listened. There was a faint sound of snoring, tremulous, desultory.

The rats advanced, nostrils open. Scrambling on to the trunk, they moved quietly along it. *Zzzzz* . . . The weasel-hole whistled. In its depths, the shrew slumbered. He stirred, a chill in the den, and jumped up with a shudder. The sun had gone from the hole. Now, where daylight had glowed, evil snouts filled the disc and the shrew glimpsed incisors.

His end had come – he was trapped! Scrat shrank back and stood shaking, the wall firmly against him. In the shadows, he gulped. It was no good, they would smell him; a poor smell, to be sure, but they were rats and not fussy. He saw the dark noses twitch.

Silently, the shrew pleaded. No one eats me, he reasoned, no one of good taste, only owls, feathered fiends. Only ogres and demons. He viewed the snouts again, quaking. What else were these callers?

It was his own fault, Scrat snivelled. He had no business to be there. Kine himself had reproved him for using the hollow, the shrine in the Life Tree. It was sacred to weasels. Now he faced retribution, a rough and terrible justice for ignoring the warning.

He heard the drone of rat voices. 'Where's Kine?' they demanded.

'K-Kine?' breathed Scrat. 'Kine's not here.'

'Where *is* Kine?'

'G-gone away.'

'He was wise,' said the voices. They paused then rasped, 'Salute Rattun! We of the new breed hail Rattun! If Kine returns, dwarf, you'll tell us – tell or die.'

'I . . .'

'Hail Rattun!'

Scrat choked, saying nothing. He set his jaw, the hush chilling. Tell or die! He felt giddy.

'Scrat, come out!'

The hole brightened. It was blue again, shining.

'It's Farthing, Scrat. Are you there?'

'*Farthing*?' Scrat was still shaking. 'But the rats . . .'

'What rats?' Flit said.

'They were here, Rattun's minions!'

'Well, they've gone. Buck up, Scrat,' chirped the sparrows, 'we're back from the hill search.'

They hopped down through the branches. 'Never mind Rattun's minions.'

'They're going to kill me,' Scrat anguished.

'No they won't, you're too useful. It's Kine they want – information.'

'I can't betray him!'

'Why should you?' The sparrows sighed.

'You're Kine's agent. Don't you see? It's a gift – spread false news, disinform them! Your role could be crucial.'

'Doom!' wailed Scrat.

Farthing fluttered. 'There's word of Watchman,' the bird said.

'What word?'

Flit was sombre. 'He's been spotted in trouble.'

'We'll have to go,' Farthing added. 'We'll have to travel long-distance. We've drawn a blank in the hills. We'll have to take on the rook's job.'

Flit said gravely, 'For Peck's sake.'

Farthing said, 'For the valley.'

'For the weasel,' cried Flit. 'For the rat-fighter, midget!'

Kine went down to the creek. It was low tide and dry. Small boats lay on the mud; rock pools drowsed on the fringes. It was a new world to Kine, one half-awake, in suspension, a place awaiting the sea. When it came, things would change: boats would bob, rocks submerge. Then the mudflats would drown and the foot-crossing vanish.

For now, the air was relaxing, the sights novel to him. Tiny crabs scurried round, little bigger than spiders. Bubbleweed dried and popped. He put his ear to a shell and it roared like the ocean.

Far away, a dog barked while its master dug lugworms. The man's spade left black castles, great bulwarks of mud by the holes he was making. But man and dog were remote and Kine browsed undisturbed, the creek's langour contagious. The sun was high, the rocks warm. The small traveller lingered.

In a pool, an old crab, sandy-green, fanned the water. Kine watched it crawl out, its smooth body-shield dripping.

For fun, he pounced then danced back, the crab's anger amusing. Legs bent, it took guard, pincers raised, black eyes beady. Kine jigged. It stepped sideways. At length, twigging a hoax, the crab scorned its molester, stalking off on the mud towards the creek's empty centre.

Kine gave chase but lost interest. A stranded marker-buoy loomed and he considered his bearings. The creek was all very well but was it part of his journey? Where were the lands Watchman mentioned? Where was the Land of White Death? He was crossing smooth flats, a rill or two to his front where a small outflow trickled, an anchor embedded. Boats, moorings, quiet shores – where was the test in this passage? Where, he mused, was the challenge?

He watched the crab march on stiffly. Once or twice, it stood still, then pressed on with firm purpose. That, thought Kine, was the way – banish doubt, hasten forward. And yet the weasel held back, lurking in the buoy's shadow.

A small pied shore bird passed near on the trail of sandhoppers. With its beak, it turned stones, peering quickly beneath them. For a moment, Kine watched then asked the turnstone a question – 'Where is the Land of White Death?' – to which it answered, 'Right here. Don't you know?'

'*Here?*'

'You're in it.'

'Pah!' said Kine.

'Where've you been?' The bird took off, calling pertly, '*Everybody* knows that much!'

'*Tchkkk*,' snarled Kine, his pride ruffled. He eyed the creek. 'Where's the danger?' It was serene, smooth and shiny. 'It's an amble, that crossing. Produce the danger to stop me, for I am Kine the bold dancer, Kine the facer of peril!'

'Watch the crab,' called the turnstone.

Kine watched, losing patience. If he was really on track, he should be moving on bravely, not observing the shore life. He heard the cry of a gull. The seabird wheeled in the sun. Circling, it slid lower, another gull diving past it. Screaming, both spiralled downwards, a third and fourth swooping near them.

The crab had stopped and was digging. As the gulls made their plunge, it tried to sink in the mud but the leading bird snatched it up, promptly robbed by a rival. Jockeying, the birds whirled, each intent on the trophy.

Soon, several more had joined in, their harsh mewing aggressive. Overhead, scores were turning. There were common gulls, blackheads, herring gulls, grey-backed brigands. In groups, they banked, scudding down, pitching into the scrimmage. It seemed to grow as it wheeled, a great snowball of wings, each bird bent on predation. There must, at last, have been hundreds.

By now, the crab was in parts, torn, scattered, contested. Ferociously, the gulls harried. They were a cloud, a white swarm; the creek rang with their screaming. They seemed to fill the whole sky, blotting out the far shore and commanding the crossing.

'The White Death,' piped the turnstone.

Kine looked grim. 'Kine is speedy.'

'The gulls are faster, voracious!'

'I'll get across . . .'

'In small pieces – they'll pull you limb from limb, weasel!'

15

The weasel peered round the buoy. There was no doubt of
it now – he was on course for the valley. This was the
second ordeal, this land of mud flats ahead. The tide had
changed, a breeze rising. Meanwhile, the gulls had dispersed, scattered far round the creek. He would show them
his speed, show them Kine was no shore crab.

'White Death!' he laughed fiercely. 'Let them do their
worst, turnstone!'

'They'll do that.'

'If they catch me!'

'And they'll do *that*.'

'We'll see,' Kine said. Poised to sprint, he was terse. 'I'm
no shuffling crustacean. Watch me, turnstone, I dart – I am
Kine the snake-headed!'

'*Thick*-headed,' the bird said, but Kine had gone, dashing
forward, the brisk, lean form undulating. The weasel's rush
was in leaps, each bound growing bolder. He had to beat
the marauders. Once across, there was cover. He had to
conquer the creek before the gulls could remuster.

A single scout sailed aloft. Scarcely moving its wings, it
seemed to float in the sky, a white and beautiful craft as it
soared, rocking gently. A hovering pirate. So far, blind to
the race, the gull cruised without sound, but it could bring
the mob screaming and Kine galloped faster.

On he chased, skimming wildly. He passed a lop-sided
anchor. A length of chain was beside it; a small red dinghy
lay stranded. Kine gained ground, leaping nimbly, barely
touching the mud, taking off and volplaning, touching down
with a splash where fresh water ran thinly, diffused from
an outflow.

Seaweed-clad, a post reared, a black diving-bird on it.
One wing raised, the shag preened, a pale eye on the weasel.
The weasel's eye sought the gull. Still, its languid hull

soared, but now closer, more threatening. Kine redoubled his efforts.

Past a fragment of crab shell, past a flat rock he surged, on to firm, stony roads at the heart of the creek then to silt, half-way over. There was a screech and Kine swerved. The gull shot by with a yell, hurled a wing up and turned, then drove back at him, gaping.

He could see its red gullet.

As it came, he reared up, teeth displayed, and it flapped, losing nerve, and climbed quickly. The draught from beating wings struck him. Kine raced on, the gull swearing. Now, the weasel was jinking, eyeing two more marauders, herring gulls, closing swiftly. The big, raucous birds plunged and a curved beak stabbed at him.

He felt the wrench on his skin. A sharp pain tore his flank and he swung his neck backwards, grabbing, tugging at feathers. The bird yelped and released him. He saw the second gull loom, overshoot, flutter upwards.

Spitting feathers, he sprinted. He managed three bounds and fell, tackled now from behind, webbed feet straddling his shoulders, great wings beating round him. A glancing blow caught his head and he rolled, dazed but kicking. A yellow eye was above him. Its small black pupil was lustful. Again, a stout bill descended.

Kine felt consciousness ebbing. He fought to stave off the darkness. He had to get off his back and, as the bird settled on him, the weasel clawed at its breast. It rose angrily, screaming. Suddenly, sight returning, Kine looked up at the heavens – the whole blue vault seethed with pinions, scores of gulls stacked above him, a whirling horde, white and brilliant.

'They'll pull you limb from limb, weasel!' The turnstone's prophecy echoed.

Kine jumped up and lurched forward. The birds were squabbling aloft, jostling to get at him. Several came in a bunch. Again, the traveller went down, saved this time by their feuding. As they bickered for rights, Kine squirmed free, once more running. A skimming grey-backed gull struck him, skittling the small mammal. Struggling up, he cast round, desperate to find shelter.

An ancient lobster-pot beckoned. It lay marooned on the mud and somehow Kine scrambled to it, besieged by the gull mob.

Squeezing into the cage, he peered out at the rabble. Seabirds thronged overhead. Many stood on the mud and several perched on his refuge. Gulls stared in through the canes, scrutinizing the quarry. For the time, he was safe, but the tide was approaching and Kine's hunters waited.

There was an ominous hissing. The smell of brine had grown strong; now, the charge of waves sounded, each creaming surge louder. All Kine could see was a wall, a ring of gulls. He glared at them.

'*Tchkkk*,' he snarled.

'Run,' they taunted.

From the back, a screech mounted, then oaths. Heads were bobbing. There was a flurry of wings and Kine, facing the rumpus, saw something hurtle towards him and fall in the prison. Lithe and sleek, it shook fiercely. 'Gulls!' it cried, dark eyes flashing. 'Kine, don't gawp, time is precious!'

'*Chukra*.' Kine was astounded.

'Two are safer than one, Kine!'

'Are you *mad*?'

'We agreed. Besides,' she purred, 'it's three this time. See – up there, Kine, a guardian!' He raised his head. Gulls were swirling. Higher still, the rook hovered, fingered wings tilting slowly. 'It's your friend, he recovered!'

A tongue of salt-water drenched them. It ebbed.

Kine said, 'Watchman . . .'

Another wave approached, frothing. It made the lobster-pot judder.

'He's coming down,' exclaimed Chukra. The rook had dropped his grey nose. 'Like a hawk,' sighed the female.

'Like an old fool!' Kine shuddered.

They stared as Watchman descended. He fell with his wings closed. Down he plunged through the horde, black through white, seagulls screeching, startled by the intruder. Milling round, they swore harshly. Down he dropped

121

without caution. Angry birds swerved to miss him; others stabbed as they passed, driving at the dark meddler. At last, the veteran pulled out, zooming low up the creek, mobbed by half the gulls present. The rest were distracted.

'Now *run*,' Chukra squealed. 'Now's our chance – stop for nothing!'

Side by side, they sprang forward. Gulls were still on the mud. The two weasels leaped at them. Caught off guard, the birds rose, wheeling round. Kine's glance darted. 'Watch your flank! Faster, Chukra!' They spat and snapped as the gulls dived. 'Straight ashore – keep together!'

A creaming wave stole Kine's breath. As it died, he looked round. Now behind, Chukra struggled, mobbed by birds, her neck twisting. He sprang back, grabbing feathers.

'Don't stop, Kine.'

'Are you hurt?'

'I'm all right.' She rejoined him. 'Keep going, I'm with you!'

They raced the rim of the water. Several times, the surf caught them. It made the muddy sand soft and they struggled, coats sopping, no longer spring-footed. More and more, the sea threatened. The gulls had grown less determined. One, however, persisted, turning Kine on his back, and suddenly he was gasping, an ochre beak jabbing.

'Hold on, Kine!' Chukra floundered.

She saw the bird strike again – a herring gull, large and powerful. Kine writhed. She moiled forward. Then, as the gull raised his head, Chukra lunged, her teeth snapping. Kine jumped up. The bird screamed. Wings fanning, it towered, drifting angrily seaward, the weasels left swimming.

A creamer broke. Kine touched bottom. 'This way – *hurry* Chukra!' Near the shore were some dinghies. A new wave surged. He was tumbled, cartwheeled by its force, swept along like a pebble. Now, the boats were behind him. Still, the wave bore him forward.

And then was gone, Kine left stranded. He shook his head, high and dry. Chukra lay close beside him. She sat up.

'Kine, we've made it!'

They were on a small beach. A wizened tree cast a shadow. 'You're right,' he said, 'we're across – across the creek! They can't stop us!' He blinked and said, 'Where's the rook?'

'In the tree,' a voice rasped. 'Watching over you, braggart!'

'Brrr – it's cold,' said the big lad.

The youths were pushing a handcart. On the ridge the wind pierced, their thin clothes poor protection. A sudden frost had brought change, stripped the leaves from young ash, made the track hard and lumpy. It rocked the cart's frail suspension.

Down the lane, small wild apples, blown from trees, lay in ruts. Creaking wheels squashed the windfalls. On the cart, timber wobbled. Autumn flared in the woods; the boys wiped their grey noses. At the cottage, they knocked. 'Brought the planks up,' they called, and the girl said, 'You're frozen.'

She made them hot drinks to warm them.

'The wood can go in the shed, but thaw out first,' she ordered.

'Aye.' They sat in the kitchen.

'I hope it's good wood?'

They nodded. 'It's good, all right.'

'That's important.'

They clasped their mugs. 'What's he building?'

'Guess,' the girl said.

'A hen coop?'

'No, a playhouse,' she told them.

'Ah . . .' Their mouths opened vaguely.

She gave the baby a beaker. 'A Wendy House in the garden. By spring, the child will be toddling. He'll have his very own den.' The girl laughed at their faces. 'His very own little mansion!'

'Ah . . .' they said, their eyes travelling, admiring the parlour: pastel paint, polished brasses. From a pot, gold leaves fountained, autumn snatched from the draughts, set to glow in a corner. He had a mansion already. Poacher would not have known it.

The youths recalled *Poacher's* parlour, the dump it had once been, walls blackened by smoke, brambles over the windows. You could barely see out. And the stuff on the table – gun shells, traps, dirty crocks!

A shadow fell on the garden.

'You've a caller,' the lads said.

'Who is it?'

Their eyes met. 'Her we saw by the Witchwood.'

'Her?'

'. . . who's back in the village.'

'God, the witch!' The girl hissed it. Her son looked up, spilling juice, and she stooped with a handcloth.

The big, ungainly lad grinned. 'Heck,' he crowed, 'and she cursed us!'

'Well, you cheeked her,' his friend said.

They dropped their jaws in mock terror. Hands to mouths, they stood cackling.

'That's enough!' The girl straightened. 'Stop the clowning and listen. Go and send the witch packing. Tell her nobody's home. Is that clear? Go and do it. Tell the hag I'm out somewhere.'

She watched their faces grow puzzled.

'Tell her *something*,' the girl said.

'Right.' They rose to obey her. She felt the wind through the door and drew back, the child cuddled. It was instinctive, unreasoned. She had no time for the woman. She sensed the creature could harm her – nothing she could explain. A wild fear. They were talking. The voices droned for a while then the gate was closed loudly. The youths returned.

They were laughing. 'Now we're *twice* cursed.' they hooted.

'She's gone?'

'She's gone, missus.'

'That's good!'

'It was easy.' They stood and grinned.

'Well?' the girl drawled.

'We told her we were the rat men.' They liked the joke.

'It was simple. We said the place was infested. Rats like ponies – man-eaters. We said we'd cleared the old barn but they were after the cottage.'

'And she believed you?'

'She's gone!'

'It wasn't far from the truth.' The girl shrugged. 'Stack the wood, then. Come on, child, time to clean you, we'll soon have your dad home.' She eyed the faraway pump, its brick shell on the marsh, and perked up at the prospect. Her man would not stand for witches; her man would comfort her, hold her . . .

Within the cell, he worked briskly. Striplights glared on blind walls and the glazed floor was spotless. It was, he sometimes imagined, a space station he captained, kept gleaming and shipshape, on an alien planet. The engineer whistled quietly. His job made him happy.

The great metal-clad motor stirred a special pride in him. When he had checked the time-boxes, he cleaned and serviced the engine. He kept the oil in it perfect. At length, he stood and admired it. One day, before long, he would bring his son to the pumphouse. Meanwhile . . .

He grinned broadly. From the back of a clipboard, he took a sheet of graph-paper and studied his scribblings. His first plans for the playhouse! Was the sketch too austere? Should the door be on *that* side? Did it need extra windows? Maybe . . . He scrawled quickly. He thought the changes not bad and put the sheet in his pocket.

The man went out to the river. The discharge valve there was closed. When the floodwater gushed, it would force the valve open and spill to the current. He stepped to the flood-dyke. The level was normal – just below the electrodes which governed the switches. He tossed a stone in the water. At once, the ripples made contact; the engine roared deeply.

Suddenly dykes were swirling, water sucked to the pump where foaming tons every second were forced to the river. The boy would marvel at that – at the power, the concept. Swift, efficient, unfailing! You could trust the pump system;

trust it more, thought the townsman, than the whims of the valley. He cast his gaze through the mizzle. That was a place of excesses, unpredictable happenings.

When the wind blew the reeds, you could fancy you saw things, strange forces in motion. You could fancy eyes watching, damp heads, tails that slithered. The pump shut off, the dykes settling. The young man laughed. Idle nonsense! Fantasies were *her* province; they were his country girl's talent!

16

With Watchman scouting ahead, Kine and Chukra went forward. The rook was ill-humoured. The creek had sapped his reserves and the bird muttered and croaked, glad to rest on a post or low bough when he reached one. Chukra said, 'The rook's weary – we're all tired. And he's hungry. He needs a day's pause to feed.'

'A day!' Kine cried.

'Yes, he needs it.'

'He's old, Chukra, he dawdles.'

'We could rest while he foraged.'

'*He* can stop, I'm not stopping. The rook can stop then catch up. He can fly. Kine keeps going!'

They had come to a beech wood. By dusk, its copper hues glowed and a floor of leaves rustled, small birds scratching in them. Tortoiseshell in the gloom, flocks of bramblings gleaned mast, the beech fruit that had fallen. Others joined them in supper. Kine plunged on and the bramblings, disturbed, flitted spryly, their white rumps like lanterns.

Watchman pecked the ground crossly. 'Squirrel leavings.' he groused. 'I can't march on mere trifles, I need something substantial.'

'You're the guide,' Kine said sharply.

'Thank your luck,' grunted Watchman.

'Yes, yes – let's get on!' Sniffing, Kine probed the gloaming. The wood was eerie; leaves ghosted. The draughts brought scents that perplexed, conjured nothing on earth – nothing Kine had encountered. The brambling lanterns had gone, twinkling off into space, and he said, 'Well, where are we? You're the guide, Watchman, tell us.'

'We're near the Land of the Shadow.'

'What shadow?'

'Bah, *questions*!'

'You don't know,' Kine retorted.

'It's just the Land of the Shadow.' The rook perched above him. 'It's Wonder's name for the kingdom. I'm not omniscient, Kine, just far wiser than you are.'

'Oh, you two,' despaired Chukra. 'This is no place to squabble.' She paused, peering forward. Within the wood, it was dim; through the trees, the sky glittered. She said, 'The scents here are strange, I think the place is unnatural. Perhaps we've reached the earth's limits . . .'

'That's rubbish,' huffed Watchman.

'He could've lost the way,' Kine said. He reached the wood's fringe and squinted. The afterglow pricked his eyes, a rosy-silver effulgence in which a great herd was grazing, standing hock-high in mist as if browsing on cloudbanks. He turned to Chukra and gulped. 'You're right,' he breathed, 'it's not earthly.'

'They're like horses with stripes . . .'

'Black and white – they're unreal. This is somewhere abnormal; such beasts are prodigious.'

'Let's go, Kine,' urged the female.

They picked their way round a fence and stole through thickening twilight. Now, the zebras were grey. Farther on, bison grazed and a rhino was stirring. As dusk fell on the Zoo Park, rare creatures grew active, ratels and snow leopards. Wolves howled; monkeys chattered. 'What was that?' Chukra stopped. 'I don't like it,' she whispered.

'Devil voices,' hissed Kine. 'The world's end swarms with demons.'

'World's end!' the rook snorted.

A chimpanzee grunted. 'There,' said Chukra, 'what's that? That was nothing on earth, rook!'

'There's no *end*,' he demurred, 'it goes on, for I've crossed it – crossed the world on my own. To find Kine,' the bird carped. 'And made no fuss about noises.'

Chukra snapped, '*You* were flying.'

A monstrous cackle exploded. When the hyena laughter had stopped, Kine exclaimed, 'The rook's safe. The rook sits on a branch; we're down here with . . .' What? Kine thought. There was no word for the creatures. 'With these *things*,' he said grimly.

'Kine is fearless,' sneered Watchman.

'I'm not old and decrepit!'

'Nor hungry,' the rook sighed.

'Oh, poor Watchman,' cried Chukra. 'You really can't travel empty!' She took a bound, her nose working. Yelps and screeches resounded, sounds beyond comprehension. Anxiously, she explored, coming soon to a space where a great tree towered darkly. Near its foot, like a rock, lay the largest raw joint – a red and reeking meat-boulder – ever seen by the weasel. 'Food – I've found you food, Watchman!'

The bird descended. He blinked.

'Peck at that,' Chukra told him. 'That'll give you strength, Watchman.'

'You could be right.' His eye brightened.

'The strength,' she urged, 'to move on.' She glanced nervously round. 'Never mind what it's called, this is no place to idle. Hear those screams – it's uncanny.'

Kine said, 'Come on, let's leave him.'

'We ought to wait while he feeds.'

'Then he'll roost. Let's keep moving.' He watched the rook tug at the joint. 'He can find us tomorrow.'

'Will he be safe in the tree?'

'It's big enough.'

They glanced upwards. Its massive vaults embraced gloom, each ascending bough dim, lost at last in a void that was as black as the corvid. 'Kine,' the female said quietly, 'can you see something moving?'

'In the tree?'

'In the dark. Way on high, where it's darkest.'

'Yes . . .' A shadow had shifted. The tree was still, the air calm, and yet something had stirred. 'Something,' Kine hissed, 'and nothing.' A shade, obscure, formless. It moved again, this time lower. It seemed to ooze, as if viscous, sliding down through the tree, a shade of black in the darkness, both inky and supple.

'Run,' cried Kine, 'it's descending!'

'What is it?'

'A shadow . . .'

'Of course.' Chukra was sprinting. 'The Land of the Shadow!'

Kine stopped suddenly. Watchman! He had forgotten the rook and turned to find their guide eating. The old corvid was stuffing. Head down, he was feasting, unaware of the danger. At his back, the shade paused, detached now from the tree, crouched with jewel-bright eyes gleaming, appraising its dinner.

'Fly!' screamed Kine, rushing back.

He saw Watchman take off and a vast paw curl slowly. The panther yawned. Its coat rippled. The beast had spent the day sleeping, sprawling high in the tree; now, it stretched, still lethargic. Black as coal, it slouched forward.

'Kine, come out!' Chukra shouted.

He eyed the fence of the compound. He would not make it, he thought – the shadow would catch him. Instead, he ducked round the tree, desperate for a bolt-hole. It offered no refuge. Foiled, he watched Chukra sally. 'Kine, I'll dance a distraction!' She skipped and whirled but gained nothing. The panther's yawn widened.

From a branch, the rook cackled. 'You need a lesson, you weasels.' He fluttered down with a flounce. 'You need an old fowl to show you . . .' He strutted past the great cat. The beast ignored him and rolled. The rook resumed his feast calmly.

Soon, the shadow was purring. It licked its paws like a Persian.

'You see,' said Watchman, 'it's harmless.'

'We're safe then?' said Chukra.

Kine felt tricked. 'I'd not trust it . . .'

Watchman gorged, his eye crafty. 'The rook,' he bragged, 'has learned wisdom. The truth is there to be seen, Kine; the truth is there for the wise.' He cocked his head at a board on which a printed card stated: *Panther* (Panthera pardus) – *a natural mutant of the leopard – not uncommon in south-east Asia*.

'What does it say?' Kine demanded.

Watchman pondered it sagely. It was gibberish to him. 'It says a weasel is nothing in the Land of the Shadow. It

130

says a sprat is a sprat – and such, here, is the weasel. A weasel has no importance. That's why the shadow is indifferent.'

'And a rook?'

'A rook's a guru.'

'Right, let's march,' Kine said, bristling.

A single shot rocked the evening.

Pigeons streaked from the fields and the rooks flew up, cawing.

Ploughman came from his garden. At the back door, he went in and put the gun in the kitchen. Reappearing, he sniffed. Chilly clouds crossed the sky and he buttoned his collar.

For a moment, he paused, then took a spade from the shed and returned to the garden. Grey-faced in the gloom, he went down to the bottom. It was tidy but bare, a cold bonfire in ashes, some winter greens planted.

And, he mused, it was silent. No more pitiful cries, no more agonized mewing. The old cat's pain was over. He could have done nothing else, only spare it the torment. He rammed the spade in the soil. Icy rain swept the valley.

He stooped and turned the limp body. He would miss the old mouser. It had, he knew, captured rats, for he had seen it rat-bitten, an occasional tooth-mark – but these were horrific.

In the sleet, the man straightened.

Thank God, the girl had not seen it. He dug the hole without pause then squinted, viewing the Witchwood. At least, the cat had lived fully. The man was less pained than puzzled. What devil's brood had the wood hatched. What kind of rats were cat-killers?

The cold wind blew against them; flecks of ice stung their faces. Flit and Farthing pressed on, spurred by Scrat's parting message. 'Tell Kine there's not long, Rattun's minions are breeding. Tell Kine,' Scrat had quaked, 'I'll be dead soon. I'm doomed. We're all doomed if he fails us.'

Chilled, the sparrows flew faster. Since dawn, they had

winged, tumbling down to the heath, batting over charred gorse, bustling low across heather, rarely spotting a soul in that realm of lean pickings. Now, the sleet smashed against them.

'Farthing,' Flit bawled. 'I'm blinded. It's no good, we must shelter.'

'Where? I can't see a shelter.'

'There's a hawthorn ahead. If we pass it, there's nothing.'

They pitched downwards and perched. The tree was full of damp birds, migrating fieldfares and redwings. Smart globe-trotting thrushes, they gobbled haws and talked loudly. 'No room,' clacked the fieldfares. 'There's no room for sparrows.'

'Dowdy pests,' lisped a redwing. It flashed an elegant eye-stripe.

'Well, don't worry,' Flit bridled, 'we're not staying with you lot. When the sleet stops we're going.'

'We're not tramps,' added Farthing. 'We're long-range seek and guide agents. A land depends on our mission – the life and death of a valley.'

'That's a laugh,' said the redwing. 'You? Parochial vermin!'

'Stuck-up thrush!' Flit -cat countered. The sparrows glared at the bird which leered back, pinions flicking. Its underwing was vermilion. It made the sparrows seem drab. 'Tykes,' it drawled. 'Gutter dwellers!'

'That does it . . .'

They tussled.

'Dust him up,' blurted Farthing.

They fell to earth, feathers flying. 'Clack!' the fieldfares cried, staring. 'You might have guessed it – gatecrashers!' A brief and tumbling brawl followed from which the redwing soon fled, its sleek livery ruffled.

'That'll teach him,' chirped Flit. 'We'd have murdered the chicken!' They hopped about with their wings spread. The squall had passed and they flapped, making ready for take-off.

'Did you hear something?' Flit said.

132

Voices came from the heather. Farthing-feather turned quickly. 'I could swear – weasel chatter!'

Four small heads rose in concert. 'We'd have killed him,' piped one. 'We let *nothing* escape us.'

'Kitts,' gasped Flit. 'Little dandies!'

'We're fully qualified hunters.'

Flit-cat placed them. 'You're Wonder's!'

'So?' they challenged.

'Heath's offspring! Wonder came from the vale, born in the Life Tree – Kine's daughter. We know Wonder,' cried Farthing.

'Well, we don't know *you*, do we? You're just birds,' sulked the kitts. 'We don't know any sparrows.'

'You've still got your milk teeth,' snapped Farthing. He plumped his neck, his crown bristling. 'You're barely dry from the womb. Now hear this, it's important. Have you seen the rat killer? Have you seen Kine, your grandsire?'

'No.' Their heads shook.

'Or Watchman?'

They eyed each other. 'The fossil? The creaking fowl?'

'The rook,' Flit rapped. 'Your elder and better.'

'The fowl went *that* way,' they chorused, 'towards the plain, the old fossil.' They viewed the sparrows straight-faced. 'Across the Land of Lost Dreams. You can't miss the way forward. We'll give you a landmark – the thing to watch for,' they chimed, 'is the Invisible Peril!'

17

Dabbing its rear to a twig, the spider oozed liquid silk. The silk immediately hardened. Then with an end firmly anchored, the creature let out its line, squirting jets from its glands on the bristle-like spools which spun thread as it descended. In mid-air, the spinner stopped, dangling over the weasels.

When Kine snapped in annoyance, it promptly yo-yoed back up, coiling thread as it did so. Kine looked down at the gorge. He said, 'Invisible Peril? But *most* perils are hidden.'

'Not,' said Watchman, 'when they strike.' He sat over the spider which, once more, descended.

Chukra frowned. 'Are you sure? You mean, you don't see it coming?'

'I mean,' the rook explained slowly, 'that *nobody's* seen it. That's what I'm told. It's your skin, though; you needn't believe it.' He got no answer and added, 'Go on down and find out. At least, you won't see it coming. Or so I hear. Please yourselves, though.'

'Must we cross the gorge?' Kine asked.

'It's not a gorge, it's a cutting. And yes, you must,' the rook told him.

The spider tickled Kine's neck, reeling up when he shook. Chukra said, 'Gorge or cutting, it's steep.' They gazed downwards. Sets of lines ran below, like a toy electric railway. Kine agreed, 'It's a long drop.'

'I wouldn't know,' Watchman wheezed. 'I'll be doing it my way – flying over,' he teased them.

'We'll do it *our* way,' purred Chukra. She glanced at Kine. 'Are we ready?'

'What way's that?'

'Like the spider. We'll make the ivy our lifeline . . .' Its glossy leaves grew beneath them, smothering the escarpment. Tendrils climbed the face rope-like. Chukra said, 'Come, I'll show you.' She slithered down on the stems, using feet and teeth nimbly. Kine went with her, head reeling. 'There,' the female smiled, landing, 'wings aren't everything, are they?'

He laughed. She was splendid. 'Spin a web for me, Chukra!'

'You think I couldn't?' she answered.

They hid themselves in long grass and contemplated the railroad. The metals loomed like great walls, the far embankment a blur as wind howled down the tracks, roughing up the wild growth there. Small heads raised, they peered sharply.

'What d'you make of it?' Kine said. 'Does it strike you as dangerous?'

'The rook should know.'

'Maybe,' Kine said.

'We have to take the risk, don't we? There's still a long way to go. Our ordeals haven't ended.'

No, he thought, that was certain! He looked askance at the other. She was alert, uncomplaining. His conscience pricked at her loyalty; it made him feel guilty. 'I wish I'd not brought you, Chukra, I'd no right to involve you. You could be safely at home.'

She said, 'I made my own choice. I want to see this fine valley.'

'I hope you will.'

'Kine, who'll stop us?' She tossed her head. 'It *is* real? You've not imagined it, have you?'

'It's real,' he smiled, eyes reflective. As real as bluebells in spring, golden mice in the covert, sun-drenched slopes and the perfume: meadowsweet, elder blossom. He would show her lush pastures, cool ditches of yarrow. The sigh was nostalgic. 'I'll show you dykes where the frogs croak and fat bank-voles dabble. You'll see the Moon Pond and Life Tree. And bright arcades in the brakes strolled by scarlet-tabbed pheasants. The best of places, Kia thought it.'

'So shall I,' Chukra whispered.

'Then we'd better get moving.'

'We're going to make it,' she told him. 'You'll slay the Rat King - you must!'

'Rattun's doomed,' Kine assured her.

They stepped into the wind and picked their way across stones to the great concrete sleepers. The whistling draught was unsettling; it almost shoved them off balance. As they drew near a rail, something flicked and they halted. 'It's a tail.' Chukra bristled.

'Fox,' rasped Kine. 'I can smell it. Don't move till it passes.'

They froze on hard, sharp-edged ballast. The wind was droning in cables. When a long minute was up, Chukra murmured, 'It's sleeping.'

'Sleeping!' Kine shuffled closer. He said, 'It's never asleep, not out here. It's dead, Chukra!'

The fox was stiff, its brush moving, the tail-hairs wind-ruffled. A handsome mask lay cheek downwards, rudely cushioned on stones. It was a bleak place to die. There was a rail alongside and a sleeper-end jutted. The weasels stared, drawing back.

'D'you think . . .' said Kine.

Chukra shrugged.

The Invisible Peril?

They cocked their heads. The lines juddered. The near-side track was vibrating and Kine looked up, his gaze urgent. 'Run,' he cried, 'run for cover!' Chukra turned, her glance startled. Leaping back to the verge, they heard a thunderous roar and a train hurtled past them. It raced away up the track, showering sparks from the power-rail.

Kine was dazed. They stared dumbly. Presently, he inched forward. 'Well,' he croaked. 'there's our *peril*.'

'Hardly invisible, was it?'

'A killer – a whirlwind!'

'I'm not so sure,' Chukra pondered.

'Ask the fox!'

She looked thoughtful. 'The fox says this,' she responded, 'that it is dead but undamaged.' She watched the speeding train vanish. 'If *that* hit you . . .' She shuddered.

'All right,' Kine said, 'let's scout. Before we cross, let's look further. Perhaps this isn't the best place.'

They prowled by the railway. Nothing changed, it stretched drearily, each length replicated, each bolt, every detail. Only the bodies were different. 'See – over there,' Chukra whispered. 'This time it's a badger.' Again, it lay by the rail; again, it might have been sleeping. They crept up close. Kine was watchful; he kept an eye on the track. There was no sign on the corpse of a struggle or impact.

'You're right,' he said, 'I don't like it. There's something here we can't see.'

'Something lethal,' said Chukra.

Black sails flapped. 'You're convinced, then?' Watchman hovered above them.

Kine ignored the bird, brooding. 'It's the rail,' he said slowly. 'The bodies lie by the rail.'

'Pah,' the rook said, 'that's nonsense.' He winnowed down, perching on it. 'There,' he growled, hopping sideways, balancing on the metal. 'It's not the first line I've sat on.'

'All the same . . .' Kine was cautious. The nearby tracks were vibrating and Watchman rose quickly. Chukra stood on hindlegs. Her neck was raised, her head twisting. 'Kine, watch out!' She was peering. He saw her sway in the wind, touch the live rail and jerk. As the voltage earthed through her, a train thundered past them.

Kine stood stunned, his jaw shaking. The ground itself seemed to quake as the tracks groaned and shuddered. The sudden air-lash was violent. Speeding Pullmans rocked wildly. Then they were gone and he quivered. Chukra's slim form was limp. Gently, Kine nosed the female. She was warm but inert. He nudged her flank, disbelieving. She was as still as the fox. He stepped backwards. She was as dead as the badger.

'You'll slay the Rat King – you must.' Her rousing words kept returning. They contradicted his heart, the dull weight in his breast that declared everything pointless. What was the point of endeavour with life itself so uncaring, so carelessly wasteful?

Kine looked back at the track. He had at last crossed alone, simply hurdling the metals. It was the least of the ordeals, yet it had claimed the bold female, the bravest of spirits – scourge of farm cat and mink – who had flouted all dangers. The irony pierced him.

'That's it,' Kine said, 'it's over.' An Odyssey finished. 'I can't leave her, Watchman.'

'You can't stay,' the rook mumbled.

'It's all I *can* do,' Kine told him. 'But for me, she'd not be here, she'd be hunting the plain still, a flame, a bright dancer. At least, the crows shan't defile her.'

'Death passes,' the rook said. 'It's the living who need you.'

'I've lost heart.'

'Kine the valiant?'

'First Kia and now Chukra – both dead. I'm jinxed, Watchman.'

'Kine the braggart?' the rook said. He laughed, harsh to be kind, to strike a spark in the weasel. 'A pair of summer-bright partners! What did they see in you, faint-heart?'

'What, indeed!' Kine said sadly.

'Fire,' the rook snapped, 'and fury. Where's the Blood Fury now, Kine?'

Kine's head dropped. 'Rook, I killed her.'

A pang stabbed the corvid. He had proclaimed the rail safe, had stood on it to prove it. Should he have doubted his wits? 'No,' he said, 'guilt's no answer; neither of us killed Chukra. She knew the risks she was taking. It was *her* choice, Kine, don't steal it. Don't diminish her courage.'

They sat together and brooded.

'Think of your own, Kine, there's Wonder. You haven't seen Wonder's kitts yet.'

'What are they like?'

'Cheeky devils. As impudent as their grandsire.'

The weasel straightened. 'You watched her – you saw how Chukra fought, Watchman. You saw her scatter the gulls; she was a flame, rook, she darted. She thought that nothing would stop us. "You'll slay the Rat King – you must." That was the last thing she told me.'

'It's up to you, I'm no good. One old rook on his own . . .'

'*Tchkkk*,' said Kine. 'We're two, Watchman. We're two now for the valley – two against Rattun's forces.'

'Four!' a new voice corrected.

Kine looked up at the bank. On a thicket sat Farthing. Flit-cat fluttered beside him. 'Four,' they chirped, 'for the battle, for vengeance and freedom!'

'Bravo,' Watchman applauded.

Kine said, 'How did you find us?'

'With difficulty!' Flit twittered. The sparrows were breathless. When they had rested a moment, they burst with all that happened: their search, at first, of the hills; the news that Watchman was weak; their dogged quest for his trail. As Farthing put it with passion, 'It's getting devilish late. The rats will soon rule the valley.'

'They're multiplying,' cried Flit.

'The guards have mobbed Ploughman's cat. He was doomed – a rat killer!'

'They've put a ban on all weasels.'

'And threatened Scrat,' Farthing gabbled.

'They want to know where you are, Kine.'

'Poor old pigmy! How is he?'

'Almost dead of fright,' Flit chirped.

Kine looked back at the railway. He told them quietly, 'We're marching. Wait for me on the bank, I'll join you there very shortly.'

'*Now*,' the sparrows said. 'Hurry . . .'

Watchman scowled. 'Let him be.' He eyed Kine. 'He'll be with us. Let him do what he has to.'

On his own, Kine turned slowly. He faced the rails, his coat blowing, the chill slicing through him. He could not see Chukra's body, the tracks broke his vision, but he could sense, almost feel her. The droning wind stung his eyes. He would always remember . . . as he remembered Kia's courage. Trance-like, Kine faced the cutting. 'I promise, Chukra, I'll slay him.' The weasel's stillness was eerie. 'I'll slay the Rat King or die. I won't betray you,' he muttered.

He climbed the bank in grim silence. The rook and sparrows were waiting, looking out on the country. Flit said, 'Everyone ready?'

A quilt of fields lay before them. Little woods and farms clustered. Across it all, six lanes streaming, the motorway rumbled.

'Defer,' the rats droned, 'to Rattun! All power to the leader!'

Scrat was down by the river. The night was full of their squeals, thick with chanting and slogans. Scrat moaned, seeking bugs. The tiny tapered nose snuffled. Torn between fear and hunger, the mite searched in panic. The sky was black, rain-encumbered; the marsh, demon-haunted.

A beetle stirred. The shrew grabbed it. Crushed between tiny cusps, the meal was rapidly swallowed. In the stream, wavelets sighed. Their sock-and-suck on the bank matched Scrat's minuscule heartbeat.

'By decree . . .' the rats chanted. They were leaving the reeds, trooping past the pump-house. Murkily they formed squads, marching upstream and downstream. They were dim in the night. Here and there, a head shimmered, slick with rain; a tail slithered. They were menacing, ghoulish. 'By decree . . .' squealed a leader.

'By decree,' they intoned, 'vigilance on all borders, cross-ings barred to all weasels. By rat-law,' they chanted.

'Thugs,' groaned Scrat.

'Kine shall perish.' The border-guards were dispersing. 'Kine shall perish in exile.' Another mob was assembling. The coarse backs jostled damply. 'To the barn!' voices grunted.

Scrat watched the rats scuttle. They formed a tide on the track, the dark, whiskered crest surging. Through the marsh-gate they poured, up the slope to the covert. Well behind, the shrew followed. It was his job as a spy. More important, Scrat reckoned, the safest place when they roved was to the rear of their armies.

'Doom,' he breathed. It was inky. At the fringe of the copse, water spattered from trees and he heard the pond hissing. 'Woe,' thought Scrat, it was lonely. The rooks had gone from the oaks, roosting back in winter quarters. Not even bats braved such evenings. All he saw was the rat wave, the great tide of their shoulders, their pale, phantom rat-heels.

They stopped and Scrat froze behind them. The barn was faint, a black outline. In the night, a voice echoed.

'Advance – recapture the diggings!'

Scrat quaked. It was Rattun.

18

Like a plume of dark smoke, a great flock of birds gathered, changing shape in the distance, twisting, stretching, condensing, drifting gradually inland. The girl gazed as they sailed closer. A storm was brewing, she reckoned. She thought, 'O, winter's a-coming!' and turned to her husband.

From the door of the shed, she watched him work at the saw-bench. She thought he made it seem easy, rather like slicing bread. The smell of sawdust was pleasant. He raised his head. 'Here,' he beckoned. He fished the plan from a pocket, the drawn-on graph-paper crumpled. 'See,' he said, 'that's the layout.'

He stacked the cut wood in lengths. 'I'll put it up by the sapling. A little house,' he enthused, 'a little tree – they'll go nicely. He's going to love it next summer! I'm going to make a swing, too.' He marked a line on a board. 'There's a strong bough on the plum tree.'

She smiled.

'And maybe a sandpit.'

'He's got a good dad – I've told him.'

He grinned. 'His mum's not bad, either.'

'Oh, she can be!' the girl teased.

The birds passed. Most were plovers; there must have been many thousands, flocks of rooks and gulls with them. Their massed passage was hushed, countless wings barely sighing. Only the ducks, which came after, flying straighter and faster, cried out, pinions creaking. 'Stormy weather,' the girl said. 'I'm glad we don't need to join them. We're lucky – cosy old cottage!'

Winter nights, the logs blazing! She loved to sit in the hearth-light, the young man beside her. They were magic, those evenings. There were dreams in the fire, lands of bliss and inferno, picture-stories where flames danced. Heroes, heroines, monsters!

She eyed the graph-paper vaguely. 'What's this, where you've scribbled?'

He took the blueprint and squinted. 'I'm going to put in a window. He'll need a window to look through.'

'You won't forget that job for me?'

'To do the door by the kitchen?' He left the shed and stood with her. The old back door was rat-nibbled. Sometime, Poacher had patched it but there were signs of fresh gnawing. 'I'll put a board on the bottom; keep the worst of the draught out.'

'Yes, the draught . . .' she reflected.

'Good as done,' he assured her.

'You'll make it strong?'

The man nodded. 'I'll make you snug as a dormouse.'

'Because . . .' She left it unspoken and viewed the barn. They were back; there were new earthworks and tunnels. They would need food for the winter. The brutes got hungry and cold. The brutes got jealous of comfort.

While the rooks flew ahead, Kine moved on with the sparrows. The grass was dank, starved of sun; willow-herb, dead or dying. Partly screening the road, clumps of trees were half-bare. In patches, leaves stayed aloft, weak and limp but defiant. Others, wholly exhausted, fell with startling abruptness. They did not shift, having landed.

A man was shooting wood-pigeons. The sudden clap of the gun made Kine stop and look upwards. Blue-grey feathers were falling. The clouds were deeper in colour, a bruise-like yellowish-mauve, with rain-tails in some cases. Flit-cat perched near the weasel. He said, 'Keep on down the hedge. There's a ditch by the highway. We'll meet you there, you'll have cover.'

A dull roar signalled traffic. As Kine advanced, it grew louder, the air fume-polluted. The ditch was littered with junk: wrappings, cans, human refuse. He poked his head up then ducked. The monstrous multi-lane joust hurled chaotic shapes past him. Cars and buses stampeded. Massive trucks thundered headlong, charging both ways, their mad progress earth-shaking.

The sparrows perched near the trench. 'What d' you make of it?' Flit said.

'It's hopeless,' Kine told him. 'Use your sense,' he demanded, 'there's not a chance of surviving.' He swung his head. 'Where's the rook?'

A horn blared. Lights were flashing; juggernauts sped like race-cars. Drivers' faces stared briefly, pale and mesmerized, speed-doped.

Farthing shrugged. 'Forget Watchman. You heard the gun – he'll be hiding. The sound of gunfire upsets him.'

'The sound of gunfire!' Kine snorted.

'It's Watchman's job to spot guns, that's the job of a Watchman.'

'And a guide's to guide,' Kine snarled. 'What kind of guide hides when needed?'

Farthing scratched. 'He'll come back.'

'When he's ready,' chirped Flit. '*We* can guide you till then; we know the way from here on.'

Kine looked fierce. 'And the road?'

'Oh, you'll have to cross that . . .'

'*Tchkkk*,' he spat. They were dense. He paced and counter-paced grimly, working out his frustration. 'All you're good for is sparring! Brawling urchins,' he muttered. 'Watch the juggernauts rampage! Are you saying you'll stop them, hold them up while Kine passes?' He grunted, casting his mind back. 'There *was* a way – Watchman knew it. He told me how. I've forgotten.'

When they had paused for reflection, Flit-cat said, 'We've a problem . . .'

'We have indeed.'

'Not the road, Kine.'

'No,' chimed Farthing, 'not that.'

'It's the ditch . . .'

'What about it?'

'The signs,' said Flit.

'Show the weasel.' Farthing peered. 'He can read them. Kine knows the signs backwards. He knows the print of the fox, the hare's trod, the deer's foiling.'

'Yes,' said Flit, 'he's an expert. He knows a hundred signs, Kine does.'

'Yes, yes,' Kine snapped, 'just show me.' He viewed the shallow impressions of pads and claws in the mud. There were faint fan-marks between them. 'Webbing,' Kine said. 'An otter . . .'

'There, you see, that means danger!'

'Follow the path of the otter . . .' Kine looked up. 'That was it! That was what the rook told us.' He thought of Chukra and paused. 'He was exhausted, all-in. He blurted out some directions, the lands to cross on the journey, then – yes, follow the otter. He said to follow the otter.' He eyed the tracks in the ditch.

'Come on,' Kine rapped, 'it's this way!' He bounded off down the trench, leaping debris and brambles. The otter's spore disappeared; then, where silt made a bank, a fresh seal was imprinted. As Kine raced, the birds fluttered. 'You'd best take care,' called the sparrows, 'it's a big brute, an otter.'

There was a right-angled turn. The ditch ran straight for the road, vanishing into darkness. Kine stopped dead. 'It's a tunnel!'

'You wouldn't get us down there.' The sparrows sat near the culvert.

'I'm going in,' said the weasel.

'Is that wise?'

Kine braced quickly. 'Wise?' he said. 'Ask the rook!' He plunged into the pipe. There was no time for wisdom. He was Kine the risk-taker and had to beat the road somehow.

All the same, he slowed down, nosing cautiously forward. It was dim and smelled rank, a thick sludge in the bottom. Twigs and broken stems rotted, swept in during flooding. A glistening newt watched, unmoving. Its tiny orange eyes glowed. Suppose he met something larger; suppose an otter was waiting? He would, he thought, stand no chance – journey's end would be sudden. Darkness deepened. The earth shook.

Overhead, trucks were rumbling.

Kine felt cold. Something touched him. A coiling tentacle

groped and he jinked as it dragged – an old tree root left stranded. The thunder grew. It was constant, tremors drubbing his bones, beating down from the lanes through the concrete above him. He struck a pool of trapped bilge and spat slime. The taste sickened. He stopped a moment, head splitting. Again, he ventured on blindly.

He seemed to travel an age. This was no earthy burrow, the work of rabbit or mole. Theirs were short, twisting pipes. This great tube was remorseless, man-made and unbending. It was a black throat to . . . where? Should he turn and go back? No, he thought, otters used it. He was as fearless as they; he was small but undaunted. The tremors lessened. Kine listened. He thought he heard a faint splash. The stale air became fresh, and far off, the light glimmered.

He scurried on, now with vision. At first, the image was round, a full moon in the murk. Then, the tunnel's end closer, walls and floor grew in detail. Prudently, he took stock. The sound of water was clear and, as he stole the last inches, he saw a quiet bank of scrub, a swift stream at its bottom.

The sound of traffic had dropped. It hummed softly behind while he rested, elated.

'Flit,' bawled Farthing, 'he's made it!' They had located the exit. 'Flit, our champion's made it!'

Water swirled through tall reeds. Its slick tongues skirted boulders. Kine was hypnotized by it. 'The river – our stream!' It had grown since the downs, filled and broadened, gained muscle. 'The stream's returned,' churred the weasel.

'What stream *is* it?' Flit queried.

'*Our* stream. Don't you see?' Kine went down to the water. 'It'll lead to the valley.'

The sparrows mused. 'Are you certain? We didn't pass any rivers.'

'You fly too low, you see nothing.' The weasel dunked, rinsing briskly. The tunnel's stench had been strong. He frisked, telling them rudely, 'All you see are the daisies.'

'*You* can talk!' They puffed up.

'Ask the rook,' he said, drying. 'That's if he deigns to rejoin us. He flies high – see what *he* says.'

Not far off, reeds were swaying; a sloshing noise stopped their chatter. There was a sizeable splash and something moved underwater. 'It's a big fish,' Flit muttered. Farthing gawped. 'That's no fish, Flit!' The surface heaved. Kine lay flat. A broad head rose, peering sharply, eyes wide, the skull streaming. The otter saw him and huffed. Its wild snort was not friendly.

'Run!' cheeped Flit. The birds quivered. 'Buzz the water-beast, Farthing . . .'

The sparrows whirled from their perch, skimmed the river and wheeled. Hovering, they chirped fiercely. Kine had dived for the rushes. He found their feet in the tide and floundered, seeking a raft. Scrambling on to a log, he peeped out from the reed-bed. The stream was clear save for bubbles, and Farthing whisked past him. 'Did you see that?' he twittered.

'He fled,' whooped Flit. 'He dived under!'

'We confused him!' piped Farthing.

'He lost his nerve.'

'We'd've pooped him . . .'

Kine was not listening to them. The reeds were moving beside him, gliding past in long columns. Or so it seemed. He rocked gently. It was the *log* that was shifting, the rushes were static. His wooden platform was floating, being nudged by the current, eased out from the bank. ·

'Kine, get off!' bawled the sparrows.

He viewed his raft. It was sturdy. The stream was smooth, running swiftly.

'I'll get off,' he called back, 'when I get to the valley.'

Watchman stretched a wing slowly. He thought he must have drowsed off, for he was still in the tree and could hear traffic rumbling, the shooting now over. The rook had veered from the shots, seeking cover by habit, a perch to spy out from. Yes, he must have snoozed off – tiredness ambushed him nowadays.

Other rooks shared the branches, an unfamiliar crowd, a young hen-bird perched near him. She preened herself, her plumes flashing. 'Are you all right?' she demanded, his decrepitude striking. 'You're very old to be travelling.'

And she, he thought, was very handsome. He slid a leery eye open. She was, he guessed, full of mischief, full of ardour and passion. Erstwhile mates came to mind, days of strutting and courtship.

'Not *that* old,' Watchman quibbled. Not too old for adventure! 'Old enough to have lived, to know a fine head of feathers.'

'Oh yes . . .' she said primly.

'To be a judge of good style.' He arched his neck and posed grandly. The hoary sight made her wince. 'In fact, you're lucky to meet me, I'm famed,' rattled Watchman. 'I've crossed a dozen lands lately; my travels are epic.'

The other shrugged, her glance cool. 'Then you'll need the rest, won't you?'

'I could help you,' he promised. He sidled closer, wings twitching. It was madness, he thought, the 'false spring' of October, when corvids felt bouncy.

The female added, 'You *old* ones – you'll have a stroke any moment!'

'My revelations would thrill you . . .'

'I've heard it all.'

'And my daring.'

'I know,' she drawled, 'you're an eagle!'

It was, he saw, fizzling out, an abortive flirtation. 'Of course,' he told her, 'I'm fussy. I doubt you're ready for fame, for Watchman the sagacious, the guiding eye of the just, the eye of Kine the avenger, challenger of the despot.'

She cackled. *What* despot?'

'Lord Rattun, the Rat King.'

The female scoffed. 'That's a new one! And you'll be Lord Geriatric – and me, I'm bored. Push off, dry-bones!'

Watchman glowered. The common hen! The bird was blind to distinction, a rook of class, when she met it.

A brash young male caught her eye.

No doubt her friends were as coarse! Watchman scowled his disdain. As if he cared for such fowl! As if he fell for such females! He shook his wings and took flight. She had a nerve to think he meant it! The motorway sprawled below. He flew higher. The hussy!

Beneath him, twin specks were bustling. They looked like ants from his viewpoint. As they grew, scrambling upwards, he could see they were sparrows.

'Hey, Watchman . . .' they twittered.

The rook nursed his chagrin. He should have taught her a lesson, set some 'dry bones' about her – he should have plucked her fine feathers! Farthing flew alongside. He dipped and rolled for attention. Flit-cat joined the formation.

'Watchman, Kine's on the stream . . . he's sailed off . . . we can't stop him . . .'

'On the stream?' Watchman glared. He stalled and pulled out abruptly.

'On a raft,' Flit said glumly.

'*Raft!*' The rook squinted forward. The countryside rolled ahead, darkly daubed by cloud-shadows. Gleaming strips marked the stream – curves, a reach and then nothing, the flow lost in forest. Again, it shone, now far distant, a match-stick log on its crest, a weasel dot on the splinter.

'You let him go?' the rook ranted.

'We couldn't stop him.'

They side-slipped. Watchman flopped to a bridge. It was of grey stone construction with two graceful arches. The rook sat there and brooded. 'You let him go,' he repeated. 'Now no one can stop him.' He eyed the flow. 'The stream's got him.'

'It could lead back to the valley.'

'Or *anywhere.*' Did it matter? Watchman shook his head slowly. Where it went was academic. Kine would drown, that was certain.

19

Kine walked the length of the log then returned to the middle. The vessel was stable. It had a habit of swinging, sometimes turning right round so prow and stern interchanged, but the deck remained steady. A beetle pottered about, reassuringly lively. Cruising home! Kine clung tightly. He was hardly a sailor.

Suppose the otter returned? It was equipped for the river, like the mink. They were pirates. Kine's domain was the land. Suppose the weather turned rough? The clouds were dirty-grey sheets, full of rain. If a storm broke . . .

He eyed the so-far smooth stream and hoped the voyage would be short. Fleets of smaller craft drifted, bronze armadas of leaves, broken twigs, fallen berries. Amid the dross of past seasons, a plastic pop-bottle sailed until, snatched by an eddy, it lodged in the bank-growth.

At that point, there were reeds. Further on, Kine passed coves, hoof-pocked bays where steers watered from close-bitten pastures. Elsewhere, bluffs rose above him, scaffolded with tree-roots. Wisps of dead vegetation, bleached near-white, marked a floodline.

Here and there, a great stone, rising out of the stream, ploughed the flow into lanes and the log took its choice, slewing off to one side, again slowly gyrating creating merry-go-round spectators from staring black cattle, drab-faced ewes with long faces.

An old and broken-down pony watched the stream, melancholy.

Kine sat up. 'Can you hear me?' He strained his voice. 'Are you *listening*? Am I right for the valley?'

The pony lowered its eyelids and said nothing.

Kine cursed it.

Ahead, the stream's surface ruffled. A bustling brook joined the flood, the main current edged sideways, and now the log pitched abruptly. The weasel braced, feet spread widely. He saw the beetle plod forward, slither backwards, keep plodding. A bank of nettles was looming. He thought the raft must strike ground, then the confluence passed and the curling flow centred.

The log crept round, gliding sideways. Little fish swam beside it. Dozens of them shoaled dimly, one or two squirming up, goggled-eyed, to mouth leaves. A larger shape ghosted near, olive-backed, and they fled, scattering like shell-shrapnel. As Kine watched, the pike prowled. It returned to the shadows.

Not far off, a man fished, his keep-net in the rushes. He was hunched on the bank, heron-still, and Kine groaned for it seemed luck had left him. He almost jumped from the log. Instead, he made himself flat while the craft, cruising slowly, perversely steered for the angler. It had a mind of its own and looked set on disaster – on running down the man's float, on compelling attention.

Scarcely daring to look, Kine tried hard to be wooden. He glimpsed the rod, its length threatening. It lifted back, poised above him. He glimpsed the man. The man rose. This was it, thought the weasel. He clenched his teeth. Nothing happened. He eyed the rod: it was bent, the line taut. He heard reeling.

The pike heaved up, lashed and plunged. As it fought, the man played it. His concentration was total. A *fleet* of weasels on logs could have proceeded unnoticed. Kine looked back, his chest swelling. He felt the old braggart in him, a sprite of the stream now.

He shot a couple of bridges. Their stony vaults echoed. Then, whirled deep into forest, the weasel faced darker shadows, gloomy tunnels of trees, and his doubts were rekindled. Black boughs swept the water. There were gurgles from caverns, unaccountable *plops* that startled and haunted. Kine was suddenly lonely. He wished the sparrows were there but knew they would not have followed. They had not held with the river.

Perhaps he ought to have listened. Suppose it *was* the wrong stream? He might sail on forever, beyond all hope of returning. So much effort for nothing – Chukra's sacrifice wasted! Flit and Farthing betrayed; Watchman left unconsulted! One impetuous stroke and his vows rendered worthless!

He paced the deck. Had he failed? 'No,' he snarled, 'trust your instinct, the divination born in you; trust the gift of your forebears.' Kine glowered at the shadows. 'Cast your gloom,' he churred grimly, 'Kine the weasel goes forward!'

As if impressed, the stream brightened. The trees had thinned and were smaller, slowly shelving to brush. Beyond the banks, dressed for winter, the land was sombre and worn, drear as Ploughman's old coat, the one he wore on the tractor. Again, the reach mirrored clouds: dull enough, to be sure, but not as black as the forest. Near a bend, swans were floating. Several youngsters gazed round, fully-grown, still buff-coloured. Nearby, swam the adults.

Another test!

Kine lay low. The raft was bobbing a little, heading straight for the cob, whose great neck was submerged, the beak dredging for stream-plants. Kine's eye caught the beetle. It had crawled into a crack on the log and was sleeping. The weasel envied its nerve – or was it simply exhausted? His own nerves were far-stretched. He was not built for quiescence.

The male swan raised his head. For a moment, he glared, the broad bill dripping weed as he regarded the weasel. Then he shook and rasped softly – a reassurance, it seemed, for the pen turned serenely, drifting off as he paddled.

The log swirled on by the cygnets. For them, its jockey was fun, a novel freak of the stream, and they crowded the traveller. Kine kept still, fuming quietly. The cob and pen, he had feared; he had not reckoned on this, a brood of overgrown nurslings. With necks craned, the group ventured, dark bills poking at him.

A flat tip gave a prod. He was almost thrown over. Another tweaked and drew back. Weasel fury exploded. Leaping up, he spat wrath, hissing straight in their faces. '*Tchkkk*,' he spat, 'I am danger!'

They stared. They were startled. But this was sport, said their eyes, and they came back, necks weaving.

A throaty growl crossed the flow. The cob's voice stopped them short, his stern summons commanding, and Kine watched with relief as the young joined their parents. They could have drowned him quite easily. He had no room on the raft; he could not dance there and fight.

The log was travelling too slowly, attracting all kinds of dangers.

Worse, it lacked any cover and storms were approaching. Dusky rods smeared the sky. Falling somewhere up-river, rain would raise the stream's level, make his highway a torrent. He watched the swans thunder up, winging into the murk. On the raft, he was helpless. Either the vale was reached soon or the spate would deluge him.

The clouds broke on the downs, dumping rain in black curtains. As it hissed on the slopes, the sheep scuttled for shelter while cattle, heads lowered, turned their tails to the downpour. Soon, the land-drains were full, gushing out into ditches. Springs grew strong, streamlets hustled. Everywhere, levels rose and the river, turned brown, stretched its shoulders and fretted.

With a rumble, it charged, swirling high up the banks, claws unsheathed as it quickened. A bolting rabbit, snatched up, tried to swim in the current. Swept away, the beast panicked, kicked briefly and vanished.

Through the bridge the flood hastened, lashing weeds to a frenzy. Here, the sparrows sat watching. Flit and Farthing had sheltered in a niche in the stonework. Looking out through the rain, they saw the slick surface froth and churn on down a reach that grew wider and wider.

'We ought to find him,' said Flit.

Farthing moped. 'In *this* weather?'

They eyed the downpour and sulked. They would be drenched if they flew, their airworthiness fleeting. Flit-cat puffed up his feathers. 'When it eases . . .' he croaked.

'*When*,' the answer came glumly. Umber vapour rolled

over. 'It's set in,' Farthing forecast. 'We warned him not to sail off. There's no hope now.'

'The thick-head!'

'We picked a dolt for our champion.'

'All the same – when it stops . . . We ought to know where he perished.'

The rain beat and they brooded.

Barging on, the flood heaved, grabbing debris from banks, tumbling it in wild currents. Fallen branches from trees writhed and reared like sea-serpents; plastic farm-bags swept past, bloated by the air in them. Where side-streams joined the flow, evil tides thick with mud raised a pudding-like foam on the breast of the torrent.

Watchman cowered alone in the fork of an alder. Though the trunk broke the rain, water trickled from twigs and the rook was bedraggled. This, he thought, was the end – the damp would get in his bones and the joints would seize solid. He would die of exposure. And in vain. Curse the weasel!

He had been mad to help Kine, to waste time on the braggart. Kine listened to no one. All weasels were rash, Kine the worst, a disaster!

'Brrr!' moaned Watchman.

He shivered. The young could stand such discomfort; he was too old to get soaked. The storm would be the death of him. And of Kine, he reflected – the fish would feed on the weasel. The thought gave brief satisfaction but hardly consoled him.

Still, the water was rising. Downstream, it lapped fields, frothing up on the grass, and a farm dog was barking. The dog bounced back from the waves, its head low, its rump wriggling. At last, a man called its name and it turned and ran swiftly, raising spume in the meadow.

Faster now, the log swirled. Drubbed by rain, the stream seethed and Kine clung to a raft that grew less and less stable. The deck was no longer dry and the beetle had floundered. Once, smoothly gyrating, the craft had taken to pitching, to violent lurches and rolls, plunging, bucking and rearing.

On a path, children shouted. 'Ma, the log, see the log . . .'

'Come away from that stream!'

'There's an animal on it . . .'

'You're getting soaked, come on home.'

The woman's stricture was terse and they passed in the downpour, young voices protesting. 'But *ma* . . .'

Kine clung grimly. At times, the deck was awash and he choked, coughing water. The log careered wildly on, the flood's volume awesome. Where gentle eddies had twirled, hungry maelstroms were churning. Kine saw one straight ahead, a great whirl gulping flotsam. Twigs and leaves vanished in it, dragged round and sucked under.

Whipping rain stung the weasel. It broke reeds with its force, spattering in the whirlpool. Kine was scrambling astern as the log entered orbit. For half a spin, the craft turned, dragged in by the vortex, then its weight snatched it free and the main current took it.

Giddily, Kine peered round. Now, the banks had grown tall, rock-walled, wet and daunting. Crags gleamed in the downpour. From the welter ahead, two great boulders loomed greyly, like fortifications, the flood forced between them. Kine caught sight of the rapids. Compressed, the flow doubled pace, spearing into the neck, the soused log driven with it.

As it plunged, Kine hung on. He thought his claws would be torn, ripped out of his feet. He thrust his teeth into bark, anchoring with a jaw-lock. *Bam!* The craft slammed a wall, ricocheted, yawed madly. *Bam!* The other wall met it. The impacts loosened his footholds. Clinging only by mouth, Kine was flailed through the chute. Teeth and neck screamed in protest. *Bam-Bam!* He leeched grimly.

Flanked by towering rocks, the weasel aquaplaned on, rising, falling, corkscrewing. Then the narrows were gone; the stream spread, became smoother. Half-drowned, Kine regained balance and gasped, his lungs heaving.

Overhead, it grew black. If anything, the rain strengthened, at last expunging the land, muffling sounds with its growl, the snarl it made on the stream as it rasped down the reach, beating paths through the reeds to expose secret closets. Here, ducks lurked for shelter, heads withdrawn, treading water. Not far off, on one leg, a heron huddled, rain-blinded.

Kine thought of the Moon Pond. How still was its surface; how scented the nights there! How securely the Life Tree spanned the stars that swam by it! True and firm was the willow – unlike the crazed log beneath him. The log he could not escape as it whirled to fresh danger!

Ahead, the water turned white; a roar drowned the rain's grumbling. As the roar grew in strength, Kine could see the dark ledge where the flood broke its back, plunging down into tumult, the froth and spume of the weir fierce as steam in the deluge. He knew his voyage had ended. Not even Kine the survivor could live in that ferment.

There were only two options: either he sailed to destruction or jumped and swam for it. He eyed the fast, muddy flow. The weasel's way was not passive; he must at least meet death striving.

The weir's deep thunder came louder.

Desperately, Kine sprang, striking out in the water. All that showed from the bank was his head, like a leaf, pointing shorewards but slipping, sliding gradually down, though he paddled with frenzy. Near the lip of the falls, he grew weak and slid faster. For one moment, he bobbed. He seemed to hang on the brink then was gone.

20

The big lad gawped at the garden. 'Next thing,' he said, 'I'll see fairies!'

With his less lubberly pal, he had mooched up the track on the look-out for rabbits. They had the dogs at their heels and could hear Ploughman's tractor, a dull, muffled throb in the rain that was falling. So far, the rain was not strong but the outlook was gloomy.

'I'll be damned . . .' They had stopped. At the first youth's surprise, the second stood on his toes, peering over the hedge which surrounded the cottage. 'He never wasted much time! Look at that . . .'

They stared damply. 'It's like in stories, *appeared*, popped up like a mushroom!'

The little Wendy House gleamed, its new timbers fine-grained and made bright by the wetness. There in Poacher's old garden, its unexpectedness startled. It had a magical impact, make-believe in dimension. Like a Gulliver figure, the man rose behind it. 'Got a moment?' he asked. 'I could do with a hand here.'

He was holding a hammer. They pushed the gate, stepping through. 'Thanks,' the engineer grinned. He drove a nail home and told them, 'I want to get the roof finished in case it rains harder.'

The youths drew near. 'You done well . . .'

He stood back. 'Not so bad.' He admired his work proudly. 'There's bits to do by and by but the structure's complete. Grab that bitumen sheet while I tack the laths, will you?' The dogs sniffed round while he hammered. At length, he said, 'That'll do – at least, she won't let the water.'

'She's all right,' said the big lad.

His comrade said, 'She's a treat.'

They contemplated the playhouse. It was agreeably rustic

and would mellow quite soon, its scale matching the sapling which grew alongside. In spring, when soft leaves were sprouting, there would be primroses near and thick grass in the orchard for toddling excursions.

'Think he'll like it?' the man said.

'Will it have television?'

They laughed and picked up the tools. 'Come indoors,' the girl called them, 'there's a fire in the cottage. You're wet.' They dried by it. Outside, it grew dull and the rain drubbed the windows. 'It's settled in,' she complained. 'That's because he's been building – it's put a jinx on the weather. Poor little palace, all soaked!'

'Soon dry up,' said the big lad. He eyed the child, who beamed back, and the youths made clown faces.

The girl looked glum. 'Don't believe it. It's going to rain now for days.'

'You can't tell.'

'*I* can tell,' she said darkly. 'I know what it's up to.'

'Yes, she does,' laughed her husband. She had an uncanny instinct, his girl of the valley. 'I'll have to look to the pumps. She'll be right, she's a deep one!'

The youths smirked. 'We'll be off, then.'

'Want a lift in the van?'

'No, we'll go by the woods – let the dogs find a rabbit.'

They shuffled out, collars raised, and whistled the terriers. As they made for the covert, the rainfall grew stronger. The large youth dragged his feet, grumbling, 'We should've taken the lift.' Then, with muted admiration, 'She wasn't wrong, his ol' missus; this lot won't stop quickly. We should've gone in the van.'

At the trees, they looked back. The weather drove from the hills, clouds capping the summits. There were few creatures about. The rabbits hated the rain; the rook nests were deserted. 'Place is dead,' said one youth. 'When d'you last see a weasel? You couldn't come here at one time and not see a weasel. Or stoat . . . My neck's sopping!'

'We could take the short cut.' But the other looked doubtful.

'Through the Witchwood? Not likely!'

'We could skirt round the side; there's a path to the village.'

'Past the rats?'

'They live deeper. Besides,' the slight lad opined, 'in this rain we won't meet them.'

'We'd best not . . .' They trudged forward. Slicing squalls drenched the woods, tearing down the last leaves. Withered burdock lurked damply, sticking seeds on their jackets. Heads down, the youths hurried, rain-blurred eyes fixed ahead, half-afraid to glance sideways. Suddenly, the dogs clamoured.

'They're in the brush – they've found something.'

The couple paused.

'Or been *found*!'

'By them monsters . . .'

The dogs ran out, wet and growling. Hackles raised, they stared back, stiff-legged, at the forest.

'Something's coming . . .'

'It's *her*.' The youths grinned. They felt better. 'Her who's after old Ploughman. It's the old biddy skulking!'

'In the Witchwood?'

'She's barmy.'

'She's a nut.' said the big lad.

Kine was falling through space. Overwheimed by the stream, he had been swept to the weir and hurled into the downpour, a sheet of vertical water which smashed to bits at its bottom. Here, a seething mass billowed, smithereens flying upwards, passing Kine as he tumbled. For one last anguished gasp, the weasel hung in suspension, then profound darkness claimed him.

Presently, a light shone – a light far-off, like dawn breaking. How long his world had been black he could not say. Time meant nothing. Only the far gleam now mattered, a pure and beckoning torch, and Kine felt oddly light-headed. He felt serene, reborn almost.

It was a buoyant sensation. No longer riding the flood, he seemed to float in thin air as if he were weightless. Somewhere, rain was still falling and, at the edge of the flood, a sodden body lay limply, washed up by the river. It could have been his own, Kine thought, but seemed unimportant. The small damp shape became dim and he was drawn by the light, which got steadily brighter.

Now, the sky had grown clear, a blissful dunnock-egg blue. He felt blithe, free of troubles. Full of joy as he watched, he saw the light slowly rise, surpass the brilliance of dawn, become the sun in its glory. Not since his first weeks of life had those rays spread such wonder. A peacock butterfly passed. Not since his nursery days had Kine noticed such colours.

The land was a picture. Trees glowed in their greenness; lush meadows were emerald. Gone was the onset of winter – this was summer eternal, the season of gladness. The warp of time appeared natural. He was in summery mood and felt young again, wide-eyed. Every wildflower was brilliant.

There were reds: banks of poppies. And pinks: mallow, loosestrife. Yellow charlock and toadflax caught the sun while blues ravished, a host of shades from cool cornflower to the bold spires of bugle. The blooms in this land were constant. It was a scene to delight, a place of sweet, heady fragrance – 'the Land of Lost Dreams?' Kine pondered.

Once, and then again briefly, he thought he heard voices calling, the squeal of weasel kitts playing. He could have sworn that he knew them, heard the chortling of brood-mates. But it was quiet when he listened. They were sounds snatched from space and did not come a third time.

Instead, where foxgloves dripped dew, a snuffling grunt broke the hush and an old wall-eyed badger, late abroad, trundled homewards full of grubs dug by starlight. The rolling, thickset beast paused, sniffed the flowers and continued.

The weasel knew the old growler. Long ago, by full moon, Kine had peered from a hedge and watched the badger at work scraping larvae from wasp-bikes. Kine was sure it was him, the first brock of his life – the boar with strange opaque eyes who had died the next winter.

A land of dreams, summer memories! An innocent

160

country – or so, thought Kine, it had seemed, for the nightmares came later: the Mink Wars then Rattun. He could
imagine no evil in this sunny idyll.

Everywhere, moisture glittered, great spiders' webs twinkling. He had not seen webs so fine since he explored as a
youngster. Little rabbits bobbed up, twitching dew from
their noses. Scarcely bigger than moles, they browsed and
sloppetted staidly, perfect miniatures of adults. Then,
jumping straight in the air, they streaked off into bushes.

In warm fields, hares were drowsing, stretched like dogs
in the hollows. Others, up on their haunches, reached for
morsels of herbage. It was, mused Kine, as it should be –
as it *had* been in those days. Simple joys filled the hedges.
There were the platforms of twigs in small trees where
doves nested. He used to climb to them sometimes and
watch the world pass beneath him.

Or he would sit on the shelves formed by huge bracket-
fungi and snap at bluebottles.

Now, the hares ambled off, their long hindlegs ungainly.
Grazing cattle ignored them, the tasselled tails of the steers
swinging loosely at insects. In a while, from the blue, a pair
of shellduck flew down, their white and chestnut plumes
shining. Surrealistically bright, the birds perched on a barn,
motionless, as if sculpted. Then they dropped to their nest
in the straw the roof sheltered.

Across a lea, in the sun, a supple beast undulated.
Another joined it. Two weasels.

Kine looked hard. They were females. He only wished
they were nearer. They had their tails turned his way and
were half-hidden by grass, but the sight was spellbinding.
The first looked round. Was it Kia? She took a step and
doubt left him. She seemed so young, a red sprite. 'Kia, it's
me – Kine! Wait for me!'

She neither heard nor perceived him.

'Kia . . .'

His heart's plea was soundless. Again, he begged, still in
vain. 'Don't go, Kia, wait for me. It's Kine – you
remember . . .' As he would always remember: summer,
birdsong, their courtship. '*Kine, I'm very fond of you.*' She

161

had laughed. *'Don't ask why – I am, really. And of the valley, I love it. Don't let anything spoil it.'*

'Nothing shall.'

'Do you promise?'

He had. Now, she shifted.

'Kia, don't go . . .'

She pranced on, her companion remaining. The second weasel glanced back. There was no mistaking Chuk-Chukra, her bright, sparkling challenge. 'You promised me, too,' her eyes said. 'Kine, your work isn't over.'

'Chukra, wait . . .'

But they faded.

'Kine, you can't die,' a voice said. It was urgent.

But I want to, he thought. I want to join Kia and Chukra. I want to live in the sun, in this land of lost summers.

'You've got to *live*,' the voice grated.

Perhaps, he thought. He *had* promised. He gave a groan. The scene misted. Something wet struck his face. It was rain. A nose nudged him. 'Come on, Kine, you can do it – you've got to move,' the voice ordered. 'The stream's still rising. Don't lie there!'

His head was sore. Shapes swam round him: dank reeds, loury clouds, the sandy face of Young Heath, Wonder's mate, looking anxious.

'Kine, wake up; you're alive, Kine!'

'Where am I?'

Rain slanted.

'On the bank by the flood. Where the weir torrent washed you. If you don't budge, you'll be flotsam.'

Kine moaned and rose slowly. Propped on two legs, he shuddered.

'There,' growled Heath, 'you can make it!'

'You went close that time,' Heath said. 'I thought you were finished.'

'Me?' said Kine. 'You know me better than that, Heath.'

They watched the flood. It was spreading.

'I know you, Kine!' Heath was smiling. 'I remember the Mink Wars.'

162

'You can't kill off old campaigners. We're two of a kind.'

'All the same, it was near. I thought you'd given up breathing.' The sandy weasel looked solemn.

'I blacked out,' Kine said, shrugging. 'You won't catch Kine giving up – not Kine the intrepid! I might give up sailing rivers, but that's something different. That's for ducks. They can keep it!'

'And the rain,' Heath said, frowning.

'How far now to the valley?'

'You'd see the hills if it cleared. It's not far to the heath, then the ground will be firmer. Wonder's there with the dandies.'

Kine drew breath. Almost home . . . 'Let's get on.'

'Can you manage?'

'Just lead the way.' Kine stretched stiffly. 'I need to loosen my joints.' He was in poor shape for Rattun. 'I need to sharpen my action. The trek will help.' He moved feebly. Life aboard had been cramping. 'A little time,' he insisted, 'I'll soon be fit.'

'Take it easy . . .'

They marched until Kine was tired then lay up in a burrow. It was a break from the deluge. When he revived, they went on, threading damply through hedges, hopping water-filled ditches. 'Look,' cried Heath. He had halted. They viewed the growth. 'There's the heather. It won't be very much longer.' He ran ahead, his nose working. 'We'll pretty soon find the others.'

They found the dandy hounds first. The young weasels were hunting, looking wet and dejected.

'Would you believe it?' sighed Heath. 'You'd never reckon I taught them!' He raised a fatherly snarl. 'Not like that, you'll catch nothing – on your toes, show some spirit!'

'Let them be.' Wonder joined them. 'Kine. you're safe!' she exulted. She was drenched but delighted. 'And Heath returned, Kine, I found him!'

'Heath found *me*.'

'It's a blessing.'

The dandies yawned.

Feathers ruffled and Kine looked up, sneezing loudly.

Flit and Farthing scowled back, huddled close in the scrub. 'Caught a cold?' Farthing censured. 'That's what comes of not listening, sailing off. Now he's sneezing!'

'He's not fit,' Flit-cat added. 'We've a snuffling fighter.'

'On the eve of the contest!'

'The fight of fights,' Flit said glumly.

'You can forget it,' snapped Wonder. 'Kine stays here. He needs rest. There'll be no fight with the Rat King.'

'*Tchkkk*!' Kine's utterance startled. They hushed, growing damper. The weasels crouched in the heather. Kine reviewed the group slowly – his daughter, Wonder, then Heath, a brood of fidgeting dandies, two waterlogged sparrows. It was a force of a kind. He sniffed and asked them, 'Where's Watchman?'

Part Three

THE DEATH DANCE

21

Watchman slewed from the rain, pitching down by the sparrows. He shook his head, his beak dripping. 'They're taking over,' he wheezed, 'they're everywhere in the valley. The place is crawling with rats, plagued with great scuffling monsters. By spring, the law will be rat-law – all eggs and chicks for rat stomachs; all domains rat-infested, mined by filthy rat-bunkers. At least, I shan't see the worst; I shan't make it through winter.'

'Come on, Watchman,' chirped Flit, 'don't be glum. You're still with us.'

'I see that *he* is,' the rook said. 'Trust Kine's luck! What preserves him?'

'Justice,' Kine bragged. 'I'm needed. Only Kine can beat Rattun.' His head had cleared. 'I'll be there, rook. So far, nothing has stopped me. I'm as good as there this time.'

'As good as home,' chimed the sparrows, now less pessimistic. 'Kine's mending, he'll make it. It's a jog through the hills now.'

Watchman scowled. 'There you're wrong. I've just come from the hills and they're swarming with rat guards, squads patrolling the passes. They're after the weasel.'

'They won't stop me,' snapped Kine. 'Rattun can't stop me that way.'

Wonder frowned. 'It's too dangerous. Kine, you can't thwart the Rat King.'

'Someone has to,' he churred.

'Why you, Kine?'

'Rattun fears me. I am bold . . .'

'Mad!' rasped Watchman.

'I am Kine the death dancer.'

'Very well,' Wonder told him, 'we'll *all* come.' It was final. Several damp faces brightened. 'You'll not go off on your own. We're your kin, we'll fight with you.'

'Yes, we'll fight!' cried the dandies. 'It'll be like the Mink Wars!'

'Huh,' the rook huffed. He squinted. 'You weren't born. What do *you* know?'

'Old fossil!' they chanted.

'Quiet,' snarled Kine, stepping forward. 'Now hear this – it's *my* battle.' His eye was fierce, his neck bristling. There was no sound from the youngsters. 'I go *alone* to the Witchwood; it's ordained – me and Rattun.'

'That may be,' Heath said gravely, 'but the hills . . .'

'I'll get through.'

'You'll need back-up,' Heath told him. 'We'll cover you through the hills. We can see you're not ambushed. Rattun's planned the reception – what we need is our own plan.'

'Heath, you're right. Let me think . . .'

'*Can* you think?' mumbled Watchman.

Kine ignored him, eyes distant. He paced a while in the rain then, half-hidden by heather, stood trance-like, reflecting. The others watched, growing damper. At last, he cried, 'Right, a plan - here it is, listen carefully. First, we misinform Rattun. We've got Scrat in the valley. He'll say I'm dead, that I drowned; that'll put them off guard. Watchman, that's *your* assignment – find the midget and brief him.'

'Bah,' the rook said. He grimaced.

'Flit and Farthing will scout, fly ahead in the hills and look out for the rat gangs.'

'That'll suit us,' said Flit. 'If we spot them, we'll buzz them. You'll be warned of the ambush.'

'Good,' growled Kine. 'I'll be leading. Here's the order of march - me, then Heath and then Wonder, single file in that order. The dandies stay in the rear, out of sight unless called for.'

'In the rear?' wailed the youngsters. 'Out of sight? But we're fighters!'

'You heard Kine,' Wonder told them. The small female looked steely.

'Right,' said Kine, 'now let's rest. Start at dawn. Any questions?'

*

At first light, Farthing stirred, jostled Flit and took wing. As they rose from the heath and set course for the hills, the rain eased, it grew colder. The rook had left them at dusk, lifting off with much grumbling. Now the sparrows flew hard, pounding air to get warm.

Climbing over the scrub, they were soon crossing hillocks, the first steps of the heights whose dark peaks raked the dawn. Streams in spate tumbled down them. One or two larger birds, early up, passed the sparrows.

'Turning chilly,' yelled Flit. 'It's no day to be idle.'

Farthing's eye gleamed. He shouted, 'It's a day for a fight, Flit!'

'It's that – a fine morning.'

'A first-class day for a broil, for a bit of a warm-up!'

The sun rose, pale and wintry. Below, a fox made for home, winding up through a gully. Browsing rabbits ignored it, aware it had eaten. A fox at dawn was no threat until snow clad the uplands, then hunger would sharpen it's hunting instinct. Flit-cat banked, Farthing with him, glancing back at the heath. They could just see the weasels undulating through heather, bounding forward in file as they made for the hillside.

'Well done, Kine,' mumbled Flit. 'He's no slouch, our rat fighter!'

'Which route is he taking?'

'The grassy slope to the scree. See that thicket?' bawled Flit. 'There's a track to the top there.'

'Best gain height and observe it.' They climbed, Farthing leading. The hill was suddenly craggy, steeper as they got higher. A crow flew beneath them. The bounding weasels were tiny. 'Seems all clear.' Farthing hovered.

'The track's clear – check the thicket.'

They circled quizzing the bush, a scrubby thorn near the scree. It commanded the pathway. Shadows moved. 'Guards,' screeched Farthing. His stubby wings whirled. 'It's them, Flit . . .'

'Let's go,' Flit rapped. 'We must signal.'

They ducked their grey caps as one and power-dived, their tails streaming. Flit could see the bush plainly. The stony slope seemed to rise, thicket leaping towards him. There were two rats on watch, hairy brutes with mean snouts, sitting tight by fresh diggings. They could have comrades below, resting underground, Flit thought. He spotted earth on their whiskers. Then he had flattened his dive, skimmed the growth and zoomed up.

'There's the champ!' Farthing joined him. 'It's time we reported.'

Kine was flat in the grasses. 'How many?' he queried.

'Two in view,' Farthing told him. The sparrows ruffled, excited. They had perched near the weasel. 'There may be more down the holes.'

'Big ones?' Kine asked.

'Lean monsters. Not giants like the Rat King but hard-looking hill rats. They'll give you a fight, Kine!'

Kine laughed, his teeth glinting. Heath and Wonder crept forward. 'Fight?' drawled Kine, 'I *eat* hill rats! We'll get close in the grass then we'll rush them together. Flit and Farthing can cover; the dandies stay hidden.'

He grinned at Wonder. 'Two sentries . . . you and Heath can take one, I'll dispose of the other. Are we set? Let's start climbing.'

He watched the sparrows fly off then pushed on through the ground-growth. It was still damp from the rain and the old grass was soggy. Hollow stems of dead plants stood in hindering clusters. He could see Heath to one side and glimpsed Wonder beyond, but the weasels were deft and the stems barely shifted. The hillside air had grown still; it was cold, almost scentless.

Quietly, Kine wriggled upwards. Soon, the grass became thin, stony patches encroaching. Rocks were scattered in places. He was forced to slip round them, increasingly in the open, hidden now by mere tussocks. He touched a pebble; it moved and he froze, staring forward. The bed of scree lay ahead. Beyond the scree loomed the guards, both alert, noses twitching.

There was a sudden commotion. Fluttering from the rear, Flit and Farthing bowled over. As they passed, cheeping loudly, the rats turned to watch them.

'Now!' snapped Kine.

He sprang fiercely. Underfoot, the stones rattled. Heath and Wonder were with him. All three weasels were bounding, swift as flames in a draught, lithe as snakes, their eyes beady.

'*Tchk-kkk-chk!*' rang their war-cry.

'For the valley!' Kine shouted. He saw the first rat spin round. It confronted him, startled. It had a wild, cheated look, as if betrayed, and flinched slightly, the weasel's thrust stunning. The blow went straight to the neck where Kine's needle-fangs anchored.

The second rat, with more speed, dived below, chased by Wonder. Kine saw Heath vanish with them. Then his own victim lunged and he tightened the death-grip.

Kine was dragged by the creature. Though no giant, it was strong and fought hard to dislodge him. Twice, his back struck the stones, his spine numbed by the impact. Then, twirled near the bush, he was raked by stout branches, their gnarled edges searing. The rat had grown frenzied. The stricken beast charged and reared, quivering in its panic. Kine's head reeled. He bit deeper. The frantic struggle seemed endless.

Quite abruptly, it stopped, the rat subsiding, mouth open. When Kine stepped back, it was dead, its brief twitching a reflex.

Breathlessly, he took stock. He was alone on the slope, everything very still – rat-corpse, air, the black tunnels. Somewhere under the earth, Heath and Wonder were busy. The weasel cocked his head, listening. There was a sound far below, a faint scuffling which grew, rising up as he waited. He braced.

'Kine?' a voice said.

Heath hauled from the diggings. He shook himself. 'We found two . . .'

'Where's Wonder?'

'She's safe.' Heath looked pleased. 'She's a demon.'

Wonder followed, exhausted. She blinked in the daylight. The small female was soiled but her snort was triumphant. She said, 'Well, that's three to start with who won't take

171

the news back,' and smiled. Kine admired her. She was, he thought, Kia's daughter - another Kia to the eye-teeth.

There was a brisk sparrow-twitter. Something grey heaved and bolted.

Kine exclaimed, 'There's a fourth!' He swung round. 'We must stop him . . .'

They chased. Kine cursed softly. 'He's gaining ground,' he said, gasping. 'He's fresh, we shan't catch him.'

'Wait,' breathed Heath. They stood panting.

As they watched, the rat dithered. From the large stones around it, four slim shapes had popped up, prancing forward like veterans. Wonder beamed. 'It's the dandies!' She glanced at Kine, her face straightening. 'The brats – they've moved without orders . . .'

'Orders!' Kine crowed. 'Who needs them? Watch them dance – Kine's their grandsire! When did Kine obey orders?'

The rat went down, swamped by dandies. When it was still, Kine advanced. 'Right,' he growled, 'don't show off; you can't kill him twice over! Save your strength, kitts, you'll need it.'

'We're not kitts, we're rat fighters!'

'Oh, you think so?' Kine twinkled. He eyed the heights, his heart quickening. The path wound up, bleak and wintry, lost to view as it twisted. A pair of hawks topped the summits. There was a long climb ahead but it would be the last effort. One last slog!

Then the valley . . .

On a branch of the Life Tree, the bumble-bee waited, her last sleep approaching. Brain-fatigued, starved of nectar, the old queen had grown still, summer's industry over, her peace made with extinction. A few young queens would survive, tucked away through the winter; for her, life's business was done and the longest night beckoned.

Her season's reign had been full, her small earth-palace bustling, always busy with work, always flowing with sweetness. The nest had hummed with procreation; withstood many crises. It had escaped ant-invasion, theft by voles and, the arch-dread, a usurper-bee visit.

Now the queen bowed to winter, drowsed a while then keeled over. She fell into the pond, drifting gently legs upwards, a tiny trimaran of wings and her spent, furry body.

The covert was silent. Withered nettle leaves drooped, damp and black; paths were soggy. An icy breath through the trees made small waves on the pond where a lone reed vibrated. From somewhere deep in the wood rose a faint lamentation, the very slightest of noises – the squeak of a shrew's voice.

'Doom and woe . . .'

An owl ghosted. It seemed to hang in the vault then dissolve in columned dimness. 'Doom,' the shrew piped, then nearer, 'Grief . . . sorrow . . . affliction . . .' Scrat paused. 'Woe,' he twittered.

A heron turned. It was fishing. '*Kraak*,' it rasped. 'What now, pip-squeak?'

'Kine's dead!'

'So?'

'The bold one!'

'Bah, the *upstart*,' the bird said. 'Who cares?'

Scrat kept moving. 'Woe,' he screeched, 'Kine has perished.' He eyed the wood's shadowed cavern. Its shades spelled danger. He beetled. 'D-doom and woe,' Scrat cried, trembling. 'Mourn the weasel!' His eyes rolled.

The dwarf glanced over his shoulder. Round the pond he ran, wailing, into dank, evil places. 'Kine is dead . . .'

'*Stop and tell us.*' A horny foot pinched his tail.

'D-doom!' Scrat's legs beetled faster. They failed to carry him forward, his rear end pinned firmly.

'Tell us all,' hissed the rat voice.

'K-Kine's dead . . .'

'You're sure, midget?'

Scrat gulped. Humped shapes threatened. 'He'd better be,' one said darkly. 'Go on, shrew – what befell him?'

'He d-drowned. In the river.'

'Go on . . .'

'In the torrent. At the weir. He went over.' Scrat quaked.

The rats grunted. 'Good – that's good,' they growled, melting. 'We'll tell the Rat King. That's good, dwarf!'

'Doom,' he breathed as they vanished. His falsehoods appalled him. He searched the damp trees, eyes straining. 'Are you there, rook? They'll flay me. When they find out, they'll skin me. I'm mad, Watchman, I must be. When they learn, they'll destroy me.'

'So, who'll miss you?' the rook drawled.

22

The engineer left his van and stood, hunched, by the pump-house. The wind was easterly, bitter; the sky's hue, metallic. All its vapours had drained, swilling now through the vale, where the marsh was still brimming. Every ditch was replete, the great water-pump humming. The water poured to the river. Sucked up from the dykes, countless tons were thrust seawards, a burdened stream frothing.

Impressed, the man paused a moment. A floating log caught his eye. As it passed in the turmoil, it joined a vast foam-fringed whirl then broke free, drifting onwards. The sodden raft took him back, stirring memories of boyhood: crude boats sailed in gutters. A tractor stopped and its driver, well-wrapped, came towards him.

'Still baling?' growled Ploughman.

'Pumping flat out. She'll shift it.' It was the last of the spate. Without the pump, it would spread, the winter corn flooding.

'Let's hope she keeps running.'

The engineer's grunt was scornful. As if the pump ever failed! She was not an old tractor. He shoved the door of the house and displayed the big motor. It purred. 'That's an *engine*.' He stepped inside. 'All electric, no messing. Come on in – ever seen her?'

A long-drawn-out sigh filled the room. The pump churned slower and stopped. In the chamber below, they could hear water slopping, falling back from the spinner.

Ploughman lit his pipe slowly, one eyebrow drawn upwards. 'Croaked,' he mused.

'But she can't . . .'

'Aye, she's croaked.'

'The thing's fail-proof.' The engineer checked the fuses. They were sound. He was baffled. Striding back to the van, he used the radio in it. 'Might've known,' he called shortly, and returned. 'It's the power line. There's been a power failure somewhere.' He looked relieved. 'That pump's faultless; she's maintained to perfection.'

'Not much good without power, son.'

'They'll have it back by this evening.'

Ploughman shrugged. 'By this evening?' He watched the dyke-water rising. 'There'll be a hell of a puddle by dusk,' he said drily.

'Not for long, once the pump starts. The rain's cleared, she'll soon mop up.'

They moved their feet as the ditch brimmed. A chill breeze pinched their faces.

The veteran sniffed, his briar glowing. He eyed the sky, then the dykes. They were bleak, walled by sedges. A little tree grew lop-sided. 'Worse to come,' he drawled sagely, 'feel that air, lad, it's icy. Hear them reeds . . .' The reeds rattled. 'Sign of frost when they clack; it's marsh-talk for hard weather. You get to know what the marsh says.'

'It's damned raw.' It was biting. A few weeks back, warblers carolled and buntings had chanted. Now, the snipe foraged coldly, their slender bills silent.

'Wild old place,' muttered Ploughman. 'Like a barn cat, the marsh – think it's tamed but it isn't. Pumps or no pumps, it isn't.'

The reed-wall moaned. His eyes shifted. A tongue of water licked forward, spilling out of the ditch, and a great rat broke cover. It had a coat like a wolf's. The men stared. It paused glaring, then half a dozen more followed, shouldering from the reeds, sloping off up the marsh track. 'Flaming giants,' Ploughman blurted. He scowled and spat. 'Evil devils.'

The young man said, 'Growing bigger! I'd like your gun . . .'

'They're too clever.'

'I'd make them move!'

'Too damned knowing. They know exactly what's happening – dykes full up, pump's stopped running. They're clearing out from the marsh to the slopes where it's drier. They'll join the rest in the woods.' The farm man knocked out his pipe. 'Don't know who we can turn to,' he growled, 'but help's needed.' He clambered back on the tractor. 'Needed urgent,' he added. 'You and me can't control them.'

'*Someone's* got to.'

'Trouble is, son, who cares? There's just the youths, no one else. We're simply not on the map here.'

The tractor moved, big tyres squelching, and the engineer followed. As his van crossed the marsh, it made ripples in pools. The land was swamping already. Then the track climbed the slopes, became dry and woods thickened, stripped and bleak, void of rooks whose bare nests straggled darkly. Cold, he turned up the heat and the van's windows misted. He wiped the screen. An owl ghosted, pale as snow, swerving past him.

At the cottage, he stopped and grabbed a torch from his tool-box. There would be no lights indoors until the power was restored, and the owl presaged twilight.

'How long before it's back on?' asked the girl when he entered.

'They're working on it; not long.'

She had the fire well ablaze and he warmed, the heat tingling. 'Poor man,' she said, 'you look blue. Are you in for the evening?'

'I'll have to check things again, I've brought a decent torch for you.'

'It's going to freeze, you know that?'

'D'you reckon?'

'I'm certain. There'll be a hard frost tonight.' The girl went to the kitchen. 'You need a hot drink,' she called and he heard a pan filling. He eyed the baby and grinned. The child was propped in a chair, one small fist round a beaker.

The young man winked. 'Your mum fusses!'

The infant mewled, his eyes drowsy, then hurled the plastic mug from him. His mother clucked, coming back, and wedged the pan by the fire. 'That'll soon boil,' she purred, and when her son stretched a hand, '*You* – you're tired, my love, aren't you?'

After tea, she fetched candles. 'You never know.'

The man shrugged.

'Well, I'm ready,' she told him. She hugged the child. 'This one's weary. He's got his nightlight for bedtime.'

The engineer viewed the room: the girl embracing their son, the fireglow soft on their cheeks, chasing shadows from corners and the low, beam-spanned ceiling. He might be glimpsing the past – rustic room, cottage hearth, a girl bred in the valley. At times, he felt out of place, but then her arms drew him close and only mutual love mattered. At last, he said, 'Getting dark. I hope they soon fix the beggar.'

'The power line?'

He nodded. 'If this drags on, I'll be stumped; I'll have to wade to the pump.'

'Don't you dare in this cold!' It was fierce and she brooded. 'In any case, it'll freeze; by dawn the marsh will be solid.' She smiled and said, 'We'll skate on it. You'll see the geese land on ice – what great clowns, on their bottoms! They're worse than ducks, they slide all ways.'

He grinned.

'You'll see.' Her chin tilted. 'By dawn you'll see an ice-valley.'

'Mmm . . .' He did not dismiss it. She was too often right, as marsh-wise as old Poacher. 'Best get back, see what's happening.' He drained his cup. 'Shan't be long. You've the torch . . .'

'Keep wrapped up then.'

He left, the room briefly chilled while the door was held open. It closed and the van revved. 'Poor cold Dad,' the girl murmured. She rocked his child. 'Here's us cosy!' Ash logs flamed. 'And you're tired. Come, it's bedtime.'

She went upstairs, treading softly, tucked the babe in and kissed him. He yawned, a thumb creeping mouthwards.

'Sleep tight, angel.' She watched him. When his breathing grew steady, she turned and paused by the window. The darkening vale stretched below, a silver sheet on the marsh where the dykes had spilled over. Once, Poacher had told her, there had been floods every winter and shepherds used row-boats. Then, the carters took poles to sound depths as they travelled. All that had stopped with the pumps and she was proud of her husband.

The air had stilled, stiff with frost, and an ice-moon was rising. It gave the hills in the distance a glacial aspect. Pulling the child's blankets higher, she went downstairs and lit candles.

The room was ghostly by flamelight. Its flitting glow stirred hearth spirits, or so she imagined: Poacher's rough antecedents; short, dour men of the earth; stocky women, eyes watchful; children clustered like mice, and the hens which lived with them. She liked to summon them up, let her mind flesh the shadows. It was a game that beguiled, sometimes tended to frighten, then she would switch on the lights . . .

When they worked, she reflected.

The spell was strong, claustrophobic. They seemed to crowd her that evening, doubly impudent phantoms, aware she was powerless. She wished her husband back home, for his presence dispelled them. They fled from the townsman.

From the door, she looked out, her gaze seeking the van. A crisp coldness assailed, the front step bright with crystals. It was quiet, uncanny. The grass was white, each blade glazed, and the playhouse was frosted, sugar-iced by the rime and the moon shining on it. She saw no headlamps and waited. In a while, to pass time, she took the torch and advanced, standing now by the sapling. It was a silvery wand. The little frost palace beckoned.

The lawn crunched under her feet. She paused a second then stooped, peering in, the torch stabbing.

It caught the rats and they glared. She felt her spine crawl. Orbs glimmered. Ratlings scampered in corners, climbed walls, gazed from shadows. A newborn brood seethed and writhed, shapeless, naked, guts throbbing. Their bulbous eyes had not opened. The sightless mass heaved grotesquely. Horrified, the girl screamed, drawing back, the torch shaking. Its beam fell full on the sow, the monstrous mate of the Rat King.

She saw the van lights and ran, and was at the gate as he

reached it. 'Not much longer,' he called. 'They've been through; the line's mended.'

'God . . .' she breathed.

He came forward. 'What's up?'

'Rats,' she blurted. Her breath condensed. The cold choked her. 'Over there . . .'

'In the playhouse?'

'In the child's house – they're breeding!'

He looked amazed. 'I secured it.'

'They've broken in.' She was shaking.

The young man said, 'Where's your coat? You've no coat . . .' His hands gripped her. He forced her indoors. 'You're trembling. It's bloody freezing,' he muttered. 'Stay here, I'll do this.' He grabbed a stick and the torch.

'It's that sow!'

'There'll be slaughter.'

He started back. The girl followed. 'I've seen her round . . .'

'Stay inside.'

'She's an ogress, take care.'

'Aye,' the man hissed, 'I'll have her.' He raised the stick, creeping forward. He wrenched the door of the playhouse.

There was a blaze from the cottage. The power was back, house lights shining. They bathed the lawn. The man grunted. 'There's nothing here.' He turned slowly. 'There's nothing doing, it's empty.'

'She's got them out.' The girl joined him. 'I might've known – the sow's moved them.'

'Damn,' the man said. 'God damn them.'

A single rat crossed the mere, leaving prints in the hoar-frost. The water had frozen; the scouting rat scuttled on it. On the bank, where reeds stiffened, an anxious hedgehog sought refuge, caught out by the weather. The freeze was early and sudden, the need to hibernate urgent.

The prickly beast watched the rat. Rats did not share the problem, alert and active through winter. For others, 'sleep' had begun, the dormouse torpid already, head in paws, tail wrapped round it. So cold and stiff was the mouse, it would have rolled on a board. The hedgehog sniffed and moved on, the mere not to its liking.

Good dry hide-outs were scarce. It was all right for the carp, which simply sank in the mud, sleeping at the lake's bottom. Or for the frogs, toads and newts which could squeeze into clefts, or hibernate in the soil. A hedgehog needed more space; needed dead leaves to curl in.

The creature roamed to the woods. In their sets, badgers snored, drowsing out the hard weather. Bats hung, torpid, in trees, tucked in shadowy hollows. Some would sleep until spring; others, stir on and off, like the small pipistrelles, intermittently active.

Half-asleep, the hog scurried, vainly seeking a refuge. Here, a niche was too damp; here, a crevice constricting. Snuffling on in the gloom, the beast arrived at a coombe, missed the ledge and tipped over. In a ball, it bounced down, spines erect, shock-absorbing. *Thump-thump-thump.*

'Doom!' a voice wailed.

Scrat ducked. Stones came tumbling.

Dazed, the hedgehog uncurled. It blinked tiredly. 'Where am I?'

'You just missed me,' Scrat grumbled.

'Were you sleeping?'

'*Me?*' the shrew said. 'I'd not live long if I slept!'

'But everyone's sleeping – the Winter Sleep.' Snakes were sleeping, retired to dark corners. Caterpillars were sleeping. On a tree near the bluff, the fritillary's larva would not stir until summer, then to feed on dog-violet. Butterflies hibernated. Some, among them the brimstones, had been drowsing since August. Even snails were asleep, their shells sealed for the winter.

'Scrat asleep?' The shrew shuddered. 'Are you mad? With rats prowling?'

The hedgehog yawned. 'Well, *I'm* sleeping. All I need is dry lodgings.'

'You *can't*!'

'A quiet billet.'

'Doom,' wailed Scrat. 'You'll be needed.'

'A leafy bed.'

'Kine will need you!'

'But Kine's dead.'

'No – who says so?'

'Didn't you?'

'Yes,' the shrew moaned. 'That is – no. Well, I might have. But *you* can't sleep, you're Kine's guide; you're his lead to the Rat King. I told him: "Follow the hedgehog." You can't drowse off – *wake up!*' Scrat screamed.

23

They scaled the heights in the frost as if attacking a castle. The hard, chill ground did not daunt them; the steep paths were a challenge. On frozen scree they advanced, and shelves which dropped sheer to runnels. Motes of snow hid the peaks. Looming out of this fuzz, groups of hill-sheep descended, bent on sheltering lower.

They viewed the climbers, amazed. The sight was odd, unexampled – seven weasels ascending; a fiery band prancing upwards. Leading, now unrestrained, Wonder's dandies charged forward.

'Steady,' Kine urged, 'go easy.'

They whooped. 'It *is* easy!'

'Not so fast, it gets steep. Save some breath, you may need it.'

On they raced, now in line, a red snake as they leaped; then abreast, like small braves, each a bounding samurai. Nonplussed, the sheep blinked. For a trice, weasels bounded – lean, swift beasts – then had gone, shapes aloft blurred by whiteness. Kine peered hard. Crystals flurried. The snow was fine, mere chick-feathers; all the same, it adhered, making blobs on his nose.

Wonder puffed, snout bedizened.

'We'll break the skyline,' she warned.

'Yes, there may be rats watching.'

At length, with paws clogged, they stopped. 'Right, let's rest,' Kine commanded. 'We're almost there. Let's think calmly.'

'Oh, why stop?' moaned the dandies.

'*Down,*' growled Heath, 'and don't argue. Hear Kine's word. Get your heads down.'

'Fast!' screeched Kine.

They ducked, startled. Two buff shades sailed the slope,

were expunged by the snow-flecks. 'Hawks,' he rasped. 'They'll be hungry.'

Wonder cried, 'For young weasels – little know-alls,' she chided. 'Just take heed, we're not playing. Death can strike very quickly.'

The dandies moped. 'Hawks are nothing.'

'You'll be nothing!' Heath answered.

'But look,' squealed one, 'there's the summit. A few more steps. You can see it.' It tantalized in the fuzz, a grey ridge strewn with stones. A great outcrop bestrode it. 'Come on, Kine, can't we move?'

Heath said, 'Let me scout forward. If it's safe there, I'll fetch you.'

'Go on,' Kine said and nodded. 'No one else. This is it – one false step, we'll be spotted.'

They seemed to wait for an age, then, as Wonder grew tense, Heath returned, his eyes popping. 'You'll not believe it . . .'

Kine frowned.

'It's prodigious, astounding!'

'Safe to move?' Kine's frown deepened.

Heath drew breath. 'Safe to *look*. It's a sight! Come up quietly.' Keeping low, they crawled on, bellies pressed to cold ground. A flat stone topped the ridge and they edged to its lip, seven prone bodies wriggling. Seven heads strained for views, seven faces enquiring.

Sprawled below, lay Kine's Country, the end of his journey. It was done, terminated; dangers faced, its trials conquered: the range, the gulls, the raft peril. He was Kine the intrepid. Sleety snow smeared his gaze. He had crossed half the world, undreamed realms. Kine had triumphed. He was back – this was home. He stared down.

'There,' Heath muttered.

Wonder gulped.

It was frozen; it was stiff, an ice-valley. Hill cascades hung like glass. Blue, the far shoulder shimmered, a tundra, trees ghostly. From Poacher's cottage, smoke twisted, pearl-grey, the roof frosted. Fields and hedges were hoary, lanes blurred, their sounds muffled.

Kine gawped at the marshland. There was no sign of the dykes, of the slow, twisting river, once Caesar's *Lemanus.* The whole marsh was a rink, broken only by reeds, icy scrub and the pump-house, its flat roof white-mantled. If the old stream still flowed, there was no means of telling. The flood's roof was rigid.

Frozen, too, was the Moon Pond, the Life Tree set solid. Where gentle ripples had lapped, a cruel vice squeezed the hulk, its groans cast to the waste like an arctic-trapped ship's. Weasel eyes searched for woods. They had changed coat, stoat to ermine, copse and spinney frost-silvered, phantom forts on glazed slopes which rose, seamless, to the sky and the whirl of flakes in it.

It was magical, awesome. The vale enthralled with chill splendour, with icicled glory. The dandies marvelled. 'It's dazzling.'

'I told you,' Heath said.

Snow glittered.

Wonder said, 'It's transformed; it's an ice-realm!'

'It's *winter.*' Flit landed beside them. 'Nothing splendid in that, not for *us* – just short rations.' There was scant sign of winged life. Birds had fled to the farms, or the hamlets, for succour. Those that stayed were balled up, seeking pockets of berries; some resigned, apathetic.

Farthing perched. 'Wait for night. Nights like these swoop with talons.'

'Frost that stabs!' Flit-cat shuddered.

'Quiet,' snarled Kine, 'I can't think.' He looked out to the Witchwood. 'I need time to reflect, to consider conditions.' He paused and breathed, 'Kine is home,' an odd tremor intruding. 'Kine the bold,' he croaked fiercely, 'scourge of Rattun . . .'

'*Go get him!*'

'Hush,' hissed Wonder. 'You heard.'

'Yes,' urged Heath, 'stop the clack. Let him meditate quietly. Kine has crossed the beyond, grant him peace before battle.'

He sat a long time, eyes dreamy. They did not see an ice-valley – the ice would thaw, plant-life quicken. He thought of cuckoo-flower blooming, arrowheads in the dykes, vetches, plantains and comfrey. Spring would bring the new reeds, green of stem, purple-headed. Warm mists would drift slowly, herons spire, ducklings paddle.

For Kine, the valley was busy. Insects hummed, mallard circled, the buck hares brawled, rabbits mated. Insurgent growth ambushed paths: colt's-foot, thyme. Nettles bristled. Above a marsh where frogs wallowed, flocks of dunlin wheeled tightly, first black and then silver.

That, for Kine, was Kine Country: sun through leaves, gold of kingcup, froth of blossom in spring; hawthorn, cherry, cow-parsley. There lay his hunt-paths and tunnels, the vaulted alleys through fern, the dark plunge to mole chambers. He dreamed its smells, its earth odours. The scent of hay haunted.

He thought of Rattun and fumed. He thought of dens desecrated, glades fouled, rat-infested. The tyrant's brood drew no bounds. Nothing to them was sacred, no place, no tradition. They invaded the Life Tree and defiled Kia's memory. Rat guards trampled his birthplace. His blood boiled. Death to Rattun! Kine was back, the rat fighter. It was Kine or the Rat King!

Kine looked down. It was barren. The marsh was desolate, ice-bound. That would change, life return; he had known other winters. They called for courage and thrift, for a caution that irked but was never more crucial. There was no cover below, no concealing tone-pattern. On that white, glaring sheet, a fly that moved would stand out. And the guards would be watching.

That was the bad news, he thought. But the frost brought one blessing. For beasts of light weight, at least, the ice meant dykes could be crossed, streams traversed without problem. On the marsh, that spelled speed, the avoidance of detours.

At length, he stirred, saying crisply, 'I'm going down to find Scrat, then to follow the hedgepig.'

'Can't we come?'

'No one moves. If the rats flee, you take them.'

186

'You and me, Kine,' Heath urged.

'On my own, I'll be quicker.'

Soon the moon rose, day dying. The light did not truly go but grew lunar, ice-mirrored, webbed with long, eerie shadows which lacked definition. Kine slipped down from the hill. At first, he held to the clefts then a stiff reed-bed beckoned. He took stock of the pump-house. The place looked forsaken. As he scurried towards it, he thought of the river. Beneath his feet, dark and silent, the iced water trundled.

Snow had piled by the pump. It filled the edge of the track with a long, shining drift where the flat ground was open. There was no chance he could cross, reach Scrat's haunts undiscovered, unless . . . his eyes glinted. He was Kine the resourceful! In a flash, he had burrowed, disappeared in the drift, snorkelled up five yards distant. Again, he dived, mining forward.

Now, where dead growth lay buried, he came to snow tunnels. In sheltered caves, small plants slumbered – infant dock, tyro thistle – grubs survived, voles found refuge. A chubby shape squealed and scuttled.

'Scrat?' said Kine.

The vole bolted.

Head low, Kine continued. Beneath the snow, it felt warm, the frost's cutting-edge blunted. Tiny icicles jabbed; in one place, he smelled moisture. Farther on, a great hall, its roof beamed with bent grass seemed to end the cave complex. Kine sniffed round. It was dark. When he moved, the sound echoed, filled the chamber with whispers.

Stumped, the weasel stood still. The dim ice-palace creaked. Above, the frost must be deepening, the snow roof compacting. He felt a draught and explored. Freezing air chilled his neck. Peering up, he drew back, the cold jet in his face, its source high in the ceiling – a small, inky crevice.

With a leap, Kine squirmed in. It was tight but he climbed, straining in the snow chimney. Presently, he saw light, the moon's disc, and had surfaced.

He found himself by a hedge, out of sight of the woods. The cold was savage, transfixing. Kine gasped. He moved quickly. The hedge led up from the marsh to his first call, the covert. 'Scrat?' he churred. There was silence.

Towering oaks flanked his path, iced to windward, sap frozen. A flooding moon chilled the holly. No sound, not a movement. No owl. Batless heavens. Thin ash-masts rose starkly; firs bowed, frost-encumbered. Snow had draped withy pollard. The glades were dead and paths covered. Night played tricks with old features. Boughs of trees sagged, ice-bearded, the woodside a glacier. Everywhere, it was still, the ground veiled and unearthly.

A roosting pheasant erupted.

Kine paused. The bird honked. It flew off with a din and the night, stunned, recovered. The weasel crouched, ears alert. A new sound made him wait, a low swish, listless, dragging. The sound approached. He lay hidden. It seemed to swell and divide, coming on with dull menace.

The rat squad passed at a slouch, its mien boorish. There might have been five or six, each a heavyweight guard, arrogant, thick tails switching. They marked the snow with long stripes, unconcerned by their tracks, which fresh flakes quickly smothered.

Kine watched, temper rising. He could have taken the last, maybe two, but paid dearly. Rattun would have been warned, surprise thrown to the devil. He checked himself.

'Pssst!'

He jumped.

'Pssst,' blew Scrat. 'I've been waiting.'

'Where are you?'

'The thicket.' Scrat sneezed. He was frozen. 'Over here, but keep down, they've no mercy.'

'Nor I!' Kine stared grimly. Big snowflakes fell on him. They seemed to grow in thin air. The pond was shrouded, moon-hallowed; the fallen tree, holy. Kine was home – the crusader.

'K-Kine, you took enough time.'

'Time?' snapped Kine. 'You were lucky.'

'Alone,' the shrew squeaked, 'with *them*.' He peered round. 'No protection.'

'You're a spy, it's your business.'

188

'I'm a wreck – *what was that?*'

An iced branch shed its burden. Snow cascaded abruptly, the eased limb unbending. Kine said fiercely, 'Brace up! Did you pass on the message?'

'I t-told them. I lied.'

'That was good.'

'Woe, they'll kill me!'

'Come on, dwarf, you're with Kine. You've done well, we'll surprise them.'

'*We?*' wailed Scrat.

'I will,' Kine said. He growled. '*I'll* surprise them – Kine returned from the dead.' He smiled coldly. Death's envoy! Kill or die, he reflected. 'Scrat, your job's done, don't worry.'

Scrat brightened. 'I fooled them.'

'You were smart.'

'Scrat the f-fearless!' Scrat strutted, head lifting. His mini-feet made snow dimples then sank. The shrew wallowed. 'Kine,' he gasped, 'you'll protect me?'

'Have no fear.'

'There's one problem . . .' The midget blinked. 'Kine, the hedgehog – your guide's hibernated.'

The rook awoke. It was night. He was dying, he reckoned, chilled rigid, frost-bitten. His feet were iced to the tree. A voice called, a mad creature. What fiend would call him at roost?

'It's me, Scrat!'

The rook gritted.

'Wake up, Watchman . . .'

'I'm dying.' Watchman winced. He was dreaming, it was a nightmare. 'I'm finished.'

'*Wake up!*'

'Scrat, I'm sinking.' The bird glanced down. The snow blinded. Its sheen was everywhere, deathly. When he dropped, it would shroud him. 'It's near the end, shrew. I'm going.'

'*Kine's gone . . .*'

'Dead? ' said Watchman.

'No, wake up!'

'Fiend!'

It quietened. There was a pause. 'To the W-Witchwood.' The snow whispered. Scrat snivelled. 'He'll perish.'

'Bah,' the rook said, *'I'm* perished.' He eyed the sky. It was laden. Icy flakes landed on him. 'I've had my life, dwarf, it's over. Kine's got ten lives, he'll manage.'

'Not without a guide, Watchman.'

'The weasel's smart.'

'The snow's thickening. There'll be no tracks, rook, he'll flounder.' Scrat sobbed. 'Doom,' he blurted.

'It's night,' the rook huffed. 'Call later.' When he was dead, or in coma! He would have thought Scrat knew better – roost-rousing! What kind of fool stirred a roost? What kind of ghoul plagued the dying?

'Wake the sparrows! Disturb the riff-raff,' wheezed Watchman.

'They're on the hill.'

'Ha, they would be!'

Scrat quaked. 'Rook, I'm frightened.' He was neck deep. The snow mounted.

24

The girl had cleared the front step. The path took longer and tired her. She went in once to the child, to make sure he was sleeping. His dad had walked to the road, hoping it would be open. She wished that he had stayed home. Normally, on her own, she enjoyed the remoteness; it was the snow made her anxious. The snow frustrated, imprisoning. It knew no bounds, blurred all features.

She watched the flakes, her head aching. Their spatial whirl had no end, the chill whiteness unvaried. At first, the magic had thrilled; now, the endlessness frightened – as if the sorcerer had gone without turning the spell off. Nothing misses its attentions. Snow cloaked cottage and garden, the gate was clogged, the track smothered.

The little sapling looked sad, partly buried and frozen. She took her spade to the plant and fussed anxiously round it. When she had cleared a small space, the child's tree looked less threatened. 'There you are.' She stood back. 'Just keep strong; please don't weaken.' She mused aloud, glancing round as if, she thought, ears were listening! The quiet was eerie, unnerving.

She put the spade down and sniffed. Her nose was cold, her scarf damp. She eyed strange, festooned plants and slid her gaze to the hedge. Filled with snow, it was thick, oddly shaped, unfamiliar. Nothing moved but the flakes, which swirled softly then hid, creeping tiptoe like thieves – or worse, the girl brooded.

She stood and listened, unsettled. She had a sixth sense at times, like a wild thing's awareness. It came of roaming the vale, growing up in the country. She felt a presence unseen, a sense of stealth in the silence. Suddenly, the gate darkened.

'All right, missus? No problems?

The youths peered in.

She was startled.

'We thought you might be cut off, need some baby food – something.'

'We're all right. How's the track?'

'You couldn't drive it,' they said, 'not by van. Need a tractor.'

She said, 'My dad'll come down. He can hitch on the snow-sweep. Till then, we'll be walking.'

The big lad said, 'How's the babe?'

'Fine.' She smiled. 'He's asleep.'

'Bairns aren't daft!' The youths grinned. 'Going to make him a snowman?'

'Oh, we'll see . . .'

'She's been busy.' They viewed the path. 'That's hard work. You've took care of the willow?'

'Yes, his tree.'

They looked grave. 'From the big 'un that fell – Poacher's Life Tree.'

She nodded.

They watched her face. 'You're all right then?'

'I'm all right.'

'We'll get on.'

'Yes . . .' She felt apprehensive. She liked them round. 'I'd make chocolate – why not stop for hot chocolate?'

'Got some errands.'

'Oh, well . . .'

The girl smiled but was sorry. Alone, she gazed at their prints, all they left of their visit. Flakes were settling in them. They looked, she pondered, unnatural; like giants' footsteps, uncanny. Spoor in the snow was deceptive. It could make rabbits two-legged or turn birds into rodents. She peered more closely and frowned. She was not looking at two but three separate snow-trails.

The two were crisp, the third softer. The fall had lessened its depth but it was fresh, that was certain. It would have filled in ten minutes. The girl's eyes slewed, growing wider. The phantom prints passed the gate, tracked down the hedge to the yard and veered, rounding the cottage. Someone was still close to hand . . . in the garden.

192

She stiffened.

Behind her now . . .

She turned quickly.

'So you're the girl?' The witch squinted.

The girl stared back, her fists clenching. She had been flanked, caught unready. The woman leered, gaze malign. Her eyes were hard, cheek-bones sharp, the skin stretched like an adder's.

'I'm Ploughman's daughter,' the girl snapped.

'You poor waif.' It was sly.

It left her angry but lost. 'I know *you*,' she retorted.

'Of course, my dear, he'll have told you.'

Their eyes made war. 'You knew mum.'

'Yes, dear, well.' The tone taunted.

'A long time back . . .'

'You may think so. You'll age, it comes quickly – the winters lengthen, snow deepens. You're going to ask me indoors?'

'No,' the girl said, 'I'm busy.'

'We ought to talk.'

'There's no point.' She felt threatened, invaded. 'I don't know why you came back. I don't care; it's your business.' She took a step, her flesh crawling. 'You're wasting your time, though,' she blurted.

'With Ploughman?'

'He says so.'

'He'll find out, dear, he's slow. He never knew what he wanted.'

The girl stepped past her. 'Please leave us.'

'Oh, not so fast . . .' Snow enclosed them. It blurred the woman then cleared, her face hateful, mouth twisted. 'You can't escape the past, dearie, it's like the rats, always with us.'

The girl whipped round. 'I said go! You didn't come here invited; I'm not concerned with the past. We've all got more things to think of. He's got his own life, my dad has.'

The woman sneered. 'You're so smug. You've no doubts.'

'What does that mean?'

'I'll tell you . . .'

'No,' the girl said, 'it's evil. I know your kind, you make trouble.'

'You're very fanciful, dearie; it wasn't me made the trouble. There wasn't any at first, just us four, two young couples – me and him, her and Poacher. Until the war, then it started. Poacher left in a flash, chanced his arm. That was Poacher. Thought the war was a duck shoot!'

An east wind droned. The snow glinted. 'Did she curse him for Satan! She had a tongue, dear, your mum. A sharp tongue and big eyes – big green eyes. Soon on Ploughman. He was the one stayed to farm. Steady Ploughman. *My* fellow . . .'

'Don't go on.'

'That was it. A fairy-tale, you could call it. Within a month, they were wed, my man and your mum. Next thing, there was you, dear. Oh yes, you've got the cat's eyes; you take after her, you do!' It was hissed. 'Shame she died without telling. Of course, she might not have known. Were you Ploughman's or Poacher's? I doubt the devil knows that, dear.'

'Go!'

The girl ran inside.

She slammed the door and leaned on it. Her body was shaking. The witch was vile, steeped in rancour, a creature spurned. She was vicious.

At last, the girl raised her child. Flakes of snow melted on her. They damped his head. 'There,' she mumbled, 'it's all right, she won't stay.'

Minutes dragged. The girl listened. There was no sound from outside and she went nearer the window. The garden was empty. The spade, she thought, had been moved. It lay askew by the willow. Benumbed, she glimpsed the small tree. It had been snapped clean in two, the spade's edge swung with vengeance.

Kine charged into the Witchwood. The time for caution had gone, the time of hoping for guides. The hour of truth had arrived and he advanced without pause, as he had vowed, weasel-daring. His will was firm, his step light; he felt grimly elated.

The mere was hard and snow-quilted. He had passed Bufo's iced bones and chilled holes where toads slumbered. Now, in ossified trees, bats were still and owls stared, night and day of no count, their eyes fixed on the frost, fiercely charting each movement.

Their hungry screams flew like spears. They roused Kine's blood, spurred the weasel. He leaped and dipped, plunging forward. The days of patience were done; danger thrilled, winged his steps. The old recklessness ruled and he grew as he shafted.

He was big – big with battles. He was Kine the unconquered, Kine the slayer of tyrants, Kine the grappler with evil. And now that evil was close, his pace surged, his nose sharpened. 'Gloat not, Rattun,' he purred, 'by your stench I shall know you!'

He spanned the snow, undulating. Back arched, the sprite flew, bounding high, trailing frost. Leap by leap he swept on, penetrating the fastness. The wood grew dense; a wind moaned, tumbling snow from dead branches. At times, he paused to test scents.

Smelling snakes, he recoiled. They were snug, winter-sleeping. The female stirred.

'Kine, I waited. I meant to kill you,' she yawned.

'Later, serpent.'

'Next summer . . .'

He eyed their nest. 'Wait, don't sleep!'

'It's so cold.'

'The rats, serpent . . .'

Her head dropped.

'Where?' he whispered.

'Zzzzz,' she said.

He raced on. It was a dead place, the Witchwood, a realm of comatose creatures, owl dirges. Small eyes gleamed: elves, tree-lurkers. *'Tchkkk,'* he snarled. They shrank from him. 'Which way to the rats?'

'You can't call on the *chosen*!' The eyes were pricks. They dilated. 'You'd not survive.'

'*Tchkkk!*'

'You'll perish.'

'Which way?'

No one answered.

Through dark trees, snow-glades glimmered. In one, he saw a great log, like a corpse, frost-encrusted. Beneath its flank, in small scrapes, beasts had scratched the earth, seeking food, vegetation. Some had gnawed at the bark, ravaging the dead wood. Flecks of fur lay close by and the snow was blood-spotted.

He did not stop but doubts pestered. The wood was large and lanes forked, many alleys diverging. He was, he judged, pressing deeper, drawing nearer the gut, the chill bowel of the labyrinth. And yet . . .

His head turned, snout questing.

No sign reassured him. Only the decadence reeked: rotted stumps, frozen fungus. Withered poles leaned grotesquely, propped on festering neighbours. Macabre roots writhed from banks. Here, where snow had been foiled, ancient holes ran to earth and who knew to what dungeons?

Who knew, he thought, to what holds? Any one could house guards.

And yet he scented no rats, heard no squeals. Kine's charge faltered. A shadow swam and he craned, searching upwards for danger. On icy draughts, the owl swirled. It raked down as he bolted. He felt the wind from its wings. For three bounds, he was shadowed, outpaced by the bird. On the fourth, he veered right, touched down short and jerked left.

The owl air-braked too late. With a screech, it plunged past, struck the snow and spread-eagled. When it rose, Kine had gone.

Thus would Rattun strike air, bemused by the goblin! The weasel crowed. He was fleet! Kine was trim, fit for battle! He pranced again, with fresh bounce. He was Kine the defender. His chant would ring for the free, his dance shock the oppressor.

'*Tchkkk-kkk-chkkk* – Kine draws closer . . .'

The snow-storm swished, brambles snared. Again, the way grew obscure and he paused, contemplating. Everywhere, there were vaults; everywhere, grizzled columns. Above, the blizzard was grey, shrouding wizened tree-fingers; below, snow-tombs beckoned.

Kine marked time, cursing softly. The Witchwood moaned. He was lost. He could no longer deny it. He stamped the ground in frustration. The snow's crust creaked. He stomped wildly. After everything – *lost*! His eyes filled, burned with anger.

Shapes were perched in the trees: owls, he thought. He swore at them.

'A lot of thanks!' grunted Watchman. He shook his plumes. 'Weasel manners!'

'Who's there?'

'Kine, it's *us*.'

'Flit?' breathed Kine.

'Flit and Farthing!'

The weasel's heart thumped. 'And Watchman?'

'For my sins.'

They hopped lower. 'Watchman fetched us,' cheeped Flit.

'I thought . . .' Kine paused. They were snowswept. 'I thought you baulked at the Witchwood?'

'A fight's a fight!'

'Have you scouted?'

'We've spied the land, it's not far. We've flown over the rat camp.'

'Then lead on.' Kine's voice rang. 'Show me Rattun!'

25

The dandies chafed and Heath snarled, 'Keep your heads down, don't fidget.' The marsh below was a waste, their chill eyrie frost-blighted. He understood their impatience. He was impatient himself, tired of quizzing the snow, a frozen kingdom, and waited. He itched to join the rat fighter.

'What's happening, Heath, is he safe?' Wonder scanned the ice-valley.

He checked his fears. 'You know Kine.'

'Yes,' she mused, 'I know Kine.'

'He's a survivor, don't worry.'

'I *do*.' Her gaze lingered. The hard, flat marsh glared back coldly. Beyond the rink rose the trees, ranged in dire, huddled legions. 'Who survives in the Witchwood?'

'The birds are with him,' hedged Heath, lacking heart for the question. 'They'll let us know if he needs us.'

'You trust the birds? Urchin sparrows!' The owls would take them, thought Wonder. 'An ancient rook, fit for nothing! Let's not wait, Heath.'

'He said to. It's Kine's domain, he's the leader.'

Heath cast back to his youth. Already, Kine had been famed, the mink fighter a legend. The youthful Heath had admired him. None had fought with more daring, greater skill and sheer fury. Maybe the weasel had aged; still, the legend inspired.

'He's reckless, Heath, believe me. And he's alone.'

'By choice, Wonder.' So it had been since Kia's death. 'We must wait.'

'While he's killed?'

'It's his right.'

'To join Kia! You realize he's determined? You know he's chosen his slayer, planned the fight of fights this time? He can't survive, Kine knows that. He's planned for this all along – to dance his last dance of death with an invincible partner!'

'You're wrong. You're fraught . . .'

'Sick of waiting. I'm going down,' Wonder told him.

'We'll all go down,' Heath relented. He checked the dandies. 'But quietly. To the pump and no more. We'll be nearer if called, and we shouldn't be spotted.' He eyed his mate and she nodded.

'The pump,' she said, 'for the moment.'

They viewed the slope. Heath looked grave. 'You're wrong,' he said, 'Kine *can* win. He fought the she-mink and lived.'

'He was younger.'

'He's fit.'

'But less quick, a shade slower.'

'A shade, perhaps.'

'Speed is life, Heath.'

An iced ravine hid their movements. As they descended, they slid, making small avalanches. 'Take care,' Heath told the youngsters. They were supple, sure-footed. He had been their age when the mink came, and Kine his hero. Now, they too knew the legend. Kine *must* win; doubt was treason!

Heath paused, Wonder calling. 'Stop,' she hissed, 'something's happening.'

'Where?' The weasels were statues.

They heard the click of a gate. In the silence, sound carried. 'It's far away,' Heath said quietly. All the same, he held still, for the whiteness endangered. The dandies twitched. 'Hush . . .' They waited.

Glacial, the slopes brooded. Their emptiness disconcerted. The woods were secretive, frightening. On the ridge by the barn, a dark figure paused, witch-like, then fled from the cottage.

'This way, Kine,' sang the sparrows, fluttering in the branches.

'Round the thorns,' twittered Farthing.

'And down the bank.' Flit-cat hovered.

'Riff-raff sparrows,' growled Watchman, 'you'd wake the dead!'

The path vanished – the drop was sheer.

'As you go, Kine.'

Kine sprang down. Snow encased him. Shoulder-deep, he ploughed onwards. The drifts were high in the hollow. At its end, he climbed out using bare roots as holds, shook the snow off and spluttered.

'Watchman's right,' Flit reflected, 'there could be guards. Best go quietly.'

'How much longer?'

'Soon be there. The next bit's thick then it opens. The citadel's in the clearing.'

'Let's get on.' Kine leaped forward.

The bird was right, it was dense. Fallen trees lay in brush, their limbs snapped, decomposing. From the rot, in fierce thongs, coiled immense bramble thickets, barbed briars and black nightshade. Partly covered by snow, the entanglement menaced, embroiled the weasel, who laboured. The hidden stems grabbed his legs; he could feel the spines scratching. Impatiently, he made ground, reduced at times to mere wriggling. It was awkward and painful.

And then the worst growth relented. A passage opened ahead and he peered, hesitating. A loop of wire broke the snow. It was old and corroding. A wooden peg held it down.

'Bah, a fool's game!' croaked Watchman. He had perched, a bleak figure. The misplaced snare drew his scorn. 'Hunting rabbits in here! They've never entered the Witchwood. Got more sense. So should we have.'

Kine ignored him, nose twitching. The scent of rats reached him thinly, then stronger. He cleared the noose with a bound, paused and sniffed, this time deeply.

'Rook, we're here!'

Watchman grunted.

'I can smell them – *rats*, Watchman!'

'Past the poles,' whispered Farthing.

'Past the masts,' echoed Flit. 'Just beyond, lies the clearing.'

Kine stole on. The trees loomed: frozen larches, like gallows.

'He's mad,' the rook said.

Flit wavered.

'Best leave him to it,' gulped Farthing, 'and find a perch.'

'High,' wheezed Flit.

'Mad but brave,' the rook granted.

Kine was crouching, gaze steady. It fixed the trees as he flexed, inching slowly towards them. The poles were starved, some subsiding, one thin trunk horizontal. It just about cleared the ground, propped on withering limbs, and the weasel crawled to it. Beneath the bole, it was dark. He squeezed under and hid. A film of snow screened his view, lodged along the obstruction.

He scraped a spy-hole and squinted. The snow was light in the clearing, a frosty drift to one side, banks protecting the others. It was a court of slight charm, lawns grown rank, the paths barren. Its flanking columns were drear. Their bark peeled; they rose grimly. Icy vaults criss-crossed from them. It smelled of age – of a Dark Age. The reek was malignant.

Kine held still, his eyes darting. At first, he thought it deserted; there seemed no life in the glade, its chill evil abstruse. Nothing moved save the snow – a small wraith from the drift as a draught blew. He shifted. Easing his head round a fraction, he brought the mound into vision. The bank just there was in gloom. Galvanized, he stared harder.

The keep was vast, shelving darkly. Despite some snow on the top, its face was clear, frozen hard, a great fortress of earth buttressing the embankment. A hundred holes, each an entrance – each gained by a path – pocked the mound, leading under. It was a potentate's stronghold. And everywhere sat the guards, rough hands crooked, strong tails curled, motionless as the clod from which they might have been moulded, so well did they match it.

As he watched, Kine's heart thundered. The super-rats were enormous. A normal rat, fully grown, would have outweighed the weasel. Rattun's guards were far larger. He did not need to count heads; he was glad to be hidden. Glad, too, to be leeward, for time to think must be gained and his scent gushed in anger. The rats were plainly at ease. They seemed torpid, complacent.

Perhaps the Rat King was absent? But fate, thought Kine, would not cheat, rob him now. That was nonsense, His foe would be in the mound, deep in dark, teeming chambers. The supposition raised choice: to pass the guards and break in, unsure of reaching his quarry, or wait for Rattun to surface?

A mumbled chant solved the problem. '*Defer*,' the guards droned, '*do homage . . .*' They formed two ranks. '*. . . praise the Leader!*'

Kine peered. They were scuffling, mustering near a tunnel. '*We, the chosen obey . . .*' Their snouts rose, the chant swelling. A massive form filled the hole. The mob squealed. '*Hail the Rat King!*'

Drooling, Rattun heaved forward. He dwarfed the largest rats round him, a brute of monstrous dimensions, flecked with earth from the hole, a huge, bloated gut dragging. He let his eyes absorb light. They were small, without warmth. From the nubs issued hate and his followers trembled.

He took a shambling pace then sat up, haunches bulging. The awesome boar inspired fear. His horny limbs were like talons; the gross tail was repulsive, thick with scales and black bristles. Several guards drew back from him. As they flinched, his lip curled, showing two stained incisors.

When he spoke, the mob shuddered.

'I spy strangers!' hissed Rattun. The monster glowered, his mouth closing. It snapped like a gin-trap.

The Rat King prowled, his guards cowering. At every glance from the giant, they crouched down, deferential. He cranked his head, the eyes beady. At length, he rasped, 'I spy doubters, disbelievers around me.'

'Not us,' breathed the chosen.

'Trouble-makers,' snarled Rattun.

'*Death!*' the mob droned. '*Praise Rattun! Death to all but the chosen!*'

'To slack guards,' the giant slavered. 'Death to guards who don't watch; who let strangers among us.'

The rats fell quiet. Horror gripped them, a dread that rippled their ranks. '*Defer*,' they droned, '*obey Rattun! There are strangers among us.*'

A small brown rat said, 'They're sparrows.' The creature stood at the back. 'That's all the strangers are, sparrows. They've perched above us; they're harmless.'

The Rat King turned, his lips narrow. The tip of his tail flicked.

'With an old rook,' said the speaker.

'*Defer*!' the mob squealed. '*No speeches!*'

The voice broke off. 'I just mentioned . . .'

The Rat King reared, a claw pointing. His icy eyes held the ratling. The rats had shuffled back, cringing, and formed a loose ring around him. They shoved the smaller beast forward. '*Defer*,' they mumbled like zombies. '*Death to those whose tongues waggle; who speak uncommanded.*'

The weasel watched. He was cramped. He had no head-room in hiding and felt his neck getting stiffer. And still he waited, gorge rising. As Rattun stirred, Kine's jaw tightened. He saw the ratling cringe back as the mammoth snapped down, then the victim sprawled limply. A pair of guards dragged the corpse off.

'*Defer or die*,' brayed the zombies.

Rattun grinned, his spite humoured.

Quietly, Kine eased towards him. He was behind the rat circle, the drift of snow giving cover.

Rattun laughed, his nose lofted. The brute felt better for violence, the swift execution. He twitched his snout, flushed with pleasure, lips flared, his teeth jutting. They were yellow, envenomed. They had the harshness of chisels.

Kine could feel his blood pumping. The anger swept him like fire - a reckless fire, the Blood Fury. It blinded him to the odds. Weasels roused to Blood Fury would take on dogs, even humans. Kine had come for the Rat King.

He forced himself to be cool, clear of head. That was crucial. The weasel's sword was precision. He needed fire *and* ice in him.

He heard the ringsiders chant. They were mindless, obsequious. '*Hail Rattun!*' they droned. He loosened, shedding his tension. '*Rat-tun . . . Rat-tun . . .*' they ranted. He took a step on the snow. Its frozen crust bore his weight. Then, with a single swift bound he cleared the drift and their backs and was facing the Rat King.

'You wanted news of me, Rattun!'

The mob was quiet, the glade breathless.

The Rat King stared. '*Kine?*' he muttered.

'Who else?'

'The rat fighter . . .'

'The death dancer, Rattun!'

'Fools,' the rat hissed, 'they missed you. They let you through. More will perish.'

'Come, show them your skills; dance the dance, rat!' Kine waltzed slowly. He dodged. The giant's lunge was signalled. '*Tchkkk,*' he churred, 'that was clumsy. I'll have to teach you the steps. Follow Kine, watch his rhythm!'

The brute hauled round, a paw slashing. The hand was horny, sharp-fingered. It missed, the rat blind with wrath. 'You're small and miserable, weasel.'

'I'm fast!' The sprite sallied.

Guards goggled. The stunned spectators surged in – and out again, as Kine darted. His snap drew hair and a howl, then he was off with a hop, prancing back from the danger. Rattun paused, stiff with hate. Kine could see his mind working, dismissing mere fumbling rage, growing evil, designing. His next attack was less wild. As Kine dodged, Rattun veered, anticipating the move, and the weasel was tumbled.

The Rat King's charge shook the earth. Rolling clear, Kine sprang up. He was safe, but served warning. The whiff of death had been close. He had breathed Rattun's breath, felt the spuming saliva. He could afford no mistakes, for this giant was not slow but deceptively agile, and Kine weaved with caution.

'Next time, Kine!' The rat eyed him. Beady orbs drilled the weasel. The brute came on, nostrils working. A vast back heaved, a rat-mountain. The coarse tail lashed. '*Dance,* we're watching! Duck and dodge, Kine, dance nicely. Then *I'll* dance,' leered the Rat King. 'I'll dance all over you, weasel!'

A sudden rush sent Kine reeling.

The rat guards gasped as he struck them.

'Drive him back,' rasped the tyrant.

Kine blinked. Teeth were stabbing – long, foul teeth. He swayed sideways. Instinct kept his feet moving. Claws grazed and pain seared him. He was, he knew, scrambling wildly and blood was flowing, he smelled it. Somewhere, rat guards were droning. '*Rat-tun . . . Rat-tun . . .*' they chanted.

It had been quick, he thought vaguely.

A sparrow cheeped. 'Come on, champion!'

It pulled him up. He braced, spitting.

Watchman groaned. 'That's the finish. He should've run . . .'

The birds squinted. Far below, the ring tightened, the mob pressing inwards. Flit saw a brown rope of backs, the fighters encircled. They seemed inert, briefly frozen. Slim and bloodied, Kine waited, a fragile form from above. Farthing watched as his mouth gaped. The Rat King stirred. He moved slowly, terrible in proportion. He moved inexorably forward. The rook's eyes closed.

'Run,' he mumbled.

'Come on, Kine!' thrilled the sparrows.

26

Ploughman stopped at his gate and took a spade to the snow-plough. When he had knocked off the ice, he cleared the worst from the tractor. The stuff was thick round the wheels. There was more by the porch. He kicked his boots off and entered.

The phone was ringing but stopped. He did not give it much thought – it was most likely the council to ask for more clearing. All year, they let the lanes crumble, neglected the verges, then the first fall of snow and they pestered him silly.

He put a kettle to boil and warmed up in the kitchen. He had cleared through to the village; some traffic was moving. There was the track yet to sweep, but it could wait while he thawed. Brewing tea, he spooned sugar.

The window misted. He rubbed it. The pane framed several cold pigeons, grey balls on his fence. Again, the phone rang and he answered, a steaming mug now before him. It was the girl, her voice fraught. 'Where've you been?'

He sipped slowly. She sounded distant, remote – the iced wires, he conjectured. 'You rung before?'

'I keep ringing.' The tone accused; it was shrill.

'Been clearing through to the village.' He tolerated her manner.

'The track's not done,' she complained.

The veteran savoured his drink. 'I've not forgotten,' he growled. Stuck off the road, she was anxious. The snow could vex, he accepted.

'They can't drive up,' the voice harped. 'An ambulance couldn't get here.'

He eyed the mug, frowning slightly. 'Ambulance?'

'Or the doctor.'

He paused then asked, 'You unwell? You're not sick?'

A hush followed. She was still there, he heard breathing.

When next she spoke, it was strange, the intonation disturbing. 'No,' she said, 'it's the baby.'

'The baby's ill?'

'The tree's broken.' She paused again. 'The small tree.'

In turn, Ploughman was silent.

'Baby's Life Tree,' the girl said.

'Ah . . .' the man comprehended. *That* was it: the old story! His gaze strayed back to the garden. The pigeons flew with a clap, suddenly lean and urgent. He said, 'You'll *make* yourself ill, girl.'

'I'm here alone till this evening. I'm frightened.'

'Just calm down,' he said firmly. 'You're worse than Poacher, by heaven. It's the snow, it's bewitched you. In any case,' he reflected, 'you can't get rid of them willows; the thing will sprout again shortly. Use some sense, the child's blooming. There's nothing wrong with my grandson!'

'The bitch was here – your witch-woman.'

He swore. 'Don't worry, she's leaving, going back where she came from.' He drained his mug. 'You forget her. Just keep warm, girl, I'm coming. I'll clear the track and be with you.'

The Witchwood rang.

'*Rat-tun . . . Rat-tun . . .*'

Kine stood his ground, dazed and bleeding.

For half a second, Rattun paused, mystified by such defiance. The weasel's vision had glazed, he scarcely seemed with the living. Yet he had rounded, jaws wide, the small needle-fangs threatening. They took the monster aback and, in that fleeting reprieve, Kine's sight cleared, a thought sharpened.

It was that he could still move; his wounds could not be severe. He was Kine the unbowed – and he had a split-second.

Rattun pounced. The giant laughed. 'Die!' he sneered, reaching out, scorning puny defences. His hands bore down. 'Like the ratling!' They crooked and stabbed, horned tips grasping. But Kine had gone, slipping from them.

'Kine survives!' churred the weasel.

'Just . . .' The Rat King raged forward. But Kine's old bounce had returned and once more he dodged safely. There was a hush round the glade.

'*Tchkkk!*' cried Kine. 'We continue – Kine does not die so easily.'

'You'll die painfully, weasel.'

'We shall see . . .'

Kine was cautious, content to skip and evade. He let the giant do the chasing. The brute would tire and slow up – then watch out for the death-hold! Kine had a scorpion's patience: the sting, he mused, would come later.

'Just watch him dance!' sang the sparrows.

'See him weave . . .'

'Watch his feet!'

'That's all show,' Watchman counselled. 'He won't get anywhere that way'

They held their breath as Kine sallied – a sudden thrust at the monster. 'Won't get anywhere?' Flit cried. The sparrows cheeped their excitement. 'He's taking up the offensive; the weasel's attacking!' A tuft of rat hair came loose and blew on to the snow-drift. Kine bobbed low, disengaging, danced from reach and crowed softly.

'*Tchkkk* – you're out of step, Rattun, let me teach you the rhythm!'

'You've got a lot to repay, Kine. I'm going to skin you for this. I'm going to flay you, small dancer, and throw you live to the chosen.'

'You're evil, Rattun.'

'I'm powerful!'

'A plague,' said Kine.

'A Supremo! The rat is master from now; Kine is nothing, an outcast. Times change, little mouser, and the oppressed are the oppressors. Rattun rules; he is feared. The Lord Rattun is Terror - and you, my *friend*, have a death wish!'

'No, you're wrong.'

'No wish, weasel?'

'Yes,' said Kine, his eyes watchful, 'to wake in spring and smell blossom; to wake without smelling rats. I mean to have my wish, Rattun, to free the vale of affliction.'

'Instead,' the giant rasped, 'you'll perish!'

'*Kine will perish* . . .' the guards droned.

They let a grey shape press forward. The Rat King's spouse had been sleeping; now, she darkened the ringside. 'Slay the vermin!' the sow hissed.

'*Slay!*' the crowding rats echoed.

The Rat King charged and Kine soared, leaping high to a flank, where he crouched, his glint mocking. Rattun fumed and turned slowly. Blebs of foam flecked his lip. He was ugly with anger.

The weasel circled, eyes gleaming. 'Turn again,' he thought grimly, 'stretch your neck for me, tyrant!' But Rattun's head was drawn in, shoulders hunched, and Kine chary. A fumbled hold meant disaster, for once committed to grappling the ultimatum was final: find the nerve-hold or die – be destroyed or kill faster. 'Dance, Rattun, keep dancing!'

The tyrant lunged, missing wildly.

'Dolt!' the Sow Queen exclaimed. 'The red bug is still there. While he lives we're not safe. Slay the cockroach!' She twitched her tail and watched slyly. As Kine came round, it curled out, deftly aimed, and he stumbled. He felt the thong snatch his legs. He was teetering . . . prostrate.

'*Now* kill him,' the sow said.

Her mate did not require urging. The mob had hushed for the blow and he towered, full weight balanced, then fell on the weasel. Kine felt the breath explode in him. It seemed to grow very dark, and a strange numbness gripped him. There was a sinking sensation. Behind his eyes, as if trapped, something frantic was pounding.

Then the teeth sought his throat and he squirmed, pinned feet-upwards. In despair, he snapped back. The flesh he gripped suffocated but the weight eased a little. Desperately, he kicked, jerking up at the monster. It was like pummelling ballast. He found a mark. The rat roared. As it heaved, he writhed free, staring up at cruel fingers.

His breath returned in short gasps. The meagre fuel cleared his mind but his vision was misted. Above him, poised to lash down, the massive rat was a ghoul, a nightmare glimpsed in a fog, and he waited, impassive. He could, he thought, hear bird-voices.

'Enough,' growled Watchman, 'I'm off. He's not moving; he's finished.'

'He was fouled.' Flit stared glumly.

'Robbed,' moaned Farthing.

They brooded.

Watchman stirred. 'Move!' he blurted. His voice was cracked. He croaked hoarsely, 'You cocksure shrimp . . . you fool upstart . . .'

The sparrows eyed him, breasts ruffling. 'Yes,' they twittered, '*get moving*!' They made it louder. 'FIGHT BACK, KINE!'

It came through dimly. Kine stiffened. He had to drag himself somehow – somehow shift his weak body. He must at least make the effort. He prayed that nothing was broken then flexed his limbs. They responded.

Askance, he saw the giant strike, and Kine heaved, his teeth gritted. He felt no blow and kept going. Again, he heaved, now obliquely. It seemed a pitiful flight; a snail, he thought, would crawl faster. Yet he was scrambling, zig-zagging, and nothing had hit him. He sensed the swipes flying past and saw hard soil breaking open, ripped up by rat talons.

He could hear sparrows applauding.

Now, he rolled, spinning over. Three times – four times, he spun, white bib flashing, then halted, exhausted. He found his feet in a daze and saw Rattun haul round, for the moment out-distanced.

Kine's brain whirled. He was spent. Only courage sustained him – and his weasel-cunning. He viewed the guards and the snow. The drift was pristine behind them. It was a chance . . .

He stepped backwards. Then, wincing, Kine raised a foot.

'He's maimed!' the Sow Queen cried, gloating.

'*The weasel's maimed* . . .' the mob chanted.

Rattun's glare held no mercy. 'The running's done,' he exulted, 'we needn't hurry now, cripple!' And, watching

Kine hobble, 'You've asked for this,' hissed the Rat King. He followed viciously, adding, 'We'll have a small exhibition, a spot of three-legged dancing.' He sneered. 'Then two-legged . . .'

The crowd pressed round.

'Make an opening.' The tyrant scowled and lashed out. 'The crippled dancer needs room – he can't perform in a crush. I want to watch this performance.' He thrust a spiteful claw forward and howled as Kine shifted nimbly, all four legs back in action. They carried him to the drift and he crouched on it, panting.

The feigned limp had deceived Rattun.

'I've eluded you, tyrant!'

'No one escapes from me, weasel. You're weak, you can't run. No one lives who defies me. My decree rules the valley.'

'Your guards,' said Kine. 'Mindless minions.'

'Taught by fear to obey, to avenge and purge protest. You've no chance.'

'Catch me, rat!'

Rattun roared. 'I'll destroy you . . .' He forayed headlong, his mouth frothing. At first, the drift seemed to bear him, then his belly had vanished. He floundered on, sinking deeper. At last, submerged to the shoulders, he fought to free himself squirming. He squealed with rage and for help – the help that none moved to offer.

The weasel fell on him tiredly. Had one witnessed the duel – a hidden human observer – one might have crept a shade closer, for no one was looking. The mob had packed the snow's fringe, oblivious of the trees, of the bank, of time's passage, all eyes on the tyrant.

He gave a final heave upwards and Kine was tossed then slumped back, his foe wallowing deeper. The weasel's neck stretched and curved; slender fangs punctured hide. The rat's frenzy subsided. The smaller animal leeched, the nerve-hold tenacious. The two were still for a moment and then the rat gave a shudder. A single snowflake descended.

At last, the weasel rose slowly. 'It's done,' he breathed, 'Rattun's finished.'

There was no sound from the guards.

'Come,' hissed Kine, 'see your leader, see the Lord of the Chosen!' A hundred beady eyes glared. 'Step, if you dare, on the snow-drift!'

A muted grunt fled the mob. There was no sympathy in it, no grief for the despot. It said a terror was laid; it said the slayer was awesome. Several rats slipped away, shuffling off through the Witchwood. Others watched, in two minds, then decamped, their tails dragging. Soon, the whole crowd was leaving.

Alone, the Sow Queen remained.

'A shrimp, a cockroach!' she muttered.

'Come and join us,' said Kine. 'Come and join your Lord Rattun.'

'I'm no such fool,' said the sow. She gave a snort of disgust. 'The dead are dead, little hero.' She followed the stragglers.

There was ice on the windscreen. The wiper flapped ineffectually and Ploughman bent in the cab, peering out through a chink as the tractor chugged forward. It nudged a lane through the snow, leaving mountainous shoulders.

Once or twice, the tyres slipped and he reversed, seeking bite, then eased back at the drifts. The land was magically still, as numb, he thought, as his mind, which seemed frozen in limbo, loath to dwell on the damage.

He clambered down at the cottage. A spade lay in the garden. The little tree had been smashed. That was the least of the harm, for it should not have been planted. He would have pulled the thing up; they grew like weeds and took over. He had no time for scrub willow.

What else had the witch done? The door was shut and he paused apprehensively. You could not tell with the girl but she had been in a state. He drubbed his hands on his sides to increase circulation, as if it might thaw his wits, and called out, 'The track's clear now.'

'Come in,' she snapped, the door opening, and when he scraped snowy boots, 'Oh, come on – come in quickly.'

The girl was holding the baby. He eyed her face, which

was drawn, then the fire. The logs smouldered. Looking awkwardly round, he saw the photo of Poacher still propped up, and he scowled.

Ploughman reached for the infant. 'Give him here, let me have him. Let's see the young fellow.'

The girl drew back. 'He's in danger.'

'Bah,' he grunted, arms empty. 'It's cold here,' he shivered.

She watched him, saying, 'I'm frightened.'

'You're not a heathen,' he told her and kicked the fire, adding logs. 'Damn-fool superstitions!' It sounded harsh and he granted, 'Partly my fault, I reckon; I let you run wild too often.'

'With Poacher,' the girl said.

'Aye, with Poacher, the pagan.' Ploughman viewed her with caution. 'My fault,' he repeated.

'He said the trees held the signs. He was sure.'

'Bloody Poacher!'

'You never liked him, you're *jealous*.'

'The beggar's dead.'

'So's his tree – they died the same day,' the girl said.

The other stifled impatience. She was perverse, getting at him. He never had got her measure – come to that, any woman's. Not that he had known many, or much else beyond farm work. Soil and sweat, grease and diesel! He said, 'Coincidence, that was. He filled your head with tales, lassie.'

'You hate him. I know why you're against him.' She turned on him with resentment. What right had *he* to instruct her? '*She* told me,' the girl breathed.

'She's as bad. The cow's spiteful.' His shoulders dropped. 'Like I told you . . .'

'Like you never!' she answered and watched him shuffle, now nervous. The ice had thawed from his boots and made several small puddles. He seemed crumpled, she thought, more work-worn than she remembered. 'Like *she* told me,' the girl rasped.

'Malicious bitch – he'd've warned you,' He eyed the photograph glumly.

She sighed and said, 'You and Poacher!'

'She wants to stir things,' he grunted.

'She wants my baby to suffer.'

The farm man braced, his back straightening.

'Look,' he growled, his gaze level, 'I'll tell you this and you heed it.' He checked his brusqueness, explaining, 'The woman turned on your mother. Your ma was *good*, all I wanted. Your ma had nothing bad in her; the other envied her rotten.'

'My ma went with Poacher . . .'

'Before we wed, they'd walked out.' Ploughman shrugged. 'Aye, I grudged him. Maybe, it still bloody rankles but it's an age ago now. He was a bit of a charmer. When he was young, the girls liked him. He could talk apples from trees, climb rainbows, could Poacher.' He smiled and said, 'Well, you knew him. He gave it up and lived rough but his tongue kept its knack. He'd keep you happy for hours when you were small, yarning to you.'

About the sparrows, she mused; about the rats and the weasels . . .

Ploughman said, 'You believed him. He could spin a yarn, Poacher.'

'He wasn't dull!'

'No,' the man said. He scratched his chin and reflected, 'That was me, the dull beggar, the one who worked for a living, sat all day on a tractor to see you had what you needed.'

'Yes,' she said. She was grateful. Poacher might have amused her - it was Ploughman who fed her. The baby coughed and she stiffened.

'Give him here girl, that's nothing.'

She eyed the veteran, uncertain.

'You'd better choose,' he said gruffly, 'we'd better know where we stand.' He half-lowered his hands but she could see the rough knuckles, the toil-calloused fingers. Like his face, they were furrowed, as lined and weathered as plough-land. They had soothed her so often, bathed her grazes, calmed passions.

'Fine choice!' the girl muttered.

She loved the stupid old fool.

'Nothing's changed, girl,' he told her. 'I've not changed, nor have you. I used to hold *you* like that, like you're holding the lad. You're the same, only bigger – still as wild, still as daft. Flaming Life Trees!' he muttered. 'That's my girl, always has been . . .'

'Oh, Dad . . .' Her chin lifted. She could have strangled the witch! As if a spell had been broken, she said, 'It's time I took down that old snapshot,'

'Aye,' he grunted, 'forget it.'

'I didn't say I'd *forget* it.' The child had started to grizzle. 'Hush.' she said, free of fear, as if a demon had died 'there's no cause for that now.' She passed the infant to Ploughman. 'Here, *you* tell him,' she smiled. 'I think I need to sit down. He's your grandchild, you tell him.'

The weasels lay by the pump, Heath and Wonder uneasy. Kine had sent them no word and the dandies were fretting. The place was cold and exposed; the young bloods lusted action. Controlling them was a problem. Before much longer, thought Heath, there would be open rebellion.

'He's been a long time,' he grunted.

It seemed to Wonder forever. 'We've got to wait,' she replied, but conviction was ebbing.

A bitter wind sliced their coats, enfilading the shelter. It scurried over the marsh, chasing snow from the waste so its steely floor gleamed, smooth and bare, a vast rink. The ice sheeted the levels. There seemed no prospect of life; winter's fastness was barren.

The female weasel hung on. She sympathized with her offspring but stood by Kine's wishes. He could have asked for support, sent the birds with instructions. Unless, she thought, her mind torn, the birds had met trouble. They were not used to the Witchwood. The frost was cruel; terrors lurked there.

Heath was pacing. The dandies brawled to keep warm but he no longer bothered, doubtful secrecy mattered. Whatever else had transpired, the surprise would be over, and Heath's hopes were fading.

He said, 'It's late,' and stopped pacing.

'Yes,' growled Wonder.

They waited.

Heath regarded the female. 'Do we go in?'

She was staring. 'A moment longer,' she breathed, her gaze trained on the woods. 'I thought I saw something move. There! A smudge . . .'

'Nothing,' Heath said.

'It is,' she muttered. '*Two* smudges!'

He looked again. 'You're right, Wonder – they're coming closer.'

'The sparrows!' She was too nervous to move. 'Bringing news . . .' The dread swamped her.

The sparrows dragged, their flight dipping. As small birds will, they flew low, now just skimming the ice-field. Then they were buzzing the pump, landing where its roof ended. A wedge of snow slithered from it.

'HE WON! KINE'S THE CHAMPION!'

The female weasel sighed slowly.

'Rattun's dead,' Flit-cat clamoured.

'What a dust-up!' cried Farthing.

'A fight of fights!'

'*What a champion!*'

Wonder turned to the woods. They were hazy with distance. The dim grey crowns offered nothing. She paused then asked, her throat tightening, 'What of Kine – is he safe?'

'Weary,' Flit said.

Heath looked up. 'And the guards?'

The dandies answered him, pointing. 'Look!' they gulped. 'Heath, they're *leaving* . . .' He swung his head, gawping with them, disbelieving the vision.

In ones and twos, they were fleeing – in threes and fours, and in clusters. As they streamed from the woods, the rats spread out on the marsh like skaters in an ice-palace. Sliding, scuttling, they fled, phantom shapes in the haze, on the cold, glassy surface. The awesome rout slithered north. Already, those at its head were lost in gloom when Heath acted.

216

'Let's go,' he called, springing forward. 'Pursue and harry, you dandies, you scions of Kine! Let's get at them!'

'Warm their heels!' whooped the weasels. Wonder watched as they charged, fiery hounds in the frost, then she made for the Witchwood.

Kine emerged looking bruised.

'Are you hurt?' asked the female.

'Exhausted . . .'

'You're injured!' She licked his wounds. 'You'll recover.' Relieved, she said, 'You've been lucky.'

'The valley's safe.'

'Yes – Kine's Country!'

'Kia's land,' Kine said, at peace. 'I kept faith with her, Wonder.'

'Now, sleep . . .'

'Catch Kine sleeping!'

She smiled. 'I'll wake you next summer.'

Epilogue

It was spring. A soft rain had been falling and the pump could just be heard, humming. It stopped and the sun shone. Perched high on the ridge, a thrush started to sing. As note followed on note, another songster joined in, and soon several were calling.

The young man cantered then halted. On the engineer's shoulders, the Dream Child squealed, his face beaming. Down the track, her hair swirling, the girl ran after them, laughing. She caught them up, her voice trilling – lines still fresh from her schooldays:

> *'When daisies pied and violets blue*
> *And lady-smocks all silver white*
> *And cuckoo-buds of yellow hue*
> *Do paint the meadows with delight . . .'*

Violets flowered by the copse. She stooped, admiring their colour. Her husband grinned at her back – bare between jeans and singlet – taking up from her drily:

> *'The cuckoo then, on every tree,*
> *Mocks married men; for thus sings he,*
> > *Cuckoo;*
> *Cuckoo, cuckoo . . .'*

He pranced on, chortling.

'Oo-oo-oo,' the child echoed.

His mother chased them, arms flailing. 'I'll give you cuckoo!' she shrilled. 'Wait and see!' the girl panted. Their cries of glee filled the covert. By the Moon Pond, they paused. The child was toddling by now and they watched as he wobbled. Overhead, corvids cawed, the vexed older birds circling. On the nests, their young fluttered.

Wife and husband held hands. While they kissed, squirrels scampered, rummaging for old acorns. In a while, the

218

girl said, 'I meant to show you – come here. The fallen tree,' she directed.

The engineer viewed the willow. Through a gauze of small insects, its limbs reached up from the pool, the sun catching their fingers. He squeezed her own. 'I'll be damned . . .'

'It's in leaf.'

'Aye, it's sprouted. It must have root in the ground still.'

'Aren't you glad?' she said, smiling. She eyed the bank and the kingcups, the pale young fern and cow-parsley.

The man bent down, arms outstretched, and came up with his hands cupped. 'Look at this – where's that boy?' He showed the toddler his catch. The shrew blinked, its nose twitching. The child was quiet, stiff with rapture. At last, he moved to reach out, stroke the pebble of velvet.

'No,' the girl said, 'don't touch. There, he's gone; he was frightened.' The shrew made off, its legs beetling. 'Hear him squeak? "Doom," he's saying, "doom and woe, life's a problem – life's so hard, being tiny!" '

She laughed, her son giggling back. The child jigged and collapsed, momentarily frowning. 'Come here, love, wipe your hands!'

They strolled on, the man proud, and she mused, 'Strange things happen.'

'Like what?'

'*Things*,' she answered. They had reached the wood's end. Below them, sheep grazed the marshes. The hills were blue far away and a choir of birds warbled. 'Like the old willow sprouting. Like the rats disappearing.'

'Mmm.' He nodded in agreement. That *was* odd, the rats leaving. He said, 'Some kind of migration. There'll be a sound explanation.'

The sun was bright. The girl squinted. 'In Poacher's story . . .' she said.

'Never mind Poacher's story, *we're* going to look at the engine.'

The weasel climbed from the hole, raised a sharp head and peered. They had gone. Kine sat up. It was quiet, the pond calm. He was alone on the tree – alone, at last, where he belonged. '*Tchkkk*,' he churred, preening quickly. His wounds had healed, scars were hidden; his sleek spring coat gleamed like armour.

He took three bounds to the bank and stood still, bright eyes darting. Another summer was near, another season of growth. Kine was back in old haunts. Soon, the geese would return, honking in from the coast, and he would be a year older. A trifle slower, perhaps, but Kine the survivor.

One day, at length, death would win – he cherished no vain illusions. He thought of Kia and Chukra, of lost kitts and his parents. There was a last dance ahead, somewhere, lying in ambush. But let it catch him, thought Kine; let it catch Kine the cunning. He had a trick or two waiting!

'*Tchkkk-kkk*!' He moved on. There were old hunt-paths to survey. He moved lightly, snout weaving, half-snake, half-hobgoblin. He was free and alone. '*Tchkkk*,' he sang as he forayed. He knew the trails, the deep places, the rabbit's stop, the mole's fortress. He could interpret the signs, knew the sounds of the valley.

He knew the bark of the fox and the laugh of the yaffle.

He was unbowed; none was bolder. He was Kine the rat killer. He was small but formidable.

Author's note

In 1981, having spent most of the previous two decades working on books of history and biography, I succumbed to my lifelong love of the countryside and put together a small book about the farmland surrounding my Kentish home. A fantasy of its wild creatures, with sketches of landscape and seasonal moods, the tale had as its unlikely hero a weasel which visited my garden. I called him Kine.

Symbolically, I hoped, on the publication day of *Kine* in 1982, the weasel appeared outside the kitchen window in splendid fettle. He could scarcely have shared my professional doubts about the book – I had never before mixed business and actual *pleasure* – but he might well, a few days later, have shared my surprise at his popularity. The trappings of best-seller status are prosaic; what truly astonished was the warmth of the fan-mail Kine received.

The flow began soon after the book's appearance, emanating with such enthusiasm from across Europe, America, Africa and the Antipodes, as well as from points in Britain, that I began to suspect some long-suppressed cult of weasel-lovers had been released. Some were indeed weasel *owners*, among them the reader from Zagreb who sent a photo of his aptly named *Luka*, or Household Hurricane.

From a reader in Italy came an invitation to visit a whole family of weasels (*donolà*) living in the attic of a Florentine villa. Unfortunately, I was by then too busy answering letters. Many came from unashamedly envious readers, simply sighing to be part of the world the book described. A couple of German nature lovers actually arrived on my doorstep, having flown from Dusseldorf complete with hiking equipment, intent on exploring Kine's territory.

In the end, Kine could boast a greater and more delightful volume of correspondence than I had received as a result of all my previous books together – some twenty multinational publications at that date. A repeated theme was the hope that the weasel and his companions would turn up in another book. It is therefore, I suppose, a valid if unoriginal claim that a new adventure comes 'by popular request'.

Having said which, I would not like to neglect Kine's adversaries. In the original story, feral mink were cast as the evil foe, a slur for which I was rebuked during a visit to the University of Durham, where fascinating work has been done on mink behaviour. At that stage, feral mink had received an undeservedly bad press and my admittedly fantastic villains were not regarded as helpful.

Since then, I have myself published a factual and sympathetic appraisal of these animals – for, having watched many mink 'in the wild', I certainly prefer to see them free than in traps or cages. Nor do I regard rats, the demons of this volume, as truly villainous, though I grew up at a time when they were a serious pest on farms.

I have a vivid memory of first encountering rats in the mass. As a young boy with a new bicycle, I had cycled alone deep in the Hampshire country and paused, momentarily lost, in a lonely lane. Suddenly, I realized that the hedgerows were alive with rodents – not the odd, bolting rat to which I was accustomed, but an army of audacious, staring animals, unafraid of me. Turning round, I severely tested the speed of my new machine.

Later, as a youthful rat-catcher earning twopence a tail, I began to respect the creatures. Not only were they wily but awesomely brave, I thought. In those days of gin-traps, it was common to see three-legged rats, since they would indeed gnaw off an entrapped limb to escape capture. More-over, the sows, disturbed with young, would often risk their lives in courageous attempts to save their offspring.

Soon, the advent of Warfarin (causing death to rats by internal haemorrhaging) was to eliminate the rat population as I had known it. But Kine's super-rat adversaries are not entirely notional. More recently, rats in some areas report-edly have developed immunity to this form of control, rather as rabbits are now surviving myxomatosis in many places.

Weasels are natural rat controllers. Though Kine himself

killed nothing but voles in my sight, I once had what must be the extremely uncommon experience of watching a weasel kill a grown rat. The opportunity – made possible by a hand-reared weasel accustomed to human company – revealed the deadly efficiency of the 'nerve-hold'. Instantly employed by the weasel, it induced first paralysis then death in about, as I remember it, a minute flat.

In the wild, young weasels learn to hunt in the family group, but this killing technique for larger prey (weasels kill mice and voles by crushing their skulls) is instinctive. According to the 'tame' weasel's owner, his young and entirely uninstructed animal had without hesitation dispatched the first rat it ever met. Watching this inquisitive hunter run up my arm to my shoulder, I was relieved that its nibble at my earlobe was a friendly one.

There is little documentary material on weasels. As in the original *Kine*, such reality as may underpin the animal fantasy in this story is based on personal observation. Kine's valley, the marsh, pump-house and other immediate locations are entirely real, my home for twenty years, while barn owls, herons, rooks, mink, badgers, foxes, hedgehogs and all the rest have been my closest neighbours.

Many of the incidents in the book were suggested by wildlife scenes virtually on my doorstep. For instance, the three young foxes with the dead mole turned up one summer evening when my wife Daphne and I, together with the artist and writer Christopher Neve and his family, were watching a pair of barn owls feed their young.

The owls had nested in a disused chimney of the house and, as we trained our glasses from the corner of an adjacent field on the owlets, which had perched on the chimney-pot, we became aware of foxes running past us in the dusk. For perhaps five minutes they played within yards of us, the animal with the mole racing in circles chased by the others until they were lost in the thickening gloom.

More often, the owls nested in the old barn beside the farmhouse, where a mass of black pellets testified to their hunting prowess. A single barn owl will consume about eight vole-sized creatures every twenty-four hours – a family of adults and young can account for well over fifty small rodents in the same period.

At this rate, Scrat has good reason to be frightened, though I must confess his timidity is not typical of shrews as I sometimes find them. To judge by their squeaky battle-cries from the dry summer ditches about the farm, these tiniest of our mammals are distinctly belligerent towards their own kind in the breeding season.

Hedgehogs, a special favourite, often come round the house after dark and are easily approachable as they tend to keep still when a light falls on them. There is an old belief that they are immune to the adder's poison. This, I think, is untrue, though the hedgehog's spines are a first-class protection against its enemies. I only wish the creature had some protection against road traffic!

Finally (since this is not the place for a country memoir), I might just add, apropos Kine's escape from the heron, that herons are by no means loath to take small mammals, especially at times when fishing is difficult. Furred creatures are often dunked by the bird before it swallows them.

A. R. Lloyd
Kent, 1988

A Selection of Arrow Books

☐ No Enemy But Time	Evelyn Anthony	£2.95
☐ The Lilac Bus	Maeve Binchy	£2.99
☐ Rates of Exchange	Malcolm Bradbury	£3.50
☐ Prime Time	Joan Collins	£3.50
☐ Rosemary Conley's Complete Hip and Thigh Diet	Rosemary Conley	£2.99
☐ Staying Off the Beaten Track	Elizabeth Gundrey	£6.99
☐ Duncton Wood	William Horwood	£4.50
☐ Duncton Quest	William Horwood	£4.50
☐ A World Apart	Marie Joseph	£3.50
☐ Erin's Child	Sheelagh Kelly	£3.99
☐ Colours Aloft	Alexander Kent	£2.99
☐ Gondar	Nicholas Luard	£4.50
☐ The Ladies of Missalonghi	Colleen McCullough	£2.50
☐ The Veiled One	Ruth Rendell	£3.50
☐ Sarum	Edward Rutherfurd	£4.99
☐ Communion	Whitley Strieber	£3.99

Prices and other details are liable to change

ARROW BOOKS, BOOKSERVICE BY POST, PO BOX 29, DOUGLAS, ISLE OF MAN, BRITISH ISLES

NAME..

ADDRESS ....

....

....

Please enclose a cheque or postal order made out to Arrow Books Ltd. for the amount due and allow the following for postage and packing.

U.K. CUSTOMERS: Please allow 22p per book to a maximum of £3.00.

B.F.P.O. & EIRE: Please allow 22p per book to a maximum of £3.00.

OVERSEAS CUSTOMERS: Please allow 22p per book.

Whilst every effort is made to keep prices low it is sometimes necessary to increase cover prices at short notice. Arrow Books reserve the right to show new retail prices on covers which may differ from those previously advertised in the text or elsewhere.

Bestselling Fiction

☐ No Enemy But Time	Evelyn Anthony	£2.95
☐ The Lilac Bus	Maeve Binchy	£2.99
☐ Prime Time	Joan Collins	£3.50
☐ A World Apart	Marie Joseph	£3.50
☐ Erin's Child	Sheelagh Kelly	£3.99
☐ Colours Aloft	Alexander Kent	£2.99
☐ Gondar	Nicholas Luard	£4.50
☐ The Ladies of Missalonghi	Colleen McCullough	£2.50
☐ Lily Golightly	Pamela Oldfield	£3.50
☐ Talking to Strange Men	Ruth Rendell	£2.99
☐ The Veiled One	Ruth Rendell	£3.50
☐ Sarum	Edward Rutherfurd	£4.99
☐ The Heart of the Country	Fay Weldon	£2.50

Prices and other details are liable to change

_____

ARROW BOOKS, BOOKSERVICE BY POST, PO BOX 29, DOUGLAS, ISLE
OF MAN, BRITISH ISLES

NAME..

ADDRESS ....

....

....

Please enclose a cheque or postal order made out to Arrow Books Ltd. for the amount
due and allow the following for postage and packing.

U.K. CUSTOMERS: Please allow 22p per book to a maximum of £3.00.

B.F.P.O. & EIRE: Please allow 22p per book to a maximum of £3.00.

OVERSEAS CUSTOMERS: Please allow 22p per book.

Whilst every effort is made to keep prices low it is sometimes necessary to increase cover
prices at short notice. Arrow Books reserve the right to show new retail prices on covers
which may differ from those previously advertised in the text or elsewhere.

Bestselling General Fiction

☐ No Enemy But Time	Evelyn Anthony	£2.95
☐ Skydancer	Geoffrey Archer	£3.50
☐ The Sisters	Pat Booth	£3.50
☐ Captives of Time	Malcolm Bosse	£2.99
☐ Saudi	Laurie Devine	£2.95
☐ Duncton Wood	William Horwood	£4.50
☐ Aztec	Gary Jennings	£3.95
☐ A World Apart	Marie Joseph	£3.50
☐ The Ladies of Missalonghi	Colleen McCullough	£2.50
☐ Lily Golightly	Pamela Oldfield	£3.50
☐ Sarum	Edward Rutherfurd	£4.99
☐ Communion	Whitley Strieber	£3.99

Prices and other details are liable to change

ARROW BOOKS, BOOKSERVICE BY POST, PO BOX 29, DOUGLAS, ISLE OF MAN, BRITISH ISLES

NAME..

ADDRESS ....

....

....

Please enclose a cheque or postal order made out to Arrow Books Ltd. for the amount due and allow the following for postage and packing.

U.K. CUSTOMERS: Please allow 22p per book to a maximum of £3.00.

B.F.P.O. & EIRE: Please allow 22p per book to a maximum of £3.00.

OVERSEAS CUSTOMERS: Please allow 22p per book.

Whilst every effort is made to keep prices low it is sometimes necessary to increase cover prices at short notice. Arrow Books reserve the right to show new retail prices on covers which may differ from those previously advertised in the text or elsewhere.